Contents

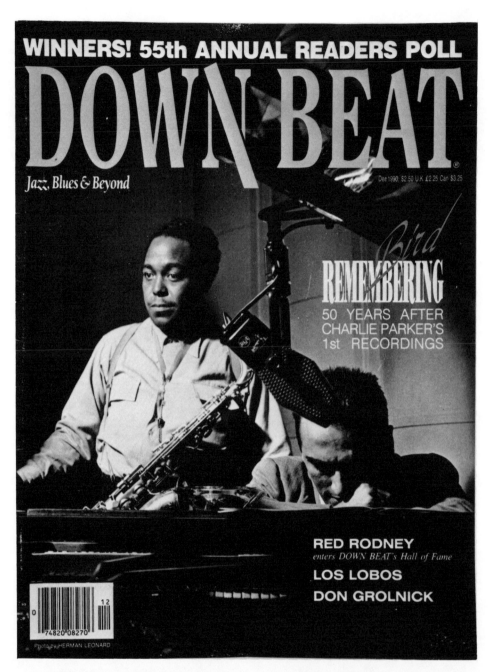

Cover of *Down Beat* for December 1990, with a photograph of Charlie Parker by Herman Leonard. This issue announces that Parker's former trumpeter, Red Rodney, has entered the magazine's Hall of Fame. Courtesy of Richard Lawn.

The Bebop Revolution
in Words and Music

Edited by Dave Oliphant
With an Introduction by Richard Lawn

Harry Ransom Humanities Research Center·The University of Texas at Austin

Cover illustration: album label for Dial recording 203-B with the Charlie Parker Sextet, featuring Miles Davis and J.J. Johnson, from 1947. Designed by David Stone Martin. *HRHRC Ross Russell Collection.*

Introduction

In 1976, Ross Russell, founder of Dial Records and author of *Bird Lives! The High Life and Hard Times of Charlie "Yardbird" Parker*, began discussions with The University of Texas at Austin about his ambitions to place his personal archive in an institution of higher learning. Russell described his collection—acquired during some 40 years and including books, records, periodicals, taped interviews, and research leading up to the publication of *Bird Lives!* and his *Jazz Style in Kansas City and the Southwest*—as "one of the finest and most complete collections in private hands in the country" and described himself as "author of 3 well-known books and over 100 articles on jazz. . . ." Negotiations were stalled between the fall of 1976 and late 1979 but were resumed in 1980. Russell explained that "litigation involving 'Bird Lives' made it impossible to make a commitment" though the legal issues had been resolved to the point that negotiations for the sale of the complete collection could now take place. Interest from the University's Department of Music and officials of the General Libraries and the Harry Ransom Humanities Research Center was further peaked by Russell's mention of additional non-jazz materials generated by the relationships and business transactions he had had, as owner of Dial Records, with classical composers Ernst Krenek, Rudolph Kolisch, and Arnold Schoenberg. Russell was anxious to part with his collection, since at the time he and his wife planned to emigrate to South Africa. An agreement was reached just days before the 1980 Christmas holiday, and the University took delivery of the Russell Collection shortly after the first of the new year.[1]

The Ross Russell Collection proved to be larger than anticipated. In addition to fifteen legal-sized boxes of correspondence, research materials, lecture notes, book manuscripts and drafts, screen plays, articles, unfinished books, photographs, materials relating to contractual arrangements, royalties,

---

[1]For a fuller account of the career of Ross Russell and of the University's acquisition of his archive, see Richard Lawn, "From Bird to Schoenberg: The Ross Russell Collection," *Perspectives on Music*, ed. Dave Oliphant and Thomas Zigal (Austin: Humanities Research Center, 1985), pp. 137-147.

mechanical rights, reviews, transcribed interviews, and promotional literature for Dial recordings, the collection had also grown to include 3,500 LP recordings and 78 RPM discs (1,500 of which are jazz related); reel-to-reel and cassette tapes; 265 books, which deal primarily with jazz and jazz-related topics; some 400 periodicals, including complete or nearly complete runs of *Jazz Review, Clef, Record Changer,* and *Jazz Record;* 200 miscellaneous booklets; incomplete articles and books (some with as many as ten chapters finished); pamphlets, programs, and record catalogues; and other memorabilia. The record collection was an unexpected bonus and included many Dial test pressings of jazz recordings by such masters as Charlie Parker, Kenny Dorham, Dexter Gordon, and Red Rodney, as well as recordings of works by Schoenberg and other mid twentieth-century classical composers.

The Harry Ransom Humanities Research Center now houses the Russell recordings—both his personal collection and those issued by Dial Records— as well as the collector's archival materials: correspondence, manuscripts, unpublished works, photographs, and all other paper items. Of special interest to jazz scholars are letters in the correspondence files from Russell's fellow jazz historians throughout the United States and Europe. These correspondents include nearly every major figure concerned with jazz criticism and history, such as Martin Williams, Whitney Balliett, Max Harrison, Charles Delauney, Rudi Blesh, Leonard Feather, Ralph Gleason, André Hodeir, Gunther Schuller, Nat Hentoff, Marshall Stearns, and Ira Gitler. There is additional correspondence from and interviews with such jazz luminaries as John Lewis, Cootie Williams, Sonny Criss, Bud Freeman, Don Lanphere, Hampton Hawes, Fats Navarro, Jessie Price, Jay McShann, Gene Ramey, Kenny Clarke, Chan Richardson, Red Rodney, and most importantly, Charlie Parker, interviewed in a backstage dressing room between sets. The Rodney letters relate to other files and notes for an uncompleted book Russell apparently planned to co-author with this Bebop trumpeter who recorded with Charlie Parker between 1949 and 1951. The Russell Collection also contains a copy of the large-format pictorial biography of Charlie Parker, compiled by Chan Richardson and Francis Paudras and entitled *To Bird With Love*. This volume, filled with photographs from every period of Parker's career and based in part on some of the holograph manuscripts from the research Russell conducted on Charlie Parker's life and music, was printed in a limited edition in Paris in 1981.

Ross Russell's personal and financial experiences with the recording and publishing business left him disenchanted and somewhat bitter. He gradually abandoned Dial Records, selling or leasing master tapes to other, more well-established companies. In the mid 1980s, Spotlight Records, under the leadership of Tony Williams, another longtime Russell correspondent, began a special limited-edition reissue series, and Williams has contacted the HRHRC on several occasions in search of original materials for this project. As the result of a lawsuit, Russell invested nearly all his royalty income from *Bird Lives!* to defend against charges of plagiarism leveled by the widow of Robert Reisner, the author of *Bird: The Legend of Charlie Parker*, published in 1962. It is no wonder that Russell decided to abandon many unfinished manuscripts which form part of his archive at the HRHRC.

The purchase of the Russell Collection by The University of Texas at Austin was timely and an important step toward furthering the institution's commitment to American studies, cultural history, and jazz scholarship. Also, the collection and the era that it represents conveniently relate to other aspects of the University's special collections, in particular the twentieth-century holdings at the Ransom Center. The wealth of materials in the Russell Collection should stand for years to come as a continuing resource for jazz scholars, casual listeners, and avid readers.

THE SYMPOSIUM

After the Russell Collection was purchased in 1981, other than to curate the archival materials, to catalogue them, and to create a partial catalogue of the recordings, the Ransom Center had been able to do little in more than a decade to expose the collection to interested scholars. In the early 1980s, there was generally in the nation little interest, money, or time for what many considered to be museum pieces or musical relics of a forgotten past. However, as the 1980s progressed into the 1990s, we witnessed a noticeable period of rebirth; an age of greater awareness of and appreciation for the rich jazz tradition. The advent of the compact disc and the countless reissued LPs and 78 RPM phonograph records is no doubt partially responsible for this rekindled interest in nostalgic jazz. Many of the new, young jazz artists began reinvestigating the repertoire from previous eras, using it as a point of departure and a basis for refining their craft. Publications also reflected this revitalized attitude toward earlier jazz styles and their masters.

It was an article by Bob Davis and the reprint of a 1949 piece by Michael Levin and John S. Wilson in the December 1990 issue of *Down Beat* magazine that triggered my own interest in sponsoring an exhibition and symposium based on the Russell Collection.[2] Fortunately, my interest in such

[2]Bob Davis, "Golden Bird, The Rediscovery of Charlie Parker's 1st Recordings 50 Years After They First Took Flight," *Down Beat*, December 1990, pp. 17-19.

a project coincided with a similar enthusiasm by curators at the HRHRC who had been working with the Russell Collection among many other archives housed in the Center. The *Down Beat* article and reprint about Charlie Parker seemed like a sign—a message to HRHRC conservationist George Leake and myself that the timing was right to publicly unveil the Russell Collection and to relate it to other items of interest representing the Bebop period in American music and literature. Leake had already considered an exhibit of materials centered around twentieth-century African-American literature housed in the Center and, after reviewing the Russell archive, he became more committed to curating an exhibit devoted to the explosive, controversial, and revolutionary music and literature from the Bebop period. Once the project was approved by Thomas Staley, Director of the HRHRC, Dell Hollingsworth, Head Music Cataloger at the Ransom Center, joined Leake as co-curator. Both George and Dell were interested in obvious ties with literature of the period—the Beat poets and similar groups influenced by the Bebop movement—and those music-related items in the Russell, Knopf, Downing, and other HRHRC Collections. The Longhorn Jazz Festival, a semi-annual event sponsored by the Department of Music, also seemed to me to offer a natural tie-in to the symposium, which eventually was designated "The Bebop Revolution in Words and Music."

Dave Oliphant, editor of the HRHRC's quarterly journal, *The Library Chronicle*, Jeff Hellmer, Associate Director of Jazz Studies at the University, Dell Hollingsworth, George Leake, and I began to meet regularly to discuss grant applications, specific plans for the symposium format, as well as appropriate speakers. Dr. Hugh Sparks from the Department of Music's External Relations and Development office was also helpful in facilitating scheduling, grant applications, and promotion. The objective was to invite those scholars and performers who had made a significant contribution to the study and performance of Bebop jazz and in particular the music of Charlie Parker, the self-styled genius of the modern jazz movement in the 1940s and 1950s. A call for papers was issued through jazz periodicals, and then months of preparation began for the mounting of the exhibition and for the presentation of the symposium.

THE PARTICIPANTS

It is quite possible that more has been written about the Bebop era and its innovators than any other period in jazz history. Perhaps this is because it was a revolutionary music that broke away from pop culture and escaped the shackles of subservient secondary functions—a role to which earlier jazz styles seemed relegated. Some viewed the music as a product of a troubled war era and those immediate postwar times. Others felt the music was a natural reflection of the Black man's quest for freedom and equality. Charlie Parker and Dizzy Gillespie, the champions of this new music, seemed determined, consciously or unconsciously, to follow in the steps of Duke Ellington and to bring the music to a new level of artistic expression and acceptance. Their music was considered by some to be controversial, destructive, and a calculated revolt against tradition. Many of these same attitudes were expressed in the non-mainstream literature by writers such as Langston Hughes and Amiri Baraka.

Ross Russell, the only living Charlie Parker biographer and close business associate, seemed to be the obvious choice as a keynote speaker for the plenary session. Unfortunately, Russell's health ultimately prohibited him from attending, so that I had the pleasure and privilege of reading his remarks at the official opening of the exhibition. Russell's comments about Bebop and Parker were as poignant as his biography *Bird Lives!* and appropriately set the tone for the four-day symposium. It is regrettable that Russell was not present to accept the proclamation from Governor Ann Richards who declared April as jazz month in the State of Texas. In part, the Governor's text reads:

> Jazz is a uniquely American musical tradition and an integral part of our nation's artistic heritage. Its influence has been felt around the world, and it has profoundly affected all other forms of music and other arts.
>
> The Harry Ransom Humanities Research Center at the University of Texas, in collaboration with the UT Department of Music, is sponsoring *The Bebop Revolution in Words and Music*, a celebration of jazz and its profound influence on our nation's culture.
>
> The people of Texas should be encouraged to recognize jazz and the tremendous influence it has had on our national culture. It is a vibrant, exciting, and dynamic form of expression which deserves to be celebrated.

I personally regretted Russell's absence since he had been so helpful in his correspondence to me during the planning stages and it was he who suggested we invite Dr. Thomas Owens as one of the symposium speakers. Owens's presentation, based in part on his doctoral dissertation, and his participation on the panel discussion (transcribed and printed here in its entirety), provided an important element of theoretical inquiry into the influence of Charlie

Parker's style on succeeding generations of jazz saxophonists. Owens's analytical approach was balanced by presentations by Dan Morgenstern and Gary Giddins, two of the most eminent contemporary jazz historians and critics.

Known for his regular contributions to *The Village Voice* and his award-winning books *Rhythm-a-Ning* and *Celebrating Bird: The Triumph of Charlie Parker*, Gary Giddins participated in the panel discussion and contributed a talk which was drawn from the article printed here, "Charlie Parker: An Overview." This piece not only offers specific evidence about the mature genius of Charlie Parker but also discusses those often overlooked details from the beginning of Parker's musical life as captured on record, in particular his early Dial recordings.

Dan Morgenstern, Director of the Rutgers Institute of Jazz Studies, past editor of *Down Beat* magazine, and noted author of numerous articles and books about jazz, spoke on and played recorded examples of Parker as a balladeer. While Bebop typically has been stereotyped as a busy music featuring breakneck tempos, complex harmonies, and rhythmically challenging melodies, in contrast to this definition, Morgenstern discussed those beautiful ballads rendered by Charlie Parker, who also demonstrated on so many occasions that he was the unquestioned master of the aforementioned pyrotechnical style.

One group of papers published here from the symposium concerns the music and aesthetics of Charlie Parker and the Bebop movement. Edward Komara's detailed history of the Dial Records Charlie Parker catalogue presented the alto saxophonist's brief but important relationship with Ross Russell's label. Komara points out that Parker enjoyed longer relationships with other recording firms (Savoy from 1944 to 1948 and Clef/Mercury/Verve from 1946 to 1954), but those sides cut by Parker for the Dial label are considered by many to be the most musically ground-breaking.

Douglass Parker, University of Texas Professor of Classics, focused on a single tune in his "*Donna Lee* and the Ironies of Bebop." This outstanding piece—itself a type of Bebop prose full of witty allusions and playful improvisations on facts and contrafacts—not only poses interesting questions about the origins of the Bebop classic, *Donna Lee*, but also clearly unearths the true oral, aural, and folk-popsong tradition which has served as the backbone for the evolution of jazz since its inception.

Bernard Gendron, who is working on a new book about the Bebop era, shared the results of his research on the acceptance and rejection of Bebop music. His paper, "A Short Stay in the Sun: The Reception of Bebop, 1944-1950," sheds light on the controversy which surrounded the music and the original artists and those imitators who created it. This piece is an important contribution to the history of jazz criticism, which in itself warrants another symposium.

José Hosiasson traveled the farthest to take part in the symposium, coming from Chile to discuss the influence that Bebop has had on Latin American musicians. In his paper he also reminds us of the mutual exchange of ideas which began during the 1940s and alludes to the concept of Cubop, which involved musicians of both the Americas.

Lorenzo Thomas, writer in residence at the University of Houston, and Nicholas Evans, University of Texas graduate student, contributed thought-provoking discussions of literary and philosophical views on jazz. Thomas, a poet and essayist, reviewed the Black intellectual tradition and asserted that "Bebop highlights the mixture of resentment and ambition, racial pride and anger, that Alain Locke so meticulously endeavored to simultaneously mask and reveal. The Beboppers both fulfilled and rejected the ideals of Harlem Renaissance intellectuals." Evans considered how literature, and in particular the poetry of Langston Hughes, is as effective as music histories and criticism in the analysis of cultural phenomenon. Evans describes Hughes as an ethnographer who, through his poems, provides us with a close look at the jazz musician subculture of the 1940s.

No symposium about Charlie Parker and his music would be complete without the presence and living example of a performing artist who was closely associated with Parker. Trumpeter Red Rodney, who performed and recorded with the Bird from late 1949 to 1951, was in residence for three days at the symposium with his own quintet. Red and his younger contemporaries provided clinics and master classes following a brilliant showcase by the quintet of what could be termed the best in neobop. Red's participation in a panel discussion with Giddins, Morgenstern, Owens, and moderated by symposium participant Carl Woidek was a high point of the symposium. The panel's topic, "Bebop in the 1990s: A Vital Form or a Museum Piece?," was timely, given Red's performance at the University, his quintet's recent recordings, and the general activities by those many younger musicians new to the scene. The panel's observations and comments bear reading and may yield some of the most accurate observations about the current state of jazz and predications about the music's future.

Looking Ahead

Jazz in recent years has come a long way from its earlier role as the ugly stepchild of modern American music. There is a long tradition, however, of rejection. Identified by a four-letter word, it is a music in a constant state of flux, caught in a rapid evolution in which recordings provide only a snapshot

13

for the historical time capsule. For many years the music was condemned by members of the social elite and, even after its relative acceptance as an original American art form, by those historians and critics who in writing about it were frequently reluctant to accept change. Bebop, which supplanted an earlier popular jazz style known as Swing, was initially given poor reviews by critics and concerned swing musicians. For example, Norman Granz, noted jazz entrepreneur and promoter, stated in a 1945 *Down Beat* article that "maybe Gillespie was great but the 'advanced' group that Charlie Parker is fronting at the Three Deuces doesn't knock me out. It's too rigid and repetitive."[3] Some years later Granz was promoting and recording concerts which featured Parker, among other beboppers. Other critics' reviews were permeated with the swingster attitude and reflected the skepticism shared by swing and traditional jazz musicians like Benny Goodman and Louis Armstrong.

Don Haynes, a regular columnist for *Down Beat* in the mid 1940s, was consistently uncomplimentary about Bird and his music. In writing about the Parker-Gillespie *Shaw 'Nuff* session, Haynes commented that "for lasting worth [the style] must rid itself of much that now clutters its true value. Dizzy's and Charlie's solos are both excellent in many ways, yet still too acrobatic and sensationalistic to be expressive in the true sense of swing."[4] This article compared to earlier discussions of Bebop is tame and nearly laudatory. For example, Haynes's 1946 review of Parker's *Billie's Bounce* and *Now's the Time* stated that "These two sides are bad taste and ill-advised fanaticism."[5] Is there any wonder that it has taken so long for academia to embrace the study of jazz when we recall earlier comments from a 1921 *Ladies Home Journal* article entitled "Unspeakable Jazz Must Go!"? Those upstanding citizens who contributed to this series of articles claimed that "Jazz is worse than the saloon. . . . It affects our young people especially. It is degrading. It lowers all moral standards. . . . It leads to undesirable things. The lower nature is stirred up as a prelude to unchaperoned adventure. The road to hell is too often paved with jazz steps."[6] This article, which now seems humorous and a bit absurd, could very well have been written in the 1960s as a reaction to rock and roll.

I do believe that it is safe to say that most of these attitudes are now behind us, and The University of Texas sponsorship of this symposium is proof of a growing recognition of the importance of jazz studies in an academic curriculum. Indeed, the October 1993 issue of *Jazz Times* includes a special feature

[3]"New York Jazz Stinks Claims Coast Promoter," *Down Beat*, August 15, 1945, p. 2.

[4]Don Haynes, "Diggin' the Discs," *Down Beat*, December 15, 1945, p. 8.

[5]Don Haynes, "Diggin' the Discs," *Down Beat*, April 22, 1946, p. 15.

[6]John R. McMahon, "Unspeakable Jazz Must Go! It is Worse than Saloon and Scarlet Vice, Professional Dance Experts—Only a Few Cities are Curbing Evil," *Ladies Home Journal*, December 1921, p. 34.

on jazz education, and the journal's directory includes no fewer than 145 schools posting jazz curricula. For that matter, The University of Texas at Austin now offers a Jazz Emphasis option for Bachelor of Music candidates and is one of a limited number of schools in the nation offering a Jazz Concentration at the Doctoral level. The jazz curriculum at the University presently includes courses in jazz theory, improvisation, history, appreciation, analysis, arranging, composition, piano, and of course participation in various small and large ensembles. The recent *Jazz Times* issue also provides comments from several jazz artists who now enjoy giving something back to their art by providing master classes, performances, and clinics at schools. While some contemporary artists express concern about the dangers of training clones and teaching dogmas rather than creativity and originality, most agree that providing jazz instruction in schools is an important step and one which they regret was unavailable to many of them. Jazz saxophonist Dave Liebman noted in his comments to *Jazz Times* about jazz education that "the ideal situation is the balance between the street and the classroom."[7] Duke Ellington said many years ago that "today you need the conservatory, with an ear to what's happening in the street."[8] For that matter, Paul Whiteman suggested in his 1923 book *Jazz* that jazz and related American musics would some day be taught in institutions of higher learning.

It may seem ironic that Bebop, a jazz style which was comparatively short lived, highly criticized, and controversial, would become the foundation on which nearly all young players are instructed and the subject of this symposium sponsored by one of America's leading research institutions. But as we train the musicians of tomorrow, it is important for them to learn about the past. They can only know where to go if they are aware of where they have come from. Paul Whiteman and Duke Ellington may be considered strange bedfellows, but their common prediction about jazz in the schools is coming true and we at the University of Texas are pleased to be part of their prophecy.

Richard Lawn, Chair
Director of Jazz Studies
Department of Music
The University of Texas at Austin

[7]Dave Liebman, "Jazz Education Directory," *Jazz Times*, October 23, 1993, p. 46.
[8]Ken Rattenbury, *Duke Ellington Jazz Composer* (New Haven: Yale University Press, 1990), p. 43.

JAZZ
HISTORY IS MADE
ON
DIAL
RECORDS

DIZZY GILLESPIE		HOWARD McGHEE	
DIAL 1001	DYNAMO	DIAL 1010	UP IN DODO'S ROOM
	'ROUND ABOUT MIDNIGHT		HIGH WIND IN HOLLYWOOD
DIAL 1005	DIGGIN' DIZ	DIAL 1011	DIALATED PUPILS
	TRUMPET AT TEMPO (McGhee)		MIDNIGHT AT MINTON'S

CHARLIE PARKER

DEXTER GORDON

DIAL 1002	ORNITHOLOGY	DIAL 1017	THE CHASE—Part One
	A NIGHT IN TUNISIA		THE CHASE—Part Two
DIAL 1003	YARDBIRD SUITE		
	MOOSE THE MOOCHE		

BILL HARRIS

DIAL 1007	BEBOP	DIAL 1009	WOODCHOPPER'S HOLIDAY
	LOVER MAN		SOMEBODY LOVES ME (trombone solo)
DIAL 1012	RELAXIN' AT CAMARILLO		
	BLUE SERGE (Serge Chaloff)		
*DIAL 1014	BIRD'S NEST		
	DARK SHADOWS		

1947 BEBOP ALBUM

DIAL D-1 ALBUM—Book Cover by Wally Berman and including

1006	CURBSTONE SCUFFLE—Sonny Berman Octet
	BIRD LORE—Charlie Parker New Stars
1007	BEBOP—Howard McGhee Quintet
	LOVER MAN—alto solo, Charlie Parker
1008	CONFIRMATION—Dizzy Gillespie Jazzmen
	DIAL-OGUE—Ralph Burns-Serge Chaloff

ERROLL GARNER

*DIAL 1016	TRIO
	PASTEL

CONTEMPORARY AMERICAN MUSIC

Publicity flyer for Ross Russell's Dial Records, with Dizzy Gillespie and Howard McGhee pictured above and some of the label's albums listed below. *HRHRC Ross Russell Collection.*

Symposium Keynote Address

Charlie Parker—?

I asked this question of many people, more than 150 while researching the biography of Charlie Parker, *Bird Lives!* I asked it of the late Russell Procope one evening in 1969 in San Diego when the Duke Ellington Orchestra had finished a concert at a local church. "Bird—!" Procope said and thought a moment and went on, "A Charlie Parker comes along once every hundred years. That's all I can tell you."

Procope had been with Duke for ten years, the pivot man in a reed section that included Barney Bigard, Johnny Hodges, and Ben Webster. Before that he had been with Jelly Roll Morton, Benny Carter, Chick Webb, Fletcher Henderson, Tiny Bradshaw, and Teddy Hill, a journeyman reed player sought after by band leaders for more than forty years and a keen student of jazz style.

Only one other musician, Louis Armstrong, brought such lasting changes to the way of playing jazz. Charlie Parker revised the 32-bar Tin Pan Alley format that served as the framework for jazz improvisation. He revised the riff. He charted a new path through the blues progression. He introduced a new concept of time. And he defined a new sound for all of the instruments of jazz. The problem he did not solve was the one of harmonic construction. That remained much as it had been when he appeared at the beginning of the 1940s. After Bird, jazz style became fragmented and went off in many directions—notably those of Ornette Coleman, Eric Dolphy, the Ayler Brothers, Cecil Taylor, and John Coltrane. It might not be much to say that the Golden Era of American Jazz music began with Louis Armstrong and ended when Bird died in 1955 at the age of 34 on the sofa in the New York apartment of a Rothschild baroness.

This Symposium proposes to explore the genius of the musician who dominated jazz in the 1940s. As a groundwork for discussions to follow I would like to take time to trace the development of formal jazz criticism. Many may be astonished to learn that until the middle of the 1930s there existed no history of Afro-American music, no work of formal criticism, no discography,

17

no trade paper, no jazz review, and no course of jazz history or jazz appreciation at any university.

Here are a few dates. The first book to deal with jazz as a serious art was *Le Jazz Hot* by Hugues Panassié which appeared in 1934. About this time Max Harrison began writing jazz pieces for *The Times* of London and in 1935 Charles Delaunay launched *Jazz Hot*, one of the first jazz reviews. *Orkester Journalen* in Sweden began publication in 1936. Delaunay's *Hot Discography*, the indispensable handbook for "collecting hot," also appeared in 1936. Like so much in American culture, the lead came from Europe.

By 1936 the jazz renaissance in America was history, unfortunately unwritten and unresearched and the great bands of the Roaring Twenties had sunk without a trace, done in by the Great Depression. It was in this period that Jelly Roll Morton recorded 56 sides for Victor with the Red Hot Peppers and Louis Armstrong recorded 63 sides with the Hot Five and Hot Seven for the Okeh label, six hours altogether, a body of music comparable in its own context to the works of Bach and Mozart. These are the roots.

That we are able to piece together a meaningful picture of early events is due to the existence of the phonograph record and those who began collecting them. Collecting led to listing band personnels, identification of soloists, classification of information, and eventually discography. In the early 1930s Hot Clubs began to appear on university campuses, especially at Ivy League schools. I belonged to one at UCLA. There were four of us, regarded as lunatics by other students. We were convinced that we had discovered a wonderful and neglected art growing up like a weed at America's back doorstep. These hot collecting clubs were kept in contact by a remarkable man with the same name as myself, William Russell, now attached to Tulane University. Bill had what must have been the most unusual job in America. He was a one-man band supplying music and sound effects for a Chinese puppet show called the Red Gate Players on tour in America in the 1930s. This work gave Bill a chance to visit junk shops and used furniture stores all over the country and amass the first important jazz record collection. He came once or twice a year and kept up our spirits and told us what to look for. The list began with Armstrong, Morton, and Bessie Smith. Bill was a partner in the United Hot Clubs of America, based in New York, an auction house which published a newsletter called the UHCA *Rag* and occasionally reissued such rarities as Armstrong's remarkable *Cornet Chop Suey*. Bill told us about *Le Jazz Hot*, which we ordered from overseas and read in French.

And what were the critical standards that existed at this time? They could be summed up as follows:

Jazz possessed three elements which made it unlike any other music in the world.

1) Jazz had a rhythmic vitality not found in European music and which was part of its African heritage. *It Don't Mean a Thing (If It Ain't Got That Swing)* according to the title of Duke Ellington's 1932 recording for Brunswick. More precisely, jazz was polyrhythmic, it had a pulse, it "swung."

2) Jazz had a unique sound ideal, a sound of its own and on all of the instruments, so that it was possible to identify the player. Each jazz musician of substance endowed his solos with a personal stamp by means of embou-chure, vibrato, attack, shake, decay, and other details that made it possible to distinguish between a trumpet solo by Louis Armstrong and one by Keppard, King Oliver, Jabbo Smith, Bubber Miley or Tommy Ladnier, and, in our own time, a solo played by Dizzy Gillespie from one by Fats Navarro, Clifford Brown or Roy Eldridge. If you couldn't make these distinctions you were new at the game of collecting hot. It added zest to the hobby and to finding such a prize as Wingy Mannone's Club Royale Orchestra on Vocalion white label with an electrifying solo by Frank Teschmacher.

3) Jazz was not a written music. That applied to arrangements. Jazz was improvised, often collectively. Jazz was the other side of the coin after European music.

These were the perceived standards. They were mine. And it has not been proven that these standards are not valid today.

Certainly they proved helpful in coming to terms with the music played at Billy Berg's in Hollywood on a December night in 1945 when bebop was heard for the first time on the West Coast. In the band, just arrived from New York, were Charlie Parker, Dizzy Gillespie, Milt Jackson, Lucky Thompson, Al Haig, Ray Brown, and Stan Levey. I went to the club that night with an advantage. Earlier that year I had opened a retail jazz record store called Tempo Music Shop. Our clientele developed along unexpected lines and the store became a hangout for young jazz musicians, people like Joe Albany, Dodo Marmarosa, Stan Getz, Dean Benedetti, and Zoot Sims. To please these misguided but well-meaning customers we half-heartedly ordered records on such East Coast labels as Comet, Guild, Continental, and Savoy. Tempo became a center for the new music and a check-in point for visiting musicians of the new persuasion. These were exciting times in Hollywood. The Boulevard swarmed with night clubs and cabarets, each with two live bands. One could hear such new voices as Howard McGhee, Teddy Edwards, Sonny Berman, Shorty Rogers, Wardell Gray, Erroll Garner, Albany, and Marmarosa. A club called The Jade Palace featured an unlikely battle of jazz between Howard McGhee's Beboppers and Kid Ory's New Orleans band. At Tempo Music Shop the shipments of new records were opened as soon as they arrived. Each record was played on a turntable built into the counter before it was sold. In this way I had constant exposure to such bebop classics as

Ross Russell's Tempo Music Shop in 1945. *HRHRC Ross Russell Collection.*

Groovin' High, Salt Peanuts, Shaw 'Nuff, and *Congo Blues*. To this was added coat pulling and patient indoctrination by young musicians who knew better than anyone else what was going on in jazz. Without this exposure I would never have understood the profound changes taking place in the 1940s and Dial would never have become a bebop-oriented label. It was a matter of luck. And of being at the right place at the right time.

Bebop set off a storm of hostile comment by established jazz musicians who should have known better. Louis Armstrong, then touring with a sextet that included Barney Bigard and Jack Teagarden, said the boppers were playing wrong chords. "Chinese music," Cab Calloway called it. "The boppers have set jazz back twenty years," came from Tommy Dorsey. The most important recording of the decade, *Now's the Time*, drew caustic reviews in the trade press. The reviewers said the musicians, Parker, Gillespie, and Roach, hadn't learned to play their instruments and were setting a bad example. Stravinsky's *Rite of Spring* received a similar reception in Paris twenty years earlier.

The social, economic, and political changes that accompanied and brought about the bebop revolution are complex and beyond the scope of the present address. It is time we had a look at the artist himself. What was Bird like? A musician as brilliant and a man as difficult as Bird, the jazzman who "comes along once every hundred years," is not likely to be described by anyone. In speaking to people who knew Bird the answers have as many facets as a diamond.

"Around Bird I had the feeling of being near an electro-magnetic field," John Lewis told me. "And that it is dangerous to get too close."

For Earl Hines he was a brilliant section man who learned new arrangements a single time through and was found asleep under the bandstand. He threw a new Selmer saxophone out of a hotel window. Urinated in the telephone booth of a Detroit night club. He was the terror of jam sessions. If he didn't like what another musician played or found it trite he would play the notes back, stand them on their head, and make them sound ridiculous. Lionel Hampton, no mean adversary, was put to flight in one such encounter.

At Billy Berg's he was erratic and undependable. That was the reason Lucky Thompson had been added to the front line. After hours Bird would jam at one of the clubs in Los Angeles' Central Avenue district, the West Coast Harlem. Then you heard what he could do, choruses piled on choruses. One night a customer named Woody Isbell brought Bird into Tempo Music Shop. Bird was glum and depressed. He found it impossible to make the kind of records he wanted. This chance meeting led to a two-year contract with Dial Records which I launched with the help of a loan from Marvin Freeman, an attorney who had been a member of the jazz record collectors group at UCLA when we were both students. The contract produced a total of 34 sides for the commercial three-minute ten-inch shellac record then in use, seven sessions

21

in all, four on the West Coast and three in New York, and ended with the AFM recording ban of 1948.

There were rehearsals for three of these sessions. At a rehearsal Bird was meticulous and demanding. At the rehearsal for the first Dial date, Joe Albany was reduced to tears by Bird's directives and had to be replaced by Dodo Marmarosa. At the rehearsal for the *Relaxin' at Camarillo* date that commemorated his release from that mental institution, Bird was supposed to furnish four originals; he showed up with one, scrawled on music paper in the cab on the way to the studio. When Howard McGhee tried to run it down the notation proved incorrect. In a fit of impatience Bird wadded up the music sheet, threw it on the floor and played the line so others could follow, and the session proceeded on that basis with excellent results. That to my knowledge is the only time I remember seeing a piece of staff paper with anything Bird had written and there may be no such artifact in existence. With Bird everything was heard, everything remembered and subject to instant recall.

There were no rehearsals necessary for the final three sessions in New York. By that time Bird had organized a quintet with sidemen of his own choosing, Miles Davis, Max Roach, Tommy Potter, and Duke Jordan, to my mind comparable to the famous Armstrong Hot Sevens with Earl Hines and Zutty Singleton. Recording the new quintet was straightforward. The group simply performed what was in their repertoire at the Three Deuces and other clubs on The Street. These sessions went quickly and yielded six sides each in less than the contract three hours.

The main thing was to have a state of the art studio and a top engineer. After making a costly mistake on the first date for Dial, one that would have included Dizzy, Bird, and Lester Young, who was a no-show, I took the greatest care to use the top studio and the top engineer. On the West Coast it was the C.P. MacGregor studio and Ben Jordan; in New York, WOR and Doug Hawkins. The engineer was instructed to cut everything, false starts, aborted and rejected takes and final cuts. Most of my troubles came from Miles Davis, Bird's choice for trumpet but slow to learn new material and given to clinkers and wrong notes. On *Night in Tunisia* Bird played a fantastic break leading into the main chorus and called for a playback. He said, "I'll never make that again." But Miles had goofed and it had to be done over and four more takes were necessary to get an acceptable cut.

The nightmarish *Lover Man* date made a few months later took place the afternoon before his breakdown and arrest for disturbing the peace in a Los Angeles hotel where he was taken following the session. This unpleasant incident led to his being confined in the psychopathic ward of the county jail and eventually sentenced to confinement at Camarillo State Hospital, an institution for the mentally disturbed.

22

Photograph of Dial recording session in the C.P. MacGregor Studios, Hollywood, on 19 February 1947. Pictured from left to right are: Charlie Parker, Ross Russell, Hal Doc West (behind Russell), Earl Coleman, and Shifty Henry. *HRHRC Ross Russell Collection*.

Leading up to this disaster was a panic on Central Avenue and interruption of Bird's customary supply of narcotics. He had taken to drinking heavily, about a quart of whiskey a day, and was in no shape to record but insisted on doing so anyway. The only coherent performance on the session was *Lover Man*, released in limited quantities some time later, perhaps inadvisedly.

If you listen to the Parker discography on Dial, now reissued by Spotlite Records of England with all of the extant takes of the original sessions, you will hear a different Bird on every one of the sessions. He was vigorous and at the full cry of his powers on *Ornithology*, a gasping very sick man on *Lover Man*. For the *Camarillo* session he was found asleep naked in a rooming house bathtub by Howard McGhee an hour after the session was supposed to start and rushed to the studio, and played with the greatest vigor and originality. There is still a different Bird on *Cool Blues*, made a short time after his release from the state hospital. Bird was then in the best health of his life, dried out, well fed, well rested, off drugs and alcohol, and this is the Bird that might have made hundreds of records. His blues line accompanied by Erroll Garner's buoyant piano is one of my favorites of all he left us.

For the first session back in New York that fall, Bird showed up at the studio disheveled and drawn, in a rumpled suit, needing money and desperate for a fix. The session had to be delayed an hour while cash was raised and a messenger sent to Harlem to find his customary supplier. When the heroin arrived Bird shot himself up in the men's room. An evil omen for a recording session? On the contrary. Within thirty minutes he was all smoothed out and recorded one of his greatest ballads, *Embraceable You*, and the up-tempo flagwaver he had promised me, *The Hymn*, which says "Get lost!" to every other saxophone player in the business. A week later, in the same studio, with the same engineer and the same quintet from The Deuces, suffering from no physical problems, Bird cut six more sides, among them *My Old Flame* and *Klact-oveeseds-tene*, which might have been called "The Shape of Things to Come," a conundrum for every jazz musician who followed.

By his own account Bird was self-taught. When he set out he knew by ear three pieces of music, the blues, *I Got Rhythm*, and *Cherokee*. Bird started out in the natural key of the old saxophone his mother had bought for him. Proceeding half a tone at a time he worked his way back to the starting point, and when he could play each of the three pieces he knew in all twelve of the steps, he felt that he was ready. This is the way he mastered the system of harmony that had come down from Bach and the European masters. And in this way he became a modally-oriented musician and familiar with keys never used in jazz.

Bird went to high school in Kansas City for three years and wound up a freshman. He was addicted to hard drugs in his teens, and probably never freed himself from the habit. Unlike most drug users, he drank, sometimes heavily, as he had during the panic in Los Angeles in 1946 before the *Lover Man* date. Unlike most drug users, he had a voracious appetite. On occasion he ordered two meals at a sitting, consuming each, course by course, from soup to dessert and back to soup the second time around. He was a sexual athlete who sometimes locked himself into a hotel suite with two or three women. By the end of the 1940s he had played his best music. He was a middle-aged man at thirty, beset with stomach ulcers and a heart condition.

Bird made a lot of money, perhaps three hundred thousand dollars in a time when taxes and inflation were low, and that was a great deal. He could have made a lot more. Most of the money went for drugs. He was always broke. He told another musician, pointing to the needle marks on his forearm, "This is my Cadillac. This is my wardrobe with a mess of suits in it. This is my retirement home. This is my bank account."

In 1937 and quite by chance I had an opportunity to hear veterans of the Golden Era of jazz. Because his name was the same as my own and we had become friendly, a band leader named Luis Russell invited me to accompany his orchestra on a week's tour of one-nighters in Northern California. This was the Luis Russell Orchestra of that period and its sections included Zutty Singleton, Pops Foster, the de Paris brothers, J.C. Higginbotham, and Red Allen. The band was fronted by Louis Armstrong himself.

Louis was no longer the trail-blazing musician of Hot Five days. He had become a sustained high C virtuoso but his playing still had an electric quality and the vocals were as good as ever. Years later the opportunity to work closely with Charlie Parker completed a privileged involvement with Afro-American music. For me those two figures loom largest in the history of that remarkable art which had its origins in Africa and was possible only in America where two streams of musical culture collided and merged. Armstrong and Parker were the great innovators of jazz. We must be grateful for the phonograph record and those pioneers who began collecting them before there were discographies or books about jazz or courses in jazz history or jazz appreciation. In addition to the commercial recordings, all of them originally intended for ten inch shellacs with their three minute time limitation, additional material is coming to us in the form of air checks and amateur recordings made in odd venues. These are being cleaned up by state of the art engineering techniques and offered to the public. There are more of these to come, closely held in private stashes in various parts of the world and by various people, all part of the legacy of the musician Russell Procope said comes along once every hundred years.

Exhibition poster designed by Martha Dillon, University Publications, 1992.

The Bebop Revolution in Words and Music: An Exhibition

CURATED BY DELL HOLLINGSWORTH AND GEORGE LEAKE

On display from 20 April through 18 September 1992 , "The Bebop Revolution in Words and Music" was an exhibition mounted by the Harry Ransom Humanities Research Center to showcase the wealth of jazz-related materials in its archive of author and record producer Ross Russell. One of the exhibition's primary goals was to explore the connections between jazz and modern American literature, seeking in the process to create among students, scholars, and the community at large a greater awareness of the Ransom Center's significant holdings in the area of African-American literature and music.

In order to achieve both a sound and visual presentation, tapes of jazz performances and interviews with musicians and critics were played continuously in the reception area of the Leeds Gallery in The University of Texas at Austin's Flawn Academic Center. The official opening of the exhibition on April 22nd featured a live performance by Jamad, a local combo, and the Ransom Center also sponsored another local group, the Martin Banks Quartet, in a gallery concert in July. Throughout the summer, the Center screened a series of videos ranging from jazz and blues documentaries to filmed readings by poets influenced by jazz. The exhibit proper consisted of nine flat cases and eight wall cases, each of the latter provided with a didactic panel providing a general historical overview of the period covered by the materials on display. The texts from these didactic panels are reproduced below and each is followed by sample labels from the more than 400 items originally on exhibit.

The roots of jazz originated in the music of Africans, whose traditions were oral rather than literate. When Africans were brought to America as slaves, their masters often denied to them the practice of important elements of their culture—the use of their native tongue, the playing of their indigenous instruments (particularly the drum), and their religious rituals. However, these Africans did preserve a number of their essentially native traditions. Spirituals, shouts, and trance states all became a part of the Christian church services in which slaves found a source of solace; work songs and field hollers lightened back-breaking work, gave vent to emotions, and reinforced the sense of community. The call-and-response form found in all these types of songs stems directly from African music (which is evident today in the songs of South Africa's Ladysmith Black Mambazo). Other essential musical features transplanted intact to America were a preference for syncopations and complex polyrhythms, the use of non-Western scales and flexible pitch (blue notes), the instrumental imitation of speech, a highly personal approach to timbre (the tonal "color" of a voice or instrument), and the vital role of improvisation. Gradually these elements blended with European musical traditions, to which the slaves were introduced in the South.

The Emancipation, Civil War, and Reconstruction made promises of freedom and social equality to blacks, but these promises were not delivered. Most former slaves remained on farms in the South as sharecroppers. From the dashed hopes of the Reconstruction era came the birth of the blues as we know it. However, with time there were some economic improvements for African Americans, allowing more freedom to those who wished to travel and the wherewithal to acquire musical instruments. Many became professional musicians and entertainers, particularly in New Orleans, which had a very active musical life and a long tradition of African-American participation in musical events. By the latter part of the nineteenth century there was a large body of black musicians in New Orleans who were familiar with a variety of musical genres—the blues (directly descended from work songs and field hollers), rags, marches, popular songs, European dances (such as the quadrille), and themes from overtures and operas. From the convergence of these various styles and the "Africanization" of their interpretation, jazz was born.

By the beginning of the twentieth century, African Americans had begun a mass migration to large industrialized centers such as Chicago, Philadelphia, and New York. With every wave of black immigrants came musicians playing closer to the roots of jazz and blues. Arriving along with other musicians was the great Louis Armstrong, who would become jazz ambassador to the world at large. The development of recording technology suddenly made this regional improvised music available to listeners throughout America and Europe, and jazz took the world by storm. The 1920s saw a period of deepening interest in black music and culture, especially in Europe, but in America as well. At the same time, white dance bands began to offer a commercialized, watered-down style of jazz that nonetheless helped to popularize this important American music.

*   *   *

W.C. Handy, trumpeter, composer, and bandleader, played a key role in bringing the blues to the attention of the general public. One of his first publications, *St. Louis Blues*, would become one of the most widely performed American songs in history.

Photograph of W.C. Handy by Carl Van Vechten, 17 July 1941. *HRHRC Robert Downing Collection.*

Photograph of Bessie Smith by Carl Van Vechten, 3 February 1936. *HRHRC Robert Downing Collection*. Reproduced by permission of the Carl Van Vechten Estate, Joseph Solomon Executor.

W.C. Handy. *St. Louis Blues, Featured in Lew Leslie's "Blackbirds" of 1928.* New York: Handy Bros. Music Co., copyright 1914. Ross Russell Collection.

W.C. Handy. *St. Louis Blues (lyrics).* Typewritten manuscript, signed and dated, January 1, 1942.

W.C. Handy. *Blues: An Anthology.* Illustrations by Miguel Covarrubias. New York: Boni, 1926. Signed presentation copy from Miguel Covarrubias to Alfred Knopf, with an original drawing of a saxophone player opposite title page.

Portrait photographs, by Carl Van Vechten, of W.C. Handy holding a copy of his blues anthology (1932), and with his trumpet (1941). Robert Downing Collection.

In February of 1936 music critic and photographer Carl Van Vechten took a series of photographs of legendary blues singer Bessie Smith. In a memorial issue of *Jazz Record* he writes, "I got nearer to her real personality than I ever had before and the photographs, perhaps, are the only adequate record of her true appearance and manner that exist."

Portrait photograph of Bessie Smith, by Carl Van Vechten, February 3, 1936. Robert Downing Collection.

Carl Van Vechten. "Memories of Bessie Smith." In *Jazz Record,* no. 58, September 1947. Memorial issue devoted to Bessie Smith.

KANSAS CITY: JAZZ CENTER IN THE SOUTHWEST

Just as the Emancipation had promised social equality for blacks, the bright decade of the 1920s offered the prospect of a greater acceptance of black culture in white American society. But the same dashed hopes were to follow. The Depression years of the 1930s affected the masses of blacks in America more than any other group. Most had little education or job skills and many had pulled up roots during the previous decades to take menial jobs in the industrialized North. Black musicians were particularly hard hit by the Depression. Theaters, nightclubs, and dance halls were folding all over the country, and the few studio jobs available were usually given to white musicians. Great instrumentalists were forced to seek the most demeaning work. During the 1930s, however, there was one vibrant African-American music scene: Kansas City.

Musicians from Denver to New Orleans were drawn to Kansas City, which boasted several hundred hopping nightclubs serving up food and liquor, despite Prohibition. As a mecca for jazz, blues, and early rhythm & blues artists in the Southwest, Kansas City offered at least thirty of these clubs—and sometimes more—that featured jazz nightly. The city was run by political boss and gangster Tom Pendergast, and the nightclubs were fronts for gambling operations, bootleggers, and drug smugglers. The police department kept away from the nightclub scene, and thus a haven was provided for the best musicians from Texas, Oklahoma, Arkansas, and other nearby states who came to land gigs, refine their techniques, and learn new regional styles. The Count Basie Orchestra, Lester Young, Ben Webster, Big Joe Turner, Mary Lou Williams, Pete Johnson, Jay McShann, Jimmy Rushing, and Charlie Parker were all products of this environment.

Musicians continually challenged one another at all-night jam sessions where players would take turns soloing until they ran out of ideas. In one legendary session the best sax player of the day, Coleman Hawkins, was outplayed by three local players: Lester Young, Ben Webster, and Herschel Evans. As told in Ross Russell's biography of Charlie Parker, *Bird Lives,* it was "a session that wore on until late the next day and left Hawkins battered and defeated." It was in this highly competitive atmosphere that the young Parker learned the alto saxophone. Born in Kansas City in 1920, Bird grew up listening to the great jazz players during the golden days of the Pendergast regime, studying the styles of the masters, particularly Lester Young. After much work and several false starts, he finally landed a job with the Jay McShann Orchestra, destined to be the last of the great Kansas City bands. In January of 1942 the band was booked into the Savoy Ballroom in New York City, and thus Parker found his way to Harlem, where Bebop was taking shape.

❊   ❊   ❊

Hailed as the first jazz concert, *From Spirituals to Swing* featured recordings of African tribal music followed by performances of spirituals, blues, boogie-woogie, New Orleans jazz, and swing by such luminaries as Joe Turner, Meade "Lux" Lewis, Sidney Bechet and his New Orleans Feet Warmers, and the Count Basie Orchestra.

Concert program: *The New Masses Presents An Evening of American Negro Music: From Spirituals to Swing (Dedicated to Bessie Smith).* Carnegie Hall, New York, December 23, 1938. Ross Russell Collection.

Program for the 1938 Carnegie Hall concert, *From Spirituals to Swing (Dedicated to Bessie Smith)*.
HRHRC Ross Russell Collection.

Bop had its beginnings in after-hours jam sessions in Harlem, the most famous of which were those taking place at a club called Minton's Playhouse. Here circumstances brought together a group of musicians who had all been experimenting on their own with various new techniques that were to fuse and form the Bebop style, a style that would ultimately change the face of jazz, and the influence of which would continue to be felt fifty years later.

In 1941 ex-band leader Teddy Hill took over as manager at Henry Minton's failing nightclub and set up a house band consisting of drummer Kenny "Klook" Clarke, pianist Thelonious Monk, bassist Nick Fenton, and Joe Guy on trumpet. Dizzy Gillespie and Texas guitarist Charlie Christian soon became regulars. Word quickly spread that Minton's was a place to sit in, and within weeks the club was crowded nightly with musicians, famous and unknown alike, waiting for their turn to perform. Even such stars as Count Basie, Benny Goodman, and Duke Ellington came to play and to check out the competition.

During the late 1930s, Christian, Parker, and Gillespie, unbeknownst to one another, had all been making similar harmonic discoveries that would become characteristic of Bebop: the frequent use of ninth, eleventh, and thirteenth chords; the use of diminished seventh chords and the flatted fifth of the scale; and the technique of slipping briefly into a chord a half step away from the expected one. Already by 1937 Kenny Clarke had begun changing the standard way of drumming. In *Bird Lives* he recalls, "I took the main beat away from the bass drum and up to the top cymbal. I found I could get pitch and timbre variations up there, according to the way the stick struck the cymbal, and a pretty sound. The beat had a better flow. It was lighter and tastier. That left me free to use the bass drum, the tom-toms and snare for accents." In the fall of 1941, Clarke and Monk heard about an obscure saxophonist named Charlie Parker who was jamming at another popular night spot called Monroe's Uptown House, and they went to hear him. They were impressed; as Clarke remembers, "Bird was running the same way we were, but he was way ahead of us." Parker began jamming with the Minton's band, and the revolution was underway.

Further important characteristics of the new style were the regular use of substitute chords (a handy device at jam sessions for weeding out the inferior musicians); a greater reliance on the bass player to carry the main beat and propel the music forward; very fast tempos for up-beat numbers and quite slow tempos for ballads or blues (which nevertheless contained very fast passages); and a much greater use of off-the-beat phrasing and polyrhythms.

At first, dancers were bewildered, critics were angered, and many musicians were confused by it. Tommy Dorsey said "Bebop has set music back twenty years"; Louis Armstrong complained that the boppers were playing wrong chords; and a prominent New York critic said "Bebop sounds to me like a hardware store in an earthquake."

✿ ✿ ✿

Minton's Playhouse, a New York cabaret, was the site of after-hours jam sessions, where Dizzy Gillespie, Charlie Christian, Kenny Clarke, Thelonious Monk, Charlie Parker, and others began to develop the musical ideas that would form the bebop style. Novelist Ralph Ellison, who had known Charlie Christian in the 1930s in Oklahoma, frequented many of the jam sessions held at Minton's.

Dizzy Gillespie/Charley Christian, 1941. Esoteric Records, ESJ-4, ca. 1953. Recorded at Minton's Playhouse and Monroe's Uptown House, New York, in 1941. Ross Russell Collection.

Ralph Ellison. "Minton's." Typed manuscript with autograph corrections of an article which appeared in *Esquire,* January 1960.

Ralph Ellison. "Manners and Morals at Minton's, 1941: the Setting for a Revolution." From *Esquire,* January 1960.

BEBOP, BILLY BERG'S, AND DIAL

In 1943 and 1944 Charlie Parker and Dizzy Gillespie worked with two big bands which gave them a chance to continue developing their musical ideas and which furnished the new jazz with wider exposure: the Earl "Fatha" Hines Orchestra and the Billy Eckstine Orchestra, both of which also featured singer Sarah Vaughan. Then in 1944 Parker and Gillespie formed a quintet at the Three Deuces Club on 52nd Street in New York. Bebop began attracting more attention, both for the music itself and for the dress and manner of the key players, which were emulated by a whole group of young people known as "hipsters," sporting berets, dark glasses and goatees, and advocating drugs and free love.

At the same time, African Americans were beginning to agitate more for social change, and Bebop came to be linked with their growing sense, as a group, of pride in being black and with their rejection of the status quo. This has sometimes been interpreted in a negative way, but in Dizzy Gillespie's book *To Be, or Not . . . to Bop*, Al Fraser quizzes drummer Kenny Clarke on this topic:

> Fraser: "Bebop" was later publicized as a "fighting" word. Was this a "fighting" music?
> Clarke: No, no, by all means no!
> Gillespie: It was a love music.
> Clarke: Bebop was a label that certain journalists later gave it, but we never labeled the music. It was just modern music. . . .
> Fraser: Did this music have anything special to say to black people?
> Clarke: . . . There was a message in our music. Whatever you go into, go into it intelligently. As simple as that.

Later Gillespie makes the comment that "we didn't go out and make speeches or say, 'Let's play eight bars of protest.' We just played our music and let it go at that. The music proclaimed our identity; it made every statement we truly wanted to make."

The Parker/Gillespie quintet's success led to recording contracts, notably with Savoy. These recordings reached yet a wider audience and had a profound impact on young jazz musicians. Late in 1945 the quintet was booked into Billy Berg's in Los Angeles; the engagement was not particularly successful with the general public, but local musicians were overwhelmed. Pianist Hampton Hawes relates in *Bird Lives* that he dated his own musical awakening from the quintet's opening night. "Bird played an eight-bar channel on 'Salt Peanuts' that was so strong, so revealing, that I was molded on the spot, like a piece of clay, stamped out. Bird never once in his lifetime played a single bar of bullshit." Other lives were changed that night, among them Ross Russell's. Russell, proprietor of the Tempo Music Shop and founder of Dial Records, heard Bebop live and met Charlie Parker for the first time. Russell was to become Parker's friend, record producer, and later, biographer; he was also to become one of the most tireless and enthusiastic promoters of Bebop.

¤　¤　¤

After having signed an exclusive recording contract with Dial Records, Charlie Parker lost no time in signing another contract that turned over half of his royalties to Emery Byrd, his heroin dealer. Parker's problems with heroin and alcohol led to his being arrested and placed in a psychopathic ward and later transferred to the Camarillo State Hospital. Russell's unending difficulties in dealing with Parker are detailed in his letter to Chan Richardson, dancer and ex-model who became Parker's common-law wife.

Autograph contract between Charlie Parker and Dial Records, February 26, 1946, signed by Parker and Ross Russell. Ross Russell Collection.

Autograph contract between Charlie Parker and Emery Byrd, April 3, 1946, signed by Parker and Byrd. Ross Russell Collection.

Autograph letter signed, from Charlie Parker (during his confinement at Camarillo State Hospital) to Ross Russell, December 1, 1946. Ross Russell Collection.

Typed carbon copy letter from Ross Russell to Chan Richardson, February 1, 1947. Ross Russell Collection.

DIAL RECORDS

Ross Russell's Dial Records was extremely influential in promoting and increasing national and international awareness of the new jazz. Many of the enduring classics of the Bebop era, and in particular many of Charlie Parker's finest efforts, were recorded for Dial under Russell's supervision. Russell believed strongly, as did Teddy Reig of Savoy, that jazz musicians should be given free rein as to choice of musical material and fellow players. In *Bird Lives* he recalls that "in our experience good record sessions were put together well before the first musician arrived at the studio. There we endeavored to provide an emotional climate conducive to the creative process. This seemed to me the only logical way to record music so wholly dependent upon improvisation."

Russell, like Parker and a number of other young jazz musicians, also had a great interest in contemporary classical music and saw parallels between the two musics. Between 1949 and 1951, when larger record companies were showing very little interest in modern music, Russell accomplished a remarkable feat, producing a number of quality recordings of important works by such major composers as Schoenberg, Bartok, Berg, Webern, Stravinsky, and Messiaen. The Ross Russell archive at the Harry Ransom Humanities Research Center contains seventeen fascinating and revealing letters from Schoenberg as well as letters from Ernst Krenek and Rudolph Kolisch.

Dial also featured a catalog of ethnic music from Africa and the Caribbean.

❊   ❊   ❊

Photograph, by Ray Whitten, taken at a Dial recording session at the C.P. McGregor Studios, Los Angeles, 1947. Russell writes on the verso: "This happens to be a rare and interesting picture of a man just going into a state of morphine narcosis (Gordon, not Russell!)." Left to right: Melba Liston (trombone), Charlie Fox (piano), unidentified drummer, Ross Russell, and Dexter Gordon, tenor sax. Ross Russell Collection.

As the producer of some of the greatest bebop recording sessions, Russell was anxious that both serious jazz collectors and the general public understand the nature of the new music. In 1947 he issued a publicity flyer entitled *Bebop Jazz*. Dizzy Gillespie, pictured with Russell, is identified only as "Gabriel," due to "other contractual obligations." Ross Russell Collection.

Bird and Bebop After World War II

Through recordings on such record labels as Dial and Savoy, night club appearances at the Three Deuces in New York and Billy Berg's in Hollywood, radio shows, and coverage by printed media, Bebop's message spread across the country and reached its peak of popularity in the five years following World War II. These were Parker's most creative years.

Unfortunately, these were also times of personal upheaval for Parker. Once he went to the West Coast, he began having problems with his heroin addiction. During the trip to California in late 1945 and his appearance at Billy Berg's, Parker began to suffer withdrawal symptoms from heroin. Once in Los Angeles, he had trouble "scoring junk," and at times ended up using inferior heroin. According to Ross Russell, Parker tried to quit heroin by substituting alcohol, "which he tolerated poorly." Parker would show up late for Dial recording sessions and in no shape to play.

After one particularly disastrous recording session, the recording of *Lover Man* and other songs, his erratic behavior got the best of him. Heroin had been becoming harder to find, and as a result, Bird was suffering the torment of withdrawal and barely made it through the session. On *Lover Man*, he missed his entrance and played like an amateur, performing the tragedy of a pain-wracked soul that was sliding into oblivion. Sent to his hotel for rest, Parker caused a disturbance when he appeared naked in the lobby and, later, when he started a fire in his room by igniting his mattress. This incident led to Parker's arrest, after which he was transferred to the Psychopathic Ward of the county jail in East Los Angeles. Only Russell's intervention saved Parker from being committed to Patton, a "maximum-security institution intended for psychotics and the criminally insane" where shock therapy was imminent. Ultimately, Russell used local connections to have Parker transferred to Camarillo, the country club of mental institutions, which offered a rehabilitation program for alcoholics and addicts.

On a brighter note, after Parker's release from Camarillo, his recordings on Dial were more consistent. The masterful Charlie Parker Quintet began an extended engagement at the Three Deuces club in New York City, where Ross Russell had moved his recording operation. In *Bird Lives*, Russell writes of the Quintet:

> The new rhythm section was the best Charlie had used. Max Roach brought jazz drumming to a new level of artistry. The stick was a blur in his hand as he attacked the huge ride cymbal, filling the club with waves of airy sound. . . . Tommy Potter's bass pumped out its light, strong tone and Duke Jordan [on piano] interpolated his chords. Then Charlie and Miles Davis would spell out the ensemble line of a Bebop classic, or the newer pattern of one of the California tunes. . . . Charlie raced through *Koko* at impossible tempi. From up tunes he went to cool ones, *Now's the Time* and *Yardbird Suite*. He played long improvisations on slow ballads. He never played anything the same way twice. There were typical openings and closings, favorite turns, but no clichés. His playing came from such an excess of creativity and emotion that an extended improvisation of ten minutes seemed too short for his run of ideas.

✿ ✿ ✿

Russell scheduled three Dial recording sessions between October and December of 1947, with the aim of recording as many sides as possible before an AFM recording ban was to go into effect on January 1, 1948. Parker had a brand new Selmer alto saxophone for this session, and was accompanied by perhaps his strongest group of players: Miles Davis on trumpet, Max Roach on drums, Tommy Potter on bass, and Duke Jordan on piano, with the addition of virtuoso trombonist J.J. Johnson.

American Federation of Musicians contract, signed by Charlie Parker and Ross Russell, for Parker's last session with Dial, December 17, 1947. Ross Russell Collection.

Charlie Parker. Dial 207, ca. 1948. Ross Russell Collection.

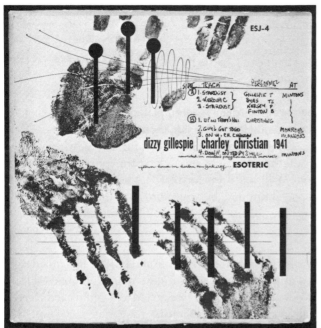

Record album covers: (above) *Dizzy Gillespie/Charley Christian, 1941*, from Esoteric Records, ca. 1953; (below) *Charlie Parker*, Dial Records 207, ca. 1948. *HRHRC Ross Russell Collection.*

The 1940s ended with one of Charlie Parker's triumphs: the opening of a jazz club named Birdland. Russell's *Bird Lives!* details this event:

> When the owners of Birdland contemplated the idea of naming the club after a practicing jazz musician, there had been no one else to consider. . . . Parker had dominated jazz since 1940, when he first appeared with the Jay McShann Orchestra, prompting veteran jazzman Cootie Williams to remark [that] "Louis [Armstrong] changed all the brass players around, but after Bird all of the instruments had to change—drums, piano, bass, trombones, trumpets, saxophones, everything."

Parker's fame had reached the shores of Europe and in 1949 he landed a gig at the International Paris Jazz Festival. The next year he embarked on a successful tour of Sweden. In Europe he was hailed as a genius and treated with the respect usually accorded classical musicians. Parker was tempted to move permanently to Europe, but he returned to the U.S. and reorganized the Quintet, only to have Red Rodney, his new trumpeter, arrested "for possession of narcotics and sentenced to five years in a federal penitentiary." Rodney's arrest frightened Parker and he started drinking again instead of taking heroin. By the early 1950s, Parker's health was beginning to fail, and he was rapidly gaining weight.

The last two years of his life were a mire of failed engagements; Parker was often late for gigs, his playing became repetitive, and his erratic behavior frequently caused embarrassing scenes. Birdland was the site of one of Parker's final performances, a botched affair where the drunk and disturbed Bud Powell got into a fight with Parker on stage. The enraged pianist smashed the keyboard with his elbow and walked off into the audience while Parker repeatedly yelled his name into the microphone.

After this incident, the ill and depressed Parker wandered the streets of New York. Complaining of ulcer pain, he was kindly taken in by a friend and jazz aficionado, the Baroness Pannonica de Koeningswarter, at her posh Manhattan apartment. The Baroness placed Parker under the care of her personal physician, who had determined that Parker was suffering from advanced cirrhosis of the liver and stomach ulcers aggravated by heavy drinking. Parker refused to go to the hospital, and the doctor finally agreed to let him stay at the Baroness's apartment. After several days, his condition seemed to improve, but on March 12, 1955, while laughing at a juggler appearing on the Tommy Dorsey show on television, Parker had a heart attack and simultaneously his stomach wall collapsed, perforated by the ulcers. The medical reports are vague on this matter, but the cause of Parker's death seems obvious. Years of hard living and abuse of his body finally caught up with the jazz musician. The Baroness's doctor estimated his age to be around 50 or 60, but Parker had died at the age of 34.

Chan, Parker's common-law wife, tried to arrange for Charlie to be buried in New York City, next to their daughter Pree, who had died two years earlier of pneumonia. Chan did not have a marriage license, so Doris Parker, Charlie's legal wife, had Charlie's body transported to Kansas City, against his stated wishes. He had grown to dislike Kansas City more with each visit, and when in 1954 a recording of his *Parker's Mood* with words added by rhythm & blues singer King Pleasure hit the top of the charts, Parker made Chan promise never to let him be buried in Kansas City. King Pleasure's lyrics were strangely prophetic:

> So long, everybody
> The time is coming, I must leave you. . .
> Don't hang your head when you see those six
> Pretty horses pullin' me.
> Put a twenty-dollar silver piece on my watch chain,
> Look at the smile on my face,
> And sing a little song,
> To let the world know,
> I'm really free.
> Don't cry for me,
> 'Cause I'm going to Kansas City.

❀   ❀   ❀

Three photographs by Frank Malcolm, of Charlie Parker at the Beehive, Chicago, February 1955 (about three weeks before Parker's death). Ross Russell Collection.

YARDBIRD I LOTUSLAND

Tredje artikeln i en serie
om Charlie Parkers äventyr
på amerikanska västkusten

av Ross Russell

MOOSE THE MOOCHE

Allt eftersom Charlie Parker–Dizzy Gillespies kvintett fortsatte sitt åtta veckors engagemang på Billy Berg's i slutet av 1945 och början av 1946 började de mer uppmärksamma bland gästerna märka en egendomlig oregelbundenhet i den lanserade altsaxofonistens uppträdande. Lyckade kvällar spelade Bird som en ängel, var glad och sorglös, tillgänglig, såg ut som sina tjugofem år och kom i tid. Men han hade också sina dåliga kvällar, som på fel sätt liknade de goda kvällarna.

De dåliga kvällarna kunde man komma till klubben och finna Parkers stol lögonenfallande tom. Av den orsaken, fick vi veta, hade Dizzy tagit med sig Milt Jackson från New York och när bandet kom till Kalifornien kallade han in Lucky Thompson för att försäkra sig om att förfoga över minst en extra stämma när den oundvikliga frånvaron skulle inträffa.

Ibland en dålig kväll vid tvåtiden strax före stängningsdags kunde en nästan oigenkännlig Charlie Parker drälla in och ändra estraden. Den ungdomlige, spänstige musiker man sett några kvällar tidigare stod inte att känna igen. Kläderna var i oordning och han såg tio, nej tjugo år äldre ut. När Charlie Parker hade en dålig kväll, var han osäker och sluten. Huden glänste av svett, ansiktet var fårat med stora ringar under ögonen. Rösten var skrovlig, ögonlocken tunga och pupillerna glasartade. Och så var han irriterad och lättretlig.

Andra kvällar kunde han komma i tid, men utan sin älskade franska Selmer-sax. Den hade han pantsatt. Ett annat instrument anskaffades och han plockade fram sitt munstycke med dess Rico-rör nr 5, vilket

han hade påtagliga svårigheter att anbringa på instrumentet. Och så spelade han som om ingenting hänt.

Dåliga kvällar, lyckade kvällar, lånat instrument eller egen Selmer spelade ingen roll. Han spelade alltid lika bra. Men visst fanns det ändå en viss skillnad i hans musik. Goda kvällar spelade han lyriskt och melodiskt, medan han dåliga kvällar lät tungsint, dyster och sprickfärdig av elakhet. Låtarna förvanskades, harmonierna försköts och rytmerna hackades sönder. Men allt utfört med utstuderat professionellt kunnande. Tonerna flödade ohämmat som från en outtömlig idéfontän. Förutom några få karaktäristiska favoritfraser var materialet alltid nytt. Han upprepade aldrig någonting, även om han spelade ett halvt dussin korus på en så enkel låt som tolvtaktersblues.

De övriga i bandet – Dizzy, Lucky Thompson, Milt Jackson, Ray Brown, Al Haig, Stan Levey – tog det hela med jämnmod. Deras spel följde ett utstakat mönster utan större toppar eller dalar. När Bird var indisponerad hade alla tempi en tendens att bli snabbare, ibland till gränsen av det musikaliskt möjliga. Goda kvällar kunde bandet spela mer avspänt och stämningen var lugnare. När han inte var där alls sjönk den musikaliska kvaliteten. Skillnaden blev inte särskilt stor, därför att det var ett mycket bra band, men det blev mindre auktoritet och geist i spelet.

Att få en förklaring på detta var inte lätt. Stan Levey stirrade, ryckte på axlarna och sa: »Bird är så där, bara.»

»Ibland är Bird lite sjuk», sa Dizzy, och tillade lakoniskt: »Att lära känna Bird, det kräver sin man».

Dean Benedetti blev lite mer mystisk: »När Bird uteblir – då har han inget budskap att ge».

Lou Gottlieb kom med en mer invecklad teori. »Efter att ha lyssnat flitigt på Charlie Parker, har jag kommit till den slutsatsen, att han troligen är det största musikaliska geniet i Amerika hittills. Det skulle vara oegentligt för en artist av Birds kaliber att fortsätta skapa, timme efter timme, kväll efter kväll, i en lokal vars huvudsakliga uppgift är att sälja whisky.»

Jag var troligen naivare än de flesta. Svaret jag sökte fick jag bland främmande människor på en främmande plats. En tisdag, bandets lediga kväll, hamnade jag i Los Angeles negerkvarter, som alltid hade fascinerat mig. Före kriget hade jag hört Fats Waller och Art Tatum spela där på en nattbysa med ett vitt miniatyrpiano. Ställets huvudnäring var att sälja illegal whisky och se till att balettbrudarna från Lincoln Theatre fick vad de ville ha. Jag förstod inte då, att vad som verkade vara »glamour» endast var en del av en i och för sig otrevlig livsstil nödvändiggjord genom segregationens maskineri.

Medlemmarna i Gillespies band, även de vita, Haig och Levey, bodde där på det främsta negerhotellet på Central Avenue, ett etablissemang som hade funnits i många år och som nu hette The Braddock. Jag kommer ihåg det från 1938, då jag hade en träff där för att följa med på busstur med Louis Armstrong, som Luis Russell hade ordnat åt mig.

Gillespies musiker disponerade ett flertal rum, mellan vilka var en ständig cirkulation av människor, musikkompisar, hipsters, bru-

Opening page of Ross Russell's serialized article, "Yardbird in Lotus Land," from the Swedish jazz magazine *Orkester Journalen* for February 1970. *HRHRC Ross Russell Collection.*

Ross Russell was one of the first writers on the Bebop style to display a knowledge of its essential elements. Russell was first inspired by Louis Armstrong, Duke Ellington, and other early jazz greats during the 1930s. In 1945, Russell opened the Tempo Music Shop in Hollywood and soon became a convert to the new style when young West Coast jazz musicians Joe Albany, Zoot Sims, Serge Chaloff, and others began coming into the shop to hear the latest Bebop recordings on such labels as Savoy, Comet, and Guild. In a letter to George Leake, Russell comments:

> It took 2-3 months of being bombarded with the new music, "hit over the head," before I stopped *hearing* the music and began *listening* to it, and listening to the young musicians to whom I was trying to sell Ellington and Armstrong. What finally did it was the opening at Billy Berg's in December 1945. Then I heard it in the round and understood that this was the extension of jazz music that began with Oliver, Morton, and Louis in New Orleans and Chicago.

As a contributor to many jazz publications, Russell focused his writings on the elements of Bebop. His series of articles on Bebop instrumental styles for *The Record Changer* was one of the first serious works of criticism on the new music and was informed by Russell's interview with Bebop drummer Denzil Best. Russell's series "Yardbird in Lotus Land" appeared in installments in the Swedish periodical *Orkester Journalen,* and was mostly based on Russell's own recollections of his years as Parker's manager on the West Coast, as Parker's record producer for Dial, and as an active member of the Bebop music scene in Los Angeles and New York. Also included is correspondence between Russell and Ralph Gleason, who was the editor of the short-lived but erudite *Jazz: a Quarterly of American Music,* and an article reprinted from Martin Williams's unsurpassed jazz journal, *Jazz Review.*

In the late 1950s, Russell began working on his jazz novel, *The Sound,* originally titled *The Hipsters.* This fictive work was loosely based on the lives of Charlie Parker and Fats Navarro. Russell's historical work, *Jazz Style in Kansas City and the Southwest,* was published in 1971. Finally, his biography, *Bird Lives! The High Life and Hard Times of Charlie "Yardbird" Parker,* was published in 1973. Russell's "Yardbird in Lotus Land" series provided a rough draft for *Bird Lives!,* which also incorporated a variety of other sources, including interviews with musicians such as Jay McShann, Jesse Price, Red Rodney, Hampton Hawes, and John Lewis.

Ross Russell. Typescript, with autograph corrections, of his novel, *The Sound* (Dutton, 1961). Ross Russell Collection.

Ross Russell. Typescript, with autograph corrections, of *Bird Lives! The High Life and Hard Times of Charlie (Yardbird) Parker* (Charterhouse, 1973). Ross Russell Collection.

Jazz and Modern American Literature

As early as the 1920s and '30s, jazz began to influence American literature. Langston Hughes, Gwendolyn Brooks, and William Carlos Williams were among the poets who attempted to capture jazz rhythms in their poems. Jazz also became a topic for fiction during this period, and some jazz criticism was produced by poets and novelists.

The "Beat Generation" writers of the 1950s, including Allen Ginsberg, Jack Kerouac, Lawrence Ferlinghetti, and Kenneth Rexroth, showed a pronounced influence from Bebop. Rexroth was a friend of Charlie Parker's and an observer of the jazz scene, and Parker would visit Rexroth on his trips to San Francisco. In *Bird Lives!*, Ross Russell quotes from some of Rexroth's views:

> Rexroth saw Charlie and Dylan Thomas as the two beleaguered, tragic giants of his time: "like pillars of Hercules, like two ruined Titans guarding the entrance to one of Dante's circles. . . . The heroes of the postwar generation, the great saxophonist Charlie Parker and Dylan Thomas. . . . As the years passed, I saw them each time in the light of an accelerated personal conflagration. . . . Both of them were overcome by the horror of the world in which they found themselves, because at last they could no longer overcome that world with the weapons of a purely lyrical art."

Besides using jazz as a theme, the Beat poets tried to infuse the spirit and rhythms of Bebop into their poetry. Lawrence Ferlinghetti and Charles Olson were advocates of a return to the oral rather than the printed tradition of poetry. They believed that there was an immediacy and musicality inherent in poetry read aloud as opposed to poetry read silently from the page. Not only did Beat poets try to work Bebop rhythms into their verse, but often writers such as Rexroth, Kerouac, Kenneth Patchen, and LeRoi Jones read along with live or recorded jazz performances before audiences in San Francisco, New York City, and elsewhere.

*   *   *

In a letter from 1951, Allen Ginsberg, the Beat Generation's most prominent poet, offers a stunning example of the use of jazz rhythm in his composition. Writing in his informal voice, Ginsberg shares with Neal Cassady different drafts of a poem which he changes from a more traditional meter to a jazzier, "downbeat" rhythm, rearranging the same words and images.

Allen Ginsberg. Typed letter signed, to Neal Cassady, March 13, 1951, page 3.

In an undated letter from the 1960s, LeRoi Jones speaks of his desire to write with the same "blocks of fire" that he hears in the jazz piano of Cecil Taylor, one of the leading proponents of the Free Jazz style, which emerged during this same period. Two other leaders of the Free Jazz movement, saxophonists John Coltrane and Ornette Coleman, both began their careers under the influence of the musical thinking of Charlie Parker.

LeRoi Jones. Typed letter, signed, to Gregory Corso, n.d., page 2.

MODERN AFRICAN-AMERICAN LITERATURE AND JAZZ

The emotional and cultural context of jazz is reflected in many works of African-American literature. Ralph Ellison's novel *Invisible Man* uses Louis Armstrong's lyric "What Did I Do / To Be So Black and Blue?" as a theme to introduce the narrative. A letter in the Ransom Center's Alfred A. Knopf Collection from James Baldwin to a Mr. Fuller, dated 17 February 1952, suggests that musicians rather than writers spoke for the African-American community, or that writers looked to musicians, particularly jazz musicians, as their cultural leaders. Hampton Hawes confirmed this view when he made a statement quoted in Russell's *Bird Lives!*:

> A jazz musician makes a total commitment, which is himself, his attitude, his sound, his story and the way he lives. Bird was like a god.

47

. . . He talked to us about things I wasn't to read until years later in books by Malcolm X and [Eldridge] Cleaver. I hear all that in his music. . . . Bird felt deeply about the black-white split. He was the first jazz musician I met who understood what was happening to his people. He couldn't come up with an answer. So he stayed high. His only outlet was his music.

Bebop and modern African-American literature both concerned themselves with the issue of an independent black cultural identity. LeRoi Jones (known as Amiri Baraka after 1967) was part of the Beat Generation until the early 1960s when he rejected the white literary avant-garde and established the Black Arts Movement, which espoused rejection of established Western literary forms, and promotion of black pride and separatism (culturally and politically).

Influenced by the Beat Generation's growing emphasis on the oral tradition in poetry, LeRoi Jones used black speech patterns and jazz rhythms in his poetry. As William J. Harris tells in his book *The Poetry and Poetics of Amiri Baraka*, "With the other members of the younger generation, Baraka inherited from the modernists the contention that the oral tradition is a principal source of poetry and the notion of verse as spoken, didactic, communicative, and political." This reliance on the oral tradition in modern literature parallels its role in jazz. In particular, horn players tried to recreate the sounds and phrasing of human speech on their instruments. In his book *Black Talk*, Ben Sidran remarks of his own experience: "The idea of considering Black music in America in light of an oral continuum evolved gradually, after years of listening to the music . . . and finally after listening to a Coltrane solo and hearing my own mother's voice." As Harris observes, John Coltrane was a major influence on Amiri Baraka:

> Because it emulates a transformation process typical of jazz revision, I call Baraka's method of transformation the *jazz aesthetic*, a procedure that uses jazz variations as paradigms for the conversion of white poetic and social ideas into black ones. . . . For Baraka, Coltrane epitomizes the *jazz aesthetic* process: he is the destroyer of Western forms. . . . By playing the notes backwards and upside down Coltrane was searching for a new non-Western self among the rubble of Western forms. . . . Baraka also wants to take weak Western forms, rip them asunder, and create something new out of the rubble. He transposes Coltrane's musical ideas to poetry, using them to turn white poetic forms backwards and upside down. This murderous impulse is behind all the forms of Baraka's aesthetic and art.

Photograph of LeRoi Jones from 1964. *HRHRC "New York Journal-American" Collection.*

This process of transformation is similar to a process described in Henry Louis Gates's *The Signifying Monkey*. "Signifying" basically involves the restatement of traditional forms, followed by their revision or reinterpretation. Gates explains that "There are so many examples of signifying in jazz that one could write a formal history of its development on this basis alone" and "improvisation, so fundamental to the very idea of jazz, is 'nothing more' than repetition and revision." Gates cites such examples as Jelly Roll Morton's version of *Maple Leaf Rag*, which signifies on Scott Joplin's song of the same title, Charlie Parker's revision of *April in Paris*, and John Coltrane's version of *My Favorite Things*.

Photograph by Benn Hall Associates of National Book Awards winners, dated 29 January 1953. Pictured from left to right are: Ralph Ellison, Archibald MacLeish, Frederick Lewis Allen (presenter), and Bernard De Voto. *HRHRC "New York Journal-American" Collection.*

Signifying is fundamental to African-American literature, and clearly LeRoi Jones signifies upon the literary traditions of the Beat Generation. The Black Arts Movement in turn was critiqued, through parody and other devices similar to the signifying process, by Ishmael Reed and Al Young. Gates discusses how Ralph Ellison in the title of his novel, *Invisible Man,* signifies on the titles of Richard Wright's novels, *Native Son* and *Black Boy.* Gates writes, "Ellison signifies upon Wright's distinctive version of naturalism with a complex rendering of modernism; Wright's re-acting protagonist, voiceless to the last, Ellison signifies upon with a nameless protagonist. Ellison's protagonist is nothing but voice, since it is he who shapes, edits, and narrates his own tale, thereby combining action with the representation of action and defining reality by its representation."

❊   ❊   ❊

The influence of bebop, blues, spirituals, folklore, and folk culture is all-pervasive in Ralph Ellison's *Invisible Man*, a modern tale of Everyman in an absurd universe, a tale based on the black experience.

Ralph Ellison. *Invisible Man*. Signed uncorrected proof.

Ralph Ellison. *Invisible Man*. New York: Random House, 1952.

Photograph, by Benn Hall Associates, of Frederick Lewis Allen presenting National Book Awards to Ralph Ellison, Archibald MacLeish, and Bernard De Voto, January 29, 1953. Left to right: Ellison, MacLeish, Allen, De Voto. From the *New York Journal-American* Archive.

Photograph of Charlie Parker at the C.P. MacGregor Studios, Hollywood, 1947, during one of his finest sessions, the *Cool Blues* date for Dial Records. *HRHRC Ross Russell Collection*.

Charlie Parker: An Overview

BY GARY GIDDINS

In 1945, just 20 years after Louis Armstrong jolted and essentially redefined jazz with his initial recordings as a bandleader, Charlie Parker made his recording debut as a leader and redefined jazz once again. A virtuoso alto saxophonist, Parker was the only musician after Armstrong to influence all of jazz and almost every aspect of American music—its instrumentalists and singers, composers and arrangers. By 1955, his innovations could be heard everywhere: in jazz, of course, but also in rock and roll, country music, film and television scores, and symphonic works. Parker altered the rhythmic and harmonic currents of music, and he produced a body of melodies—or more to the point, a way of melodic thinking—that became closely identified with the idea of jazz as a personal and intellectual modern music.

The new jazz was popularly known as *bebop,* a term of dubious origin often cited as the onomatopoeic equivalent of the two-note phrases (frequently the interval of a flatted fifth) that capped many of the melodic figures improvised by the modernists. The term may seem somewhat regrettable today, especially when a newspaper reviewer glibly pigeonholes a musician as "a bebopper," but, like the terms ragtime, jazz, and swing before it, bebop does indicate a fresh rhythmic quality. And it was the music's rhythmic quality that most distinguished it for the public. By the late '40s, the press and many musicians had established bebop, or bop, as a kind of cult, as though it were less a music than a life-style, complete with flashy clothing, dark glasses, berets, beards, secret handshakes, and an extensive lingo of jive talk.

Parker himself had little use for the word or the cult, with their implication that the new music was too esoteric for outsiders to comprehend. "It's just music," he said. "It's playing clean and looking for the pretty notes."[1] Still, unlike Armstrong, Parker created his music against a background of more than twenty years of impressive, documented jazz history, and he had to

---

[1] Mike Levin and John S. Wilson, "No Bop Roots in Jazz: Charlie Parker," *Down Beat* 16, no. 17 (September 9, 1949): 1.

53

confront not only neglect and the disparagement of a frequently hostile public, but sometimes the contempt of a jazz community reluctant to change its ways of doing or hearing things. Although the musical style he helped found soon supplanted the Swing Era with the Bop Era, Parker was celebrated chiefly by fellow musicians and a coterie of modern jazz enthusiasts. At the time of his death in 1955, at 34, Parker was arguably the most influential musician in the United States, but he never achieved the popular adulation enjoyed by Armstrong, Ellington, Basie, and other titans of the '30s and '40s.

PARKER'S BEGINNINGS

Charlie Parker was born in Kansas City, Kansas, on August 29, 1920. His father, an ex-vaudeville hoofer, left home before Charlie turned ten, and a few years later his mother leased a house on the other side of the Kaw River, in Kansas City, Missouri. The large house on Olive Street was a short walk from the dance halls and night clubs that made that city a mecca for jazz during the Depression. Parker's own immersion in music was hesitant at first. After hearing Rudy Vallee play alto sax on the radio, he asked his mother to buy him an alto, but he soon tired of the instrument and lent it to a friend. In high school, he played alto horn and then baritone horn in the school band. Encouraged by the school's bandmaster, Alonzo Lewis, he retrieved his alto sax and began to concentrate on music seriously.

By the time he was sixteen, Parker was playing in Kansas City dance halls, usually with pianist Lawrence Keys, who put together a band called the Deans of Swing, consisting mostly of former students of Alonzo Lewis. Parker dropped out of school and married—and he also began experimenting with the narcotics that were to plague his career and hasten his death. At first, he showed little inclination of having exceptional talent. On at least one occasion, he was hooted off the bandstand by other youngsters for playing in the wrong key. He took such humiliations stoically and resolved to master all the keys and ultimately win over his detractors.

Although he was not old enough to join the musicians' union, he found plenty of work in Kansas City and surrounding areas. For several months, he worked in the Ozarks with a group led by George E. Lee, for which he wrote numerous arrangements. When pianist Jay McShann heard him one night in 1937, he told Parker he sounded different from everyone else in Kansas City, and Parker explained that he had been "woodshedding" in the Ozarks, developing his style. Parker's unique approach reflected the influence of many of the musicians he heard in Kansas City and on records. Some were

54

local favorites and some were on tour with the big bands of Duke Ellington, Cab Calloway, Count Basie, and others. He is said to have learned how to double-time (phrasing at twice the stated tempo) and prepare saxophone reeds to get a hard, edgy sound from Buster "Prof" Smith, an altoist who took Parker under his wing and found him work. He was also enamored of the leading tenor saxophonists of the day, especially Lester Young and Chu Berry.

By 1938, the city fathers had begun to clamp down on crime and corruption in Kansas City, and as a side effect of this, many of the nightclubs closed. Parker found difficulty in getting work and, after an altercation with a cab driver that resulted in his arrest, he decided to leave town. He jumped a freight train to Chicago that fall, and the morning he arrived, Billy Eckstine, Budd Johnson, and few other musicians heard him at a place called the 65 Club. Parker borrowed an alto from a musician working at the club and, in the words of Eckstine, "I'm telling you he blew the hell off that thing!"[2] Within a week he took a bus to New York, where he worked for three months washing dishes at a Harlem hang-out called Jimmy's Chicken Shack so that he could hear the pianist appearing there, Art Tatum.

THE DEVELOPMENT OF PARKER'S STYLE

During his first visit to New York in 1939, Parker also became friendly with guitarist Bill "Biddy" Fleet, who instructed him in passing chords and harmonic theory. As he said later,

> I used to hang around with a guitarist named Biddy Fleet. We used to sit in the back room at Dan Wall's chili joint . . . and Biddy would run new chords. For instance, we'd find that you could play a relative major, using the right inversions, against a seventh chord, and we played around with flatted fifths.[3]

Together they would improvise on songs with challenging chord progressions—*Cherokee, Get Happy, All God's Chillun Got Rhythm*—and focus on the higher intervals of chords. Until that time, ninths, elevenths, and thirteenths were generally ignored in jazz improvisation. They were considered dissonant and obscure; the higher you played in the scale, the more likely you

[2]Billy Eckstine, quoted in *Bird: The Legend of Charlie Parker*, ed. Robert Reisner (New York: Citadel Press, 1962; rpt. Da Capo, 1985), p. 84.

[3]Leonard Feather, *Inside Bebop* (New York: J.J. Robbins, 1949), p. 12.

were to confuse the listener or, if you were improvising on a popular song, obscure the melody.

Parker also wanted, when improvising, to play through all of a tune's chord changes carefully, as Coleman Hawkins did, but as Lester Young did not. Often Parker and Fleet would practice before going to Monroe's Uptown House, where they participated in late night jam sessions. During one of those practice hours, Parker experienced the revelation that became the basis of his music. He described it this way:

> I remember one night before Monroe's I was jamming in a chili house on Seventh Avenue between 139th and 140th. It was December, 1939. Now I'd been getting bored with the stereotyped changes that were being used all the time at the time, and I kept thinking there's bound to be something else. I could hear it sometimes but I couldn't play it.
>
> Well, that night I was working over *Cherokee*, and, as I did, I found that by using the higher intervals of a chord as a melody line and backing them with appropriately related changes, I could play the thing I'd been hearing. I came alive.[4]

Shortly afterward, Parker received a telegram notifying him of his father's death, and he returned home to Kansas City. With renewed confidence, he began playing in the local big bands. He briefly toured with Harlan Leonard and His Rockets, until he was fired for habitual lateness. During that engagement, Parker met the band's pianist and arranger, Tadd Dameron, who shared many of his ideas about harmony and was to become a key figure in the bop movement. Duke Ellington, whose band passed through town, offered Parker a job, but he demurred, preferring to go on the road with his old friend Jay McShann.

It was at about this time that Parker acquired his nickname "Yardbird" or "Bird." According to McShann, the band was en route to a concert at the University of Nebraska when one of the cars hit a chicken. Parker jumped out, cradled it in his arms, and took it to their destination, where he had it cooked for dinner. Parker remained with McShann, on and off, for the next two and a half years, and made his first recordings with the band. These include some privately made transcriptions from a Wichita radio session that were released only in 1974, but which offer significant illumination of Parker's emerging style. Of particular interest are *Body and Soul* (Parker cites an eight-bar

[4]Nat Shapiro and Nat Hentoff, eds., *Hear Me Talkin' to Ya* (New York: Rinehart and Winston, 1955; rpt. Dover Publications, 1966), p. 354.

episode from Coleman Hawkins's celebrated solo on that piece); *Lady Be Good* (he pays tribute to Lester Young); a blues (later titled *Wichita Blues*) for which he scored a background from an old religious song he later used as *The Hymn*; and especially *Honeysuckle Rose*, in which, finally, we hear Parker's alto erupt in a fluent, melodic reverie that prefigures his maturity.

He also recorded with McShann for Decca Records, and those few sides had considerable effect on several younger musicians around the country. On *Hootie Blues* (Hootie was McShann's nickname), in addition to demonstrating his ease with the blues, he showed off his wit as an arranger by interpolating a phrase from *Donkey Serenade* as a background riff. On *The Jumpin' Blues*, his chorus begins with a characteristic phrase that was later expanded into the famous bop theme, *Ornithology*:[5]

The Alliance with Dizzy Gillespie

Because of a two-year ban on recordings initiated by the American Federation of Musicians, Parker was not to record again in a studio until 1945. In the interim, he had left the McShann band and joined first the Earl Hines orchestra, for which he played tenor saxophone, and then the Billy Eckstine Orchestra. In the Hines band, he associated with several young musicians who shared his interest in adventurous harmony and a new, more challenging form of jazz. Chief among them was Dizzy Gillespie, whom Parker later referred to as the other half of his heartbeat. They had first met in Kansas City when Gillespie passed through with Cab Calloway's band, but it was during the period with Hines that they really began to trade and develop ideas.

Private recordings made in a Chicago hotel room in 1943, and first released in 1986, capture Parker, on tenor, and Gillespie, accompanied by bassist Oscar Pettiford, exchanging solos on an extended version of *Sweet Georgia Brown*, and suggest that Gillespie was more at ease (on that occasion at least) with the new style than Parker, who depends on allusions to the saxophonists who influenced him. Gillespie, however, insists it was Parker who showed "how to get from one note to the next."[6] He argues that because of Parker's

[5]Thomas Owens, *Charlie Parker: Techniques of Improvisation*, Vol. 2 (Ann Arbor, MI: University Microfilms International, 1974), p. 22.
[6]Personal interview with Dizzy Gillespie, 1986.

innate ability to play blues, he was able to transcend experiments in harmony to produce a finished and convincing new way of playing.

Duke Ellington's renowned trumpet soloist Cootie Williams once observed that "every instrument in the band tried to copy Charlie Parker, and in the history of jazz there had never been one man who influenced all the instruments."[7] A similar claim could surely be made for Armstrong (Williams's own major influence), but for no one else.

By the time Parker had left the Eckstine band and returned to New York, where he appeared on 52nd Street with Gillespie, musicians of every stripe were paying close attention to him. Drummers Kenny Clarke and Max Roach shifted rhythmic accents from the skins to the cymbals, replacing the bass drum's thud-thud-thud with the lighter sound of the snare drum and the sibilant pulse of the ride cymbal. Oscar Pettiford, picking up where Ellington's bassist Jimmy Blanton left off, showed how the bass could provide more than the usual cycle of tonic notes. Bud Powell exemplified the new role of the pianist, paring down his accompaniment to a brisk, jagged series of chords, and soloing with the linearity of a wind instrument. Sarah Vaughan, who worked with Parker in the Hines and Eckstine bands, developed a virtuoso vocal style. Almost all of the best young wind players—including such influential men as trumpeters Fats Navarro and Miles Davis, tenor saxophonists Dexter Gordon and Stan Getz, trombonist J. J. Johnson, and even clarinetist Buddy DeFranco—emulated Parker's almost vibratoless, unmannered tonal production, his rhythmic and harmonic values, and his emphatically emotional melodic ideas, which transcended ground rhythms and chords and attempted to bring the listener into a more attentive and a deeper communion with the music.

In the 1940s, the years immediately following Kansas City's decline as a creative center for jazz, no community offered nearly as prestigious and challenging a home for the music than the strip of brownstones on New York's 52nd Street, between Fifth and Sixth Avenues. The Street, as it was known, was a banquet of small clubs, bars, and restaurants snuggled one against the other and spilling over with entertainment. The clubs dated back to Prohibition days and had always welcomed music.

Budd Johnson, a tireless activist for venturesome jazz, helped to get some of the modernists employed there. In 1944, with the recording ban over, he organized an important session for Coleman Hawkins that featured Gillespie, Pettiford, and Roach, and deputed Gillespie's widely noted piece, *Woody'n' You*. When those recordings were made, Parker was back in Kansas City,

---

[7]Interview with Cootie Williams conducted by Helen Dance, 1976, in Jazz Oral History Project, Institute of Jazz Studies, Rutgers University, pp. 256-57.

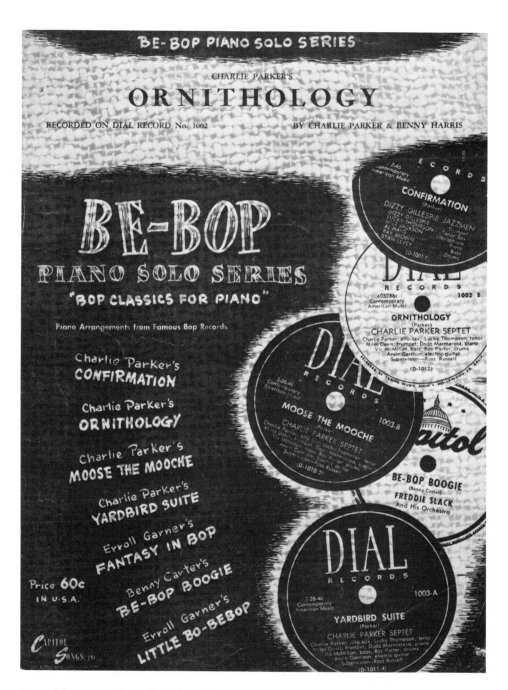

Cover of sheet music edition of Charlie Parker's *Ornithology* for piano (Capitol Songs, Inc., n.d.). *HRHRC Ross Russell Collection.*

Photograph of the Earl Hines Band from April 1943 in a performance at the Apollo Theatre, with Dizzy Gillespie pictured on the far left and Charlie Parker on the far right. *HRHRC Ross Russell Collection.*

having returned there after leaving Eckstine's band. A year later, however, Gillespie had his own band on The Street at the Three Deuces. His co-leader was Parker, and the rhythm section consisted of Al Haig on piano, Curly Russell on bass, and Stan Levey on drums.

With a seating capacity of about 125, the Deuces was usually packed, though many listeners admitted they did not understand the new music, with its often fast, barbed ensemble themes and flaring solos. Still, they found it different and compelling and they returned for more. The responsiveness between Parker and Gillespie was unlike anything in jazz since the early '20s, when King Oliver and Louis Armstrong crossed trumpets at Chicago's Lincoln Gardens. The way they enunciated theme statements was subtle and sure, and the "chase" choruses which usually consisted of four- or eight-bar exchanges by the horns and sometimes the drums were delivered at tremendous velocity, and were a kind of dazzling musical conversation.

THE FIRST RECORDINGS AND *KOKO*

An exceptional example of the Parker-Gillespie unison sound can be heard on *Shaw 'Nuff*, one of several stunning pieces recorded at a 1945 Gillespie session. The group included four out of five members of the Three Deuces band—the fifth member, Stan Levey, was replaced by Big Sid Catlett, a brilliant Swing Era drummer whose style adapted readily. The theme has three parts: an 8-bar rhythmic vamp, a 16-bar introductory theme, and the 32-bar main theme, which is loosely based on the harmonies of *I Got Rhythm* with the addition of numerous passing chords. Despite the velocity and rhythmic complexity of the theme, the trumpet and alto sax seem to breathe as one. This is especially notable on the slurred notes of the tune's roller-coaster bridge.

The performance is relatively straightforward. After the written material, Parker, Gillespie, and pianist Al Haig each improvise a full chorus. The record ends with the tripartite theme played in reverse order, from theme to vamp, providing an ironically symmetrical touch. Parker's solo is mature and authoritative, though his reliance on a series of scales during the bridge is more characteristic of his early playing than that which followed. (Incidentally, the Shaw of the piece's title was Billy Shaw, the booker-manager who helped Gillespie and Parker get work when few others showed faith in them. And the female Billie of Parker's blues, *Billie's Bounce*, was Shaw's wife.)

During 1945, Parker appeared on several record sessions as a sideman with musicians who were associated with earlier styles, including Tiny Grimes,

Clyde Hart, Sir Charles Thompson, and Red Norvo. Parker's playing is always commanding, but the general impression of the music suggests a transitional stage from swing to bop. Finally, on November 26, Parker was offered his own date by Savoy Records. Though strangely bedeviled from beginning to end, the recording session turned out to be seminal in jazz history.

Parker had been contracted to record two original blues and two variants on standard songs (*Cherokee* and *I Got Rhythm*). He hired a quintet that included Bud Powell and Miles Davis. When Powell could not make it, he recruited Argonne Thornton (aka Sadik Hakim), who was then too young to have a union card, and Gillespie, who doubled on piano and trumpet. (Davis found some of the music unfamiliar and difficult.) Parker composed most of the themes that morning, but when he started playing he was beset with technical problems and spent part of the session searching for new saxophone reeds. Still, he managed to record two F Major classic blues, *Billie's Bounce* and *Now's the Time*; extemporized memorably on the chords of *Embraceable You* (retitled *Meandering*); on the chords of *I Got Rhythm* for *Thriving on a Riff* (the piece was later called *Anthropology*) and *Warming Up a Riff*; and completed the session with the masterpiece, *Koko*, based on the *Cherokee* chords.

One reviewer at the time called the recordings "the sort of stuff that has thrown innumerable impressionable young musicians out of stride, that has harmed many of them irreparably."[8] Such comments, by no means unusual, underscored modern jazz's reputation as a revolutionary and even destructive music. It is not difficult to understand the original effect of *Koko*. Even now, decades later, unprepared listeners often respond to it as an explosion of sound, a mad scramble of notes—as listeners did in 1945. On repeated hearings, however, the logic and coherence of Parker's solo is revealed. *Koko* became the point of departure for jazz in the postwar era, having an effect that paralleled Armstrong's *West End Blues* in 1928. Armstrong's record began with a clarion cadenza and *Koko* began with an equivalent bang: an eight-bar unison theme of daunting authority, coupled with eight-bar arabesques improvised by Parker and Gillespie. Parker follows with two choruses of extraordinary originality:[9]

[8]Review, "Diggin' the Discs with Don," *Down Beat* 13, no. 9 (April 22, 1946): 15.
[9]Owens, pp. 211-227.

The tempo is brutally fast (♩ = 300-310), but despite the speed and the general impression of volatility, Parker colors his solo with ingenious conceits, such as the clanging riff in measures 5-8; the dramatic, arpeggiated figure in bars 33-34, slightly modulated in bars 37-38; the casual reference to *High Society*, or a phrase from a traditional New Orleans clarinet variation on that piece, at the outset of the second chorus (bars 1-2); the falling, chromatic arpeggios in the second bridge (bars 33-36) and the related follow-up triplets (bars 41-42); and the ebullient, breathless figure that ties the bridge to the final episode of the solo (bars 46-51).

Note, too, the extended rests, the unexpected places where phrases begin and end, and the range of the solo, which climbs to high G (bar 9 of the first chorus) and dips down to an E-flat below middle C (bar 13 of the second chorus). Parker's sound is fat and sensuous yet jagged and hard, quite unlike the cultivated approach of his great predecessors on alto, Johnny Hodges and Benny Carter.

A TRIP TO LOS ANGELES AND A PERSONAL CRISIS

Within weeks of the *Koko* session, Parker and Gillespie made their first trip to Los Angeles to play at Billy Berg's club on Sunset Strip. Many local musicians and radio jockeys dismissed their music as inscrutable, but musicians were soon converted and an audience for the new jazz grew quickly, turning Central Avenue, the city's black nightclub area, into a stomping ground for modern jazz. During that trip, Parker began recording for Ross Russell's Dial Records, an association that accounted for six important studio sessions between February 1946 and December 1947, in which we can trace his rise, fall, and resurrection during a troubled yet inspired period. In the first session, Parker produced four instant and enduring classics with a septet that included Miles Davis and tenor saxophonist Lucky Thompson: *Moose the Mooche*, a characteristic theme; *Yardbird Suite*, perhaps Parker's most lyrical composition, and one for which he also wrote a lyric (he called the vocal version *What Price Love?*); *Ornithology*, elaborated by trumpeter Benny Harris from a figure Parker had improvised on one of his first records with McShann; and Gillespie's *A Night in Tunisia*, which was much acclaimed for Parker's astounding four-bar saxophone break—a jumping-off point for his solo:[10]

---

[10]Ibid., p. 460.

This break, played in one breath, utterly confused the rhythm section at the recording date. The musicians had trouble counting the four bars and could not coordinate their reentry. After a couple of cues were missed, Miles Davis, who played trumpet on the session, agreed to count the bars and conduct. The break remains one of jazz's great virtuoso feats. It seems to burst against the bar lines. The highly original alto saxophonist Lee Konitz recently expressed amazement that Parker could have invented anything so complex yet perfectly timed.[11]

Perhaps Parker's most influential solo of the period was one recorded at a public concert in the Jazz at the Philharmonic series in March 1946, during a performance of *Lady Be Good*. Entering after a theme-statement solo by Arnold Ross, Parker plays two choruses that instantly change the character of the piece, altering a familiar Gershwin ballad into what sounds very much like the blues:[12]

[11]As reported by Martin Williams from a conversation with Lee Konitz, apparently held shortly before the great jazz critic's death in the spring of 1992.

[12]Owens, p. 435.

Charlie Parker and Dizzy Gillespie at Billy Berg's during Christmas week, 1945. *HRHRC Ross Russell Collection*.

Although Parker actually plays the first four notes of the original Gershwin *Lady Be Good* melody, he articulates them with such ardent command that the phrase is transfigured into a plea of far greater passion than anything the lyric could suggest. His opening salvo is sustained as he develops variations that are unmistakably *sui generis*. Virtually every aspect of his solo became part of the grammar of modern jazz, dissected and imitated by musicians all over the world.

At the second Dial session, in July, Parker had a mental breakdown triggered by his abuse of inferior-quality narcotics, and possibly the tensions caused by public attacks on his music. In any case, the crisis was cruelly captured by the microphones as Parker reeled around the studio. Parker considered the release of that recording humiliating, yet even here he commands our attention, climaxing awkward phrases with an emotionally devastating arpeggio at bar 24 of the first chorus. Frazzled and irrational, Parker was committed to the California State Hospital, where he was incarcerated for the next six months. He celebrated his release at another Dial session with an intricate, jaunty blues, *Relaxin' at Camarillo*, before returning to New York in apparent good health.

A RETURN TO NEW YORK

Parker's records during the next few years are remarkably consistent and they exerted incalculable influence. The press tended to harp on bebop's jargon and getups, which became emblematic of what was later tagged "the beat generation," many of whose leading poets, novelists, and painters apotheosized Parker. But musical life in postwar America had also changed radically, and Parker's imprint, though not his name, was ubiquitous. Big bands gave way to small groups, usually quintets and sextets, despite attempts by Gillespie, Woody Herman, and others to integrate bop into their orchestras. Modern jazz was associated less with dancing than intense listening. Rhythm sections grew leaner (rhythm guitar had all but disappeared) and "light" instruments, notably the clarinet, fell out of favor. Improvisors continued to focus on a song's chords rather than its melody, but now they were far more likely to superimpose their own themes in place of the original tunes. More significantly, the harmonies were increasingly broad. Chromaticism was standard; the use of bitonality, whole-tone and diminished scales, and even modality (introduced by George Russell in a piece for the Gillespie orchestra, *Cubana Be/Cubana Bop*) became common practice. Tempos grew extreme, very fast or very slow. The pulse of the music centered on sixteenth or eighth notes rather than swing's eighth and quarter notes.

EMBRACEABLE YOU

Two of Parker's greatest recordings exemplify his genius for enriching the standard material on which most jazz is based, pop songs and blues. At a 1947 Dial session, he recorded two thoroughly different takes of *Embraceable You*. The second take, though mesmerizing in its patterns of tension and release, is the more orthodox and its relationship to the original Gershwin theme is obvious. The supremely beautiful first take is also a variation on the theme, but this time Parker barely touches base with Gershwin.[13]

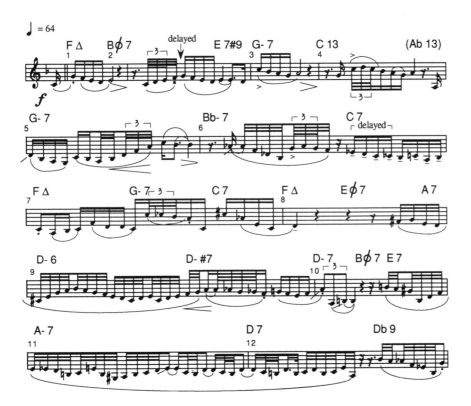

[13]Ibid., p. 330.

72

Like his *Bird of Paradise* (based on Jerome Kern's *All the Things You Are*, and recorded the same day), *Embraceable You* is so unmistakably a work of Parker's imagination that he might well have given the performance a title of his own. Indeed, had he done so, the source material, unlike that of *Bird of Paradise*, would not have been recognizable to the average listener.

Parker's earlier *Meandering* and his several subsequent improvisations on *Embraceable You* (including the superb uptempo *Quasimado*) show he was at ease with the song's harmonies. But the other performances have nothing to match the way he develops the Dial solo out of its opening six-note motif. The source of that unforgettable phrase, strangely enough, is a relatively banal pop song called *A Table in the Corner*, by Sam Coslow, best known for his scores to a few of Bing Crosby's earliest films. The song was recorded by several bandleaders in 1939, including Artie Shaw, whom Parker admired. Parker imposes the ditty's initial phrase and the first modulation as a melodic template on the Gershwin harmonies, ignoring Gershwin's melody entirely, and turning the almost ridiculous into the absolutely sublime. (The importance of Duke Jordan's piano introduction and accompaniment to the overall success of the recording can hardly be overstated.) Parker plays the opening motif five times in all, and variants on it appear throughout the solo. This is one of the slowest performances in jazz (less than ♩ = 65), and it is laced with 32nd notes. When he develops the six-note motif into a two-measure phrase (bars 6-7), imposing a triplet over an already rapid-fire figure, he runs out of breath. But not again; for the rest, his phrasing is so supple and relaxed and songful that when he winds down with a legato two-measure configuration (bars 27-28), only the listener is left breathless.

A Classic Slow Blues

The second example of Parker's ability to bring new life to overworked material is from a 1948 Savoy session and is one of his finest blues performances, *Parker's Mood*. Once again, there are two entirely different takes; both begin with a heraldic two-bar phrase that constitutes the only written material in the performances.[14]

The earlier take has a marvelous eccentric quality, as Parker slowly pokes his way through the most familiar of jazz terrains, a B-flat blues. Note the two sudden 32nd note arpeggios followed by a series of modulating triplets in bars 8-11 of his first chorus:[15]

By contrast, the later take, the one originally issued, has a relatively glossy perfection, as Parker brings together a lexicon of blues phrases, new and old, for a penetrating performance. He sounds as though he were pressing ahead with charismatic authority, as though he had no doubt about the direction in which the solo was going.[16]

[14]Ibid., p. 142.
[15]Ibid., p. 144-145.
[16]Ibid., p. 157-158.

75

He begins with four bars of tantalizingly standard blues phrases, though his slightly acrid tone and emphasis lends them startling immediacy. In the fifth measure, Parker introduces a series of repeated arpeggios, each leading with a C above middle C, in an insistent manner that is strongly reminiscent of Louis Armstrong, for example his climactic chorus on *West End Blues*. There is a conversational quality to the solo, as Parker moves from the upper register (note the little ascending figure at the beginning of the second chorus) to the lower register (the downward slurs in bars 5 and 6 of the second chorus). After a spare and worthy interlude by pianist John Lewis, Parker returns for a final chorus, which he closes on a major-second, before repeating the heraldic phrase with which the performance began.

Parker made so many notable recordings, it is difficult to choose among them. *Chasin' the Bird* and *Ah-Leu-Cha* stand out as the only pieces in which he wrote contrapuntal themes. *Kim* is an exceptional variation on *I Got Rhythm*, and *Buzzy*, *Cheryl*, *Blue Bird*, and *Barbados* are a few of his approaches to the blues. His solos on *Bird Gets the Worm*, *Crazeology* (*Little Benny*), *Klact-oveeseds-tene*, and *Klaunstance* are unrivaled examples of emotionally vital yet overwhelmingly brilliant inventions that take their structure but not their character from the harmonic contours of popular songs.

By the time most of these recordings were made, however, Parker's professional life, and that of most musicians, was changing. In New York, for example, the clubs along The Street welcomed Gillespie's 1946-47 big band, and welcomed Charlie Parker's 1947 quintet with Miles Davis. But within five years The Street was in trouble as a haven for jazz of any style; the audiences weren't there any more. New clubs sprang up over on Broadway to accommodate the modernists: The Royal Roost (which failed), Bop City (which failed), and finally Birdland, named in honor of Parker, which succeeded and lasted for a decade or so. But in midtown Manhattan, one club invariably replaced several. And Parker, because of his increasingly erratic conduct—years of addiction and riotous living were taking their toll—was banned from Birdland before his death.

In his pursuit of acceptance, Parker became involved with a string ensemble with which he recorded and toured, and which gained him greater popularity. However, most of the recorded arrangements were poor. In the '50s, he commissioned stronger arrangements from Jimmy Mundy, Gerry Mulligan, and George Russell, but these were never heard except informally at clubs and concerts. Still, at least one of the Parker with strings records qualifies as a masterpiece, *Just Friends*, for on it he allows the melody and simplicity of the orchestration to spur him to grand inventions.

Parker was intrigued by the music of many modern European composers, and it is said that had he lived he might have explored directions only hinted at in his music. He asked Edgard Varèse to take him as a student. The fact remains that when he died, in 1955, the musical community was still coming to grips with his accomplishments of the mid 1940s. No subsequent soloist to date has had a comparable effect on every aspect of jazz.

Charlie Parker with strings, at Birdland, spring 1950. *HRHRC Ross Russell Collection.*

Dial labels for recordings by the Charlie Parker Quintet with Miles Davis and the Sextet with J.J. Johnson. *HRHRC Ross Russell Collection*.

The Dial Recordings of Charlie Parker

BY EDWARD KOMARA

Charlie Parker (1920-1955) was the foremost jazz alto saxophonist from 1945 until his death, and every time Parker performed, he demonstrated his particular methods of tone production and melodic execution, which in turn shaped the jazz music of his day.[1] Together and separately, Parker and his close friend, trumpeter Dizzy Gillespie, devised original themes based on familiar songs, and they introduced new harmonies and musical phrases to jazz performing practices.[2] Parker displayed an especially musical wit, quoting melodies from other musical compositions, such as the beginning of Stravinsky's *Rite of Spring* played during a performance of *Cool Blues*.[3] Musicians of the 1940s and early '50s were attracted to Parker's new and daring music, and they took every opportunity to study it. But since Parker never wrote his solos on paper, study was possible only through his phonograph recordings, which could be played and replayed until motifs were identified and copied. The extent to which musicians studied Parker's records can be measured by bassist Charles Mingus's comment, after Parker's death, that "most of the soloists at Birdland had to wait for Parker's next record in order to find out what to play next. What will they do now?"[4]

Charlie Parker recorded for three firms: Savoy Records, from 1944 to 1948; Dial Records, from 1946 to 1947; and the Clef/Mercury/Verve labels owned by Norman Granz, from 1946 to 1954, mostly from 1948 onwards. Of the

---

[1] For an overview of Parker's life, times, and music, see Gary Giddins, *Celebrating Bird: The Triumph of Charlie Parker* (New York: Beech Tree Books, William Morrow, 1987).

[2] For Gillespie's own account of his contributions to jazz, see Dizzy Gillespie, with Al Fraser, *To Be or Not . . . To Bop* (Garden City, NY: 1979; London: W.H. Allen, 1980).

[3] The performance took place on 18 March or April 1952 at the Loew's King Theater in Brooklyn, New York. Performing with Parker were Teddy Wilson (piano), Eddie Safranski (bass), and Don Lamond (drums). For discographical details, see Piet Koster and Dick M. Bakker, *Charlie Parker 1940-1955* (Alphen aan den Rijn, Holland: Micrography, 1976), entry no. 89, or Norman Saks with Leonard Bukowski and Robert M. Bregman, *The Charlie Parker Discography* (Port Jefferson, NY: B.B.S., 1989), entry no. 167.

[4] Charles Mingus as told to Robert Reisner, *Bird: The Legend of Charlie Parker* (New York: Citadel, 1962), p. 152.

three firms, Dial Records was the smallest and was legendary among record collectors and musicians partly because its records had limited distribution in retail stores and thus were always hard to find, but also in part because its released performances were excellent, especially those by Parker. Dial owner Ross Russell by turns has confirmed, commented on, and added to the Dial Records story on several occasions,[5] not least in his biography of Charlie Parker, *Bird Lives!* (1973). Since 1980, the Dial Records business files have been housed as part of the Ross Russell Collection at the Harry Ransom Humanities Research Center on the campus of The University of Texas at Austin.[6] These business files, now available for research, lay bare the daily operations of Dial Records, and together with Ross Russell's remarks and the recorded performances themselves, these business files help explain how and why Dial record issues came to be treasured by collectors and musicians alike.

Understanding Dial Records requires an understanding of its founder, Ross Russell. Born on 18 March 1909 in Los Angeles, Ross Moody Russell graduated from Glendale High School in 1926,[7] and later attended the University of Washington, Seattle, and the University of California, Los Angeles.[8] During the 1930s, Russell wrote pulp fiction, usually about sports or on detective themes.[9] During this same time he developed an interest in jazz, not as a musician or critic but as a record collector.[10] His writing and collecting activities were momentarily suspended by World War Two, during which time he worked in the merchant marine and later at Lockheed Aircraft.[11] With the money saved from these wartime jobs, Russell opened on

[5]On at least three occasions, Ross Russell's descriptions of Dial Records sessions and musicians have been published. Russell gave one account to Martin Williams that was incorporated in Reisner, *Bird: The Legend of Charlie Parker*, pp. 196-202. A second account, again given to Martin Williams, was published in two parts as "Dial Days," *Downbeat* 31 (3 December 1964): 15-17, and *Downbeat* 31 (17 December 1964): 22-23. Also, Russell describes the Dial sessions at length in chapters 16 through 19 of his *Bird Lives!* (New York: Charterhouse, 1973).

[6]For an account of the placing of the Ross Russell Collection at The University of Texas at Austin, see Richard Lawn, "From Bird to Schoenberg: The Ross Russell Collection," in *Perspectives on Music* (Austin, TX: Humanities Research Center, 1985), pp. 137-147.

[7]See folder "Ross Russell auto bio-chronology," box 8, Ross Russell Collection, HRHRC.

[8]Ibid. The specific date of attendance at the University of Washington, Seattle, was the 1927-1928 academic year, ending with a transfer to UCLA within that time. Leaving UCLA in 1928, Russell returned there from 1930 to 1933.

[9]Ibid.

[10]For letters on record collecting, see folder "Correspondence-jazz, prior 1940," box 1, Ross Russell Collection, HRHRC.

[11]See folder "Ross Russell auto bio-chronology," box 8, Ross Russell Collection, HRHRC. Specific dates of merchant marine service were 26 February 1942-7 March 1942 (S.S. William C. Atwater); 4 April 1942-September 1942 (S.S. Olopana); June 1943-December 1943 (S.S. Paul Shouup); 3 April 1944-27 January 1945 (S.S. Samuel Seabury). Russell also earned an FCC license at Pacific Radio School in May 1943.

20 July 1945 a retail record store in Hollywood called Tempo Music Shop.[12] At first, Tempo Music Shop specialized in rare recordings of early jazz, but by the close of 1945 it was becoming involved with a new style of jazz coming out of New York City nicknamed "bebop."[13]

The "bebop" style of jazz had its origins in the early 1940s in New York City among young jazz musicians such as Dizzy Gillespie, Thelonious Monk, Kenny Clarke, Charlie Christian, and Charlie Parker. Gathering in after-hours clubs like Minton's Playhouse and Monroe's Uptown House, these musicians experimented with different chords and rhythms in place of the musical conventions associated with swing bands.[14] Gillespie and Parker continued their musical experiments while touring with Earl Hines in 1942-1943 and with Billy Eckstine in 1943-1944, but an American Federation of Musicians union ban on recording sessions prevented the new musical developments from being recorded in 1942 and 1943.[15] When Gillespie, Parker, and singer Sarah Vaughan finally recorded in 1944 and 1945, they did so on labels such as Comet, Continental, and Manor, short-lived independent companies which could afford only to have a few thousand copies pressed and issued. In the fall of 1945, none of the major labels such as RCA Victor and Columbia had yet to show interest in the new style, so these independent firms still had affordable opportunities to record major "bebop" talent. One notable opportunity was taken by Herman Lubinsky and Teddy Reig to record Charlie Parker for the Savoy label on 26 November 1945.[16] It was Parker's first time as a recording session leader with control over the participating musicians and with a choice as to the compositions to be recorded. It was also Parker's last recording session before leaving with Dizzy Gillespie for a series of performances in Los Angeles.

Meanwhile at Tempo Music Shop, Ross Russell took note of these recent musical developments and saw the opportunity for a record label specializing in this new music. Russell listened to Parker and Gillespie's performances in December 1945 at Billy Berg's club in Los Angeles, and he came away deeply

[12]See folder "Tempo Music Shop," box 4, Ross Russell Collection, HRHRC.

[13]Ross Russell, *Bird Lives!*, p. 207.

[14]An excellent discussion of the experiments at Monroe's Uptown House may be found in James Patrick's "Al Tinney, Monroe's Uptown House, and the Emergence of Modern Jazz in Harlem," *Annual Review of Jazz Studies* 2 (1983): 150-179.

[15]Parker and Gillespie made some recordings on a home disc cutter owned by Robert Redcross in a Chicago hotel room in February 1943. The surviving recordings are available now on *The Complete Birth of Bebop* (Stash ST-DC-535). Also, see Scott Deveaux, "Bebop and the Recording Industry: the 1942 AFM Recording Ban Reconsidered," *Journal of the American Musicological Society* 41 (1988): 126-165.

[16]For discographical data, see Koster and Bakker, *Charlie Parker 1940-1955*, no. 17, or Saks, *The Charlie Parker Discography*, no. 24.

impressed.[17] In January 1946 Russell founded Dial Records as an outgrowth of Tempo Music Shop, in emulation of Commodore Records run by Milt Gabler from the Commodore Record Shop in New York City.[18] Assisting Russell was Marvin Freeman, a Los Angeles attorney, who had been a fellow record collector since the 1930s and who also took note of the new jazz.[19] Freeman became Russell's financial and operational partner in the newly formed record company.[20]

Neither Russell nor Freeman had prior experience in recording jazz, and they learned an expensive lesson on how to run an orderly recording session when they were preparing for the first Dial session planned for 6 February 1946.[21] The session was to be held at Electro Broadcasting Studios, a cheap, cut-rate radio station in Glendale, California,[22] and an American Federation of Musicians union contract had to be filed before the session in order to report the participating musicians. Russell allowed George Handy, then pianist with the Boyd Raeburn Orchestra, to sign the contract as "orchestra leader." As the leader of this particular session, Handy listed on the union contract the soloists as Dizzy Gillespie (trumpet), Charlie Parker (alto saxophone), and Lester Young (tenor saxophone), with Lucky Thompson (tenor saxophone) as an alternate if Young did not appear.[23] Gillespie and Parker had just finished their last guest engagements on the West Coast and were planning to play this Dial date before catching an airplane back to New

[17]Russell, *Bird Lives!*, p. 208.

[18]Ibid.

[19]For early correspondence between Russell and Freeman, see folder "Freeman, Marvin," box 1, Ross Russell Collection, HRHRC, and for a description of Freeman, see Russell, *Bird Lives!*, p. 208.

[20]For capital contributions, see "Dial Record Company Income and Expense Statement to May 31, 1946," folder "Dial Mechanical Rights," box 6 A, Ross Russell Collection. Russell invested $500.00, Freeman $2750.00.

[21]Some doubts remain about the dates of the rehearsal and session. The AFM union contract filed on 21 January 1946 by George Handy bears no session date (see folder "Dial Mechanical Rights," box 6, Ross Russell Collection, HRHRC). Tony Williams (liner notes, *Charlie Parker on Dial*, v. 1) and Phil Schaap (liner notes, Charlie Parker, *Bird at the Roost*, v. 3) agree that the rehearsal was held on 5 February 1946. Russell, while not specifying dates, said Handy called the session to begin at 8 p.m. the day after the rehearsal (*Bird Lives!*, p. 205). Russell also told Martin Williams that the rehearsal and the session were a few days apart, again not specifying dates (Reisner, p. 197). Tony Williams has Handy calling the session to be held on February 7 at 9 p.m., yet Schaap places the recording date on February 6 due to the departure of Gillespie's band for New York on February 7. This essay accepts the rehearsal date of February 5 and uses Schaap's account of the session as held on February 6.

[22]Reisner, *Bird: The Legend of Charlie Parker*, p. 196. In his contribution, Russell describes the studio: "It took place at sort of a little offbeat studio in Glendale, California, which was part of some kind of religious network. It was actually in a wing of a church in a little park—almost a Gray's 'Elegy' setting."

[23]For the AFM union contract dated 21 January 1946, see folder "Dial Mechanical Rights," box 6 A, Ross Russell Collection, HRHRC.

82

Photograph of Dizzy Gillespie and Ross Russell, n.d. *HRHRC Ross Russell Collection*.

York.[24] Russell and Freeman were still awaiting formal legal approval to establish Dial as a business, yet they did not wish to miss this opportunity to record Gillespie and Parker. They approached Alex Compinski, owner of the Alco Recording Company, to sign the AFM union contract in their stead and to assist in the recording session. Compinski agreed, signing the AFM union contract and advising the Dial owners, receiving a fee with a sales commission in return.[25]

The recording session was preceded by a rehearsal on 5 February 1946, and this rehearsal was hampered by inexperienced studio technicians and many unwanted spectators and bystanders.[26] A test take of *Diggin' Diz* (Dial mx. D 1000), featuring Handy, Gillespie, Parker, guitarist Arvin Garrison, and Lucky Thompson filling in for the absent Lester Young, was all that was completed. The recording session on the following day was almost never held. At 7:30 p.m. on February 6, one half hour before the scheduled session time of 8 p.m., Handy told Russell on the telephone that he had lost track of Parker the previous night, that he was having trouble with the other personnel, and that he wanted to cancel the session.[27] Russell quickly enlisted the help of Dizzy Gillespie, who brought his working band, minus the still unlocated Parker, to the Glendale studio. Five pieces were recorded, among them Parker's composition *Confirmation* (Dial mx. D 1001-E), as well as *Dynamo A* (D 1003-A) and *Dynamo B* (D 1003-B) that were issued back-to-back on Dial 1001, the label's first release. Although the session's performances were acceptable for release, the recorded sound quality was slightly marred by an extra microphone inadvertently left open, resulting in some distortion.[28]

Not wishing to repeat this experience, Russell set down three rules that were enforced during future Dial sessions and that set the high standards for recorded sound quality on Dial's bestselling records. First, session leadership was to be granted only to those musicians who could be relied on to appear and to guide their supporting musicians. Second, no uninvited observers were allowed at rehearsals and recording sessions. And third, the recording sessions would be held not in cut-rate radio studios like Electro Broadcasting, but rather in professional recording studios like C.P. MacGregor and Universal Recorders, both in Los Angeles.[29] The enforcement of these regulations

[24]As stated in note 21, Phil Schaap's account (liner notes, *Bird at the Roost*, v. 3) is being followed in this essay.

[25]For typescript "Dial Records," see folder "Tempo Music Shop," box 4, Ross Russell Collection, HRHRC.

[26]Russell, *Bird Lives!*, p. 205.

[27]Ibid., pp. 205-206.

[28]For typescript "Dial Records," see folder "Tempo Music Shop," box 4, Ross Russell Collection, HRHRC.

[29]Ibid.

ensured efficient use of expensive studio time and resulted in records displaying professional musicianship and faithful sound reproduction.

Charlie Parker did not return to New York City with Dizzy Gillespie as planned, but rather he stayed behind in Los Angeles; in hindsight, Ross Russell believed that Parker had cashed his plane ticket and spent it in a single day.[30] To establish himself on the West Coast, Parker played various club dates in Los Angeles and appeared when possible in Norman Granz's Jazz At The Philharmonic shows. What led Parker to record under his own name for Dial is not known for certain, but Parker's name did need a bit more recognition on records at the time. When he signed with Dial, Parker had only one recording session to his credit as the leader who chose what to record and who recorded with him, namely the aforementioned Savoy session of November 1945 that produced two double-sided 78 rpm commercial issues. A Dial recording session or two would mean quick cash in the short term but also in the long term increased visibility in the marketplace under his own name. At that time, Parker needed whatever quick cash and visibility he could get in Los Angeles.

On 20 February 1946, Parker and Ross Russell filed an AFM union contract for a Dial session to take place on 4 March 1946;[31] there is no indication that additional sessions were planned for the future. For unknown reasons, that session was never held. However, the two men must have realized that a multi-session deal could be advantageous for both of them, for they drew up a handwritten contract on 26 February 1946.[32] Their agreement stipulated that Parker would record exclusively for Dial Records for one year; in return, Dial would make twelve ten-inch sides for that contracted year with Parker as "featured artist or band leader." Before Dial partner Marvin Freeman sent a formal version of the original handwritten contract to the AFM union, he added an option for a renewal of contract of one year.[33]

With this year-long contract agreed to and signed by Parker and the Dial owners, all turned toward the task of making records.[34] The standard recording process in 1946 was based on and intended for the 78 rpm shellac disc; magnetic tape was then in development but not yet available for professional studio use, and the microgroove long-playing record would not be invented

[30]Russell, *Bird Lives!*, p. 206.

[31]For AFM contract dated 20 February 1946, see folder "Dial Mechanical Rights," box 6 A, Ross Russell Collection, HRHRC.

[32]For contract dated 26 February 1946, see folder "Dial Mechanical Rights," box 6 A, Ross Russell Collection, HRHRC. This document has been reproduced in Russell, *Bird Lives!*, p. 210.

[33]Russell, *Bird Lives!*, p. 209.

[34]Much of this overview of studio recordings comes from the Gordon Mumma, Chris Sheridan, and Barry Kernfeld entry, "Recording," in *The New Grove Dictionary of Jazz* (London: Macmillan, 1989), 2:351-364. For a fine history of the development of recorded sound, see Roland Gelatt, *The Fabulous Phonograph* (Philadelphia, NY: J.B. Lippincott, 1955).

Contract Blank   ABORTED DATE
Local No. 767

AMERICAN FEDERATION OF MUSICIANS

THIS CONTRACT for the personal services of musicians, made this 20 day of FEBRUARY 1946

between the undersigned employer (hereinafter called the employer) and FIVE musicians (hereinafter called employees) represented by the undersigned representative. (including Leader)

WITNESSETH, That the employer employs the personal services of the employees, as musicians severally, and the employees severally, through their representative, agree to render collectively to the employer services as musicians in the orchestra under the

leadership of CHARLEY PARKER, according to the following terms and conditions:

Name and Address of Place of Engagement ELECTRO BROADCAST STUDIOS - GLENDALE

Date(s) of Employment MARCH 4 1946   MONDAY   NOON

Hours of Employment MONDAY 12 - 3 PM
7 - 10

PRICE AGREED UPON (Terms and Amount) $ 360⁰⁰   Commission $ NONE

To Be Paid to SCALE TO INDIVIDUAL MUSICIANS

Specify When Payments Are to Be Made UPON COMPLETION OF WORK

The employer shall at all times have complete control of the services which the employees will render under the specifications of this contract. On behalf of the employer the Leader will distribute amount received from the employer to the employees, including himself, as indicated on the opposite side of this contract, or in place thereof on separate memorandum supplied to the employer at or before the commencement of the employment hereunder and take and turn over to the employer receipts therefor from each employee, including himself. The amount paid to the Leader includes the cost of transportation, which will be reported by the Leader to the employer. The employer hereby authorizes the Leader on his behalf to replace any employee who by illness, absence, or for any other reason does not perform any or all of the services provided for under this contract. The agreement of the employees to perform is subject to proven detention by sickness, accidents, or accidents to means of transportation, riots, strikes, epidemics, acts of God, or any other legitimate conditions beyond the control of the employees. The employer agrees that the Business Representative of the Musicians' Local, in whose jurisdiction the musicians are playing, shall have access to the premises in which the musicians perform (except in private residences) for the purpose of conferring with the musicians. The musicians performing services under this contract must be members of the American Federation of Musicians and nothing in this contract shall ever be so construed as to interfere with any obligation which they may owe to the American Federation of Musicians.

It is agreed that all the rules, laws and regulations of the American Federation of Musicians, and all the rules, laws and regulations of the Local in whose jurisdiction the musicians perform, insofar as they are not in conflict with those of the Federation, are made part of this contract.

Any member or members who are parties to or affected by this contract, whose services thereunder or covered thereby, are prevented, suspended or stopped by reason of any strike, ban, unfair list order or requirement of the Federation shall be free to accept and engage in other employment of the same or similar character, or otherwise, for other employers or persons without any restraint, hindrance, penalty, obligation or liability whatever, any other provisions of this contract to the contrary notwithstanding.

If this contract requires or contemplates the recording, transmission or reproduction of any music by any mechanical means, then it shall not become effective unless and until it shall be approved by the International Executive Board of the American Federation of Musicians.

The employer represents that there does not exist against him, in favor of any employee-member of the American Federation of Musicians, any claim of any kind, arising out of musical services rendered for any such employer. It is agreed that no employee-member of the American Federation of Musicians will be required to perform any provisions of this contract or to render any services for said employer as long as any such claim is unsatisfied or unpaid, in whole or in part. The employer in signing this contract himself, or having same signed by a representative, acknowledges his (her or their) authority to do so and hereby assumes liability for the amount stated herein.

It is expressly agreed by all parties hereto that, pursuant to Section 1647.5 of the Labor Code of California, Chapter 454 of the Laws of 1939, all controversies arising out of this contract as to its existence, validity, construction, performance, non-performance, breach, operation, continuance, termination, or other reason shall be submitted to, heard, arbitrated and determined by the International Executive Board of the American Federation of Musicians, pursuant to and in accordance with the laws, rules and regulations of the said Federation and its rules applicable thereto and in accordance with the laws, rules and regulations of the said Federation regulating the relations of its members to employment agencies, and by which such agencies and members are governed. And the parties hereto agree to provide reasonable notice to the Labor Commissioner of the time and place of the hearing, which he shall be entitled to attend.

Name of Employer DIAL RECORDS   Accepted by Employer Ross Russell

Street Address 5946 Hollywood Blvd 28   Accepted Charlie Parker
Zone   (Orchestra Leader)

City Hollywood   State CALIF   By

Phone HI 6768   (Representatives of Employees)

10M 1/25/45   FORM B (CAL.)   5   Printed in U.S.A.

Copy of American Federation of Musicians contract between Charlie Parker and Dial Records, dated 20 February 1946 and signed by Parker and Ross Russell. *HRHRC Ross Russell Collection.*

until 1948. During a session, musicians were required to keep the length of the complete performance down to three minutes, in order to fit one side of a ten-inch 78 rpm disc. The music was recorded onto a matrix disc, from which test pressings and metal pressing stampers could be derived. No overdubs were possible, so the musicians had to be prepared, if not thoroughly rehearsed, to give a perfect ensemble performance towards a saleable commercial recording. The studio engineer was a crucial figure in the recording process, as he had to make sure the matrix disc was being etched properly during the performance. The best engineers were found not in radio studios such as Electro Broadcasting in Glendale, but in expensive professional studios equipped for processing commercial records.

Parker had to adapt the presentation of his music somewhat in order to fit the time limits of a ten-inch 78 rpm commercial record. He based his compositions on the 12-measure blues form or on the 32-measure popular song form; these forms were repeated as many times as needed to present the composition's theme and each soloist's variations on that theme. Such forms, which musicians called "choruses," served as the components by means of which performances could be improvised. A typical composition like *Moose the Mooche* has a 32-measure song "chorus." The manner in which Parker would lead his band through *Moose the Mooche* in a nightclub would be to have the whole group play the complete 32-measure theme during the first chorus, then to have each member solo during the second, third, and succeeding choruses, and finally replay the composition's theme during what would be the last chorus of the composition's performance. Performances of the same composition would vary according to the number of choruses Parker and his musicians would take in playing their solos, and their durations could last as long as 10 or 15 minutes, if not longer. For commercial records, the performance time could not exceed 3 minutes, so the number of choruses for solos between the opening and closing themes was severely limited. Before recording, then, Parker had to figure how much solo space could fit during a three-minute record, and what the order of soloists would be and for how long each would improvise.

Parker's first Dial session as leader was held on 28 March 1946 at Radio Recorders Studios in Hollywood. For his sidemen, Parker chose Miles Davis (trumpet), Lucky Thompson (tenor saxophone), Dodo Marmarosa (piano), Arvin Garrison (guitar), and Roy Porter (drums), with bassist Vic McMillan filling in at the last minute for Red Callender.[35] Parker planned to record two

[35]Callender was Parker's choice for bass, but he walked out after the rehearsal. Russell called Vic McMillan to fill in. So far as Russell believed later, the takes from the 28 March 1946 session are McMillan's only studio recordings. See typescript "Recollections of the Ornithology date" in folder "Parker unpublished reference," box 4, Ross Russell Collection, HRHRC.

pieces that he had not had a chance to record previously, *Yardbird Suite* and *Ornithology*, as well as a newly composed piece later titled *Moose the Mooche*. Recording of these three pieces went smoothly, partly because Parker reviewed them with his ensemble the previous night.[36] However, during a rest break, Russell suggested to Parker that the group record Dizzy Gillespie's *A Night in Tunisia*.[37] Parker must have known the piece from his appearances with Gillespie in New York City,[38] and he was willing to record it as the fourth title in this recording session. *A Night in Tunisia* was a difficult piece to record, not least for the virtuoso 4-measure solo "break" that Parker took between the opening theme chorus and his first solo chorus immediately following. It is difficult to describe the break in musical terms, but in a layman's parlance it is akin to watching a cat leap off a ten-storey building and execute thirteen flips before landing squarely on its feet. Parker's side musicians had trouble gauging the end of the solo "break"; in all, five takes were cut towards a satisfactory performance.

Throughout the session, Parker asked to hear a take after it was recorded, listened to it for mistakes in the ensemble performance of the theme, then either approved the take for issue or called for a new take.[39] However, Russell felt that Parker produced worthy solos in the unapproved "outtakes" and therefore saved some of those along with approved "master takes."[40] Parker rarely gave titles to his compositions, leaving it to Russell to come up with many of the titles by which Parker's music is now known.[41] Nor did Parker indicate which compositions should be released back-to-back on a 78 rpm commercial issue, leaving this matter as well to Russell. These procedures of recording, titling, and issue coupling developed during this first Parker session were continued for the other five Dial sessions that Parker was to lead.

Wages and compensation varied from session to session, with wages determined on an "as per" basis, according to the session's location and whether Parker led the session or not.[42] Also, Russell and Freeman made efforts to copyright Parker's compositions through Dial Publishing, and in fact

---

[36]Russell, *Bird Lives!*, p. 211. Russell describes the rehearsal in great detail in his typescript "Dial Records," folder "Tempo Music Shop," box 4, Ross Russell Collection, HRHRC.

[37]Russell, page 2 of typescript account of Charlie Parker, dated 3 January 1956, in folder "Tempo Music Shop," box 4, Ross Russell Collection, HRHRC.

[38]Gillespie had recorded *A Night in Tunisia* twice in New York City, the first time for Continental on 31 December 1944 in a vocal version titled *Interlude* with Sarah Vaughan; the second time for Guild on 26 or 27 January 1945 in an instrumental version also titled *Interlude* with the Boyd Raeburn Orchestra.

[39]Russell, *Bird Lives!*, p. 212.

[40]Ibid.

[41]Ibid., p. 252.

[42]The wages and deductions sheets for the Parker sessions for Dial can be located in the folder "Dial Mechanical Rights," box 6 A, Ross Russell Collection, HRHRC.

they copyrighted *Confirmation* (recorded by Dizzy Gillespie without Parker), *Moose the Mooche, Yardbird Suite*, and *Ornithology*.[43] Parker ignored such copyrighting efforts, leaving the publishing contract unsigned.[44] Russell and Freeman did not copyright any more Parker compositions, but in the future they would pay Parker the full equivalent of the mechanical right royalty.[45] Even if Parker had cooperated in protecting his music, he would have received little in the way of publication and public performance royalties.[46]

A curious episode ensued from the matter of royalties. On 3 April 1946, six days after recording *A Night in Tunisia*, Parker signed a handwritten agreement to give half of his Dial royalties to Emry "Moose the Mooche" Byrd, a narcotics dealer on Central Avenue in Los Angeles. Parker and Byrd's agreement was typed and notarized on 3 May 1946, becoming legally binding.[47] As Parker had not signed and never did sign the Dial publishing contract, he would share with Byrd only the royalties for pieces already submitted for copyrighting, namely *Confirmation, Moose the Mooche, Yardbird Suite*, and *Ornithology*.[48] Russell had to send Byrd's royalty checks to a variety of addresses, including the San Quentin Prison and the Los Angeles County Jail![49] Later, Parker's royalties for *Ornithology* were further split when Russell learned that Benny Harris had co-composed the tune with Parker, which resulted in a half share going to Byrd and a quarter each to Harris and Parker.[50] One wonders how many other people would have shared in Parker's royalties had more of his compositions been copyrighted.

The subject of royalties was the last thing on Parker's mind at his next recording session on 29 July 1946. Parker's narcotics dealer, Emry Byrd, was

[43]James Patrick, "Charlie Parker and Harmonic Sources of Bebop Composition," *Journal of Jazz Studies* 2, no. 2 (June 1975): 16.

[44]A copy of the publishing contract, in the form of a letter from Marvin Freeman to Parker dated 27 April 1946, is in the folder "Dial Mechanical Rights," box 6 A, Ross Russell Collection, HRHRC.

[45]Russell, *Bird Lives!*, p. 213.

[46]Patrick, "Charlie Parker and Harmonic Sources of Bebop Composition," p. 16. In note 19 of his article, Patrick acknowledges a taped discussion with Sanjek on 27 September 1973 about music copyrights available to Parker. Highly recommended for an historical view on the people and events that shaped music copyrights in Parker's time is the third volume of Sanjek's *American Popular Music and Its Business: The First Four Hundred Years* (New York: Oxford University Press, 1988).

[47]Both the handwritten and the typewritten versions of Parker and Byrd's agreement are reproduced in Russell, *Bird Lives!*, pp. 214, 216.

[48]In a letter to Dial dated 18 February 1947, Byrd made it clear he understood that he would share in Parker's royalties only for the four pieces already claimed by Dial Publishing. The letter is now in the folder "Dial Mechanical Rights," box 6 A, Ross Russell Collection, HRHRC.

[49]Byrd's letters to Russell are in the folders "Parker unpublished reference" and "Dial Mechanical Rights," boxes 4 and 6 A respectively, Ross Russell Collection, HRHRC.

[50]Memorandum, "Breakdown of Records Sold to Date Including 2nd Quarter 1948 Showing Royalties Earned from DIAL RECORDS by Charlie Parker," in folder "Dial Mechanical Rights," box 6 A, Ross Russell Collection, HRHRC.

in San Quentin Prison,[51] and in place of narcotics Parker relied on port wine and later whiskey.[52] Due to a lack of drugs and steady work, Parker was under severe physical and mental strain by the time he was located for the session by Ross Russell and trumpeter Howard McGhee.[53] Russell and McGhee filed an AFM union contract on the day of the session,[54] with McGhee signing as leader, which meant that Parker was merely a sideman and therefore had no power to approve the release of satisfactory takes, if any were to result.

No new pieces were composed for the session, and only those familiar to all the musicians present were recorded: Oscar Pettiford's *Max Making Wax*, Jimmy Davis's *Loverman*, Billy Reid's *The Gypsy*, and Dizzy Gillespie's *Bebop*. Parker was simply unable to play, afflicted by a spasmodic tic that was especially noticeable on *Max Making Wax* and *Loverman*; he was held still by Russell for the remaining two numbers.[55] Shortly after the session, Parker was involved in an incident of indecent exposure and arson, which eventually resulted in a six-month treatment at Camarillo State Hospital for drug addiction.[56]

Loverman and *Bebop* were immediately released on Dial 1007. On one side, Parker attempts a themeless improvisation on the *Loverman* chords but is physically unable to play. On the other side, Parker's phrases are scattershot and brief while the accompaniment is rushing along at 300 beats per minute. Undoubtedly Eliot Grennard, a witness to this session, had Dial 1007 in mind as he closed his short story "Sparrow's Last Jump," a fictionalized account of this session's events: "Yeah, Sparrow's last recording would sure make a collector's item. One buck, plus tax, is cheap enough for a guy going nuts."[57]

Parker's mental and physical health was restored during his stay at Camarillo. In the meantime, Russell sold Tempo Music Shop and bought Marvin Freeman's share of Dial. Having become the sole owner of the record company, and without the daily concerns of the music shop to distract him, Russell could devote his full energy towards developing the Dial label.[58] Russell monitored Parker's improvement at Camarillo, and with Sunset Records owner Eddie Laguna, Ross held a benefit concert to raise funds for

[51]Russell, *Bird Lives!*, p. 217.

[52]Ibid., p. 220.

[53]Ibid., pp. 219-220.

[54]AFM union contract dated 29 July 1946, in folder "Dial Mechanical Rights," box 6 A, Ross Russell Collection, HRHRC.

[55]Russell writes in *Bird Lives!* that he did so only during *Bebop* (pp. 223-224). Tony Williams states in his liner notes to *Charlie Parker on Dial*, v. 1, that Russell steadied Parker on *The Gypsy* and *Bebop*. The aural evidence supports Williams.

[56]These events are related in Russell, *Bird Lives!*, pp. 224-230.

[57]Elliott Grennard, "Sparrow's Last Jump," *Harper's Magazine* (May 1947): 419-426.

[58]Russell, *Bird Lives!*, p. 233.

Parker.[59] After Parker was released in Russell's custody from Camarillo State Hospital in late January 1947,[60] Russell exercised on 2 February 1947 the renewal option in Parker's Dial contract,[61] and within three weeks, Parker entered C.P. MacGregor Studios to record for Dial.

Parker's first session after Camarillo, on 19 February 1947, was the result of an impulsive whim. Russell was planning an all-star recording session for 26 February 1947 that was to include Parker, Howard McGhee, Wardell Gray, Dodo Marmarosa, and Barney Kessel, among others. About ten days before the session, Parker insisted that vocalist Earl Coleman be included. Russell had never signed a vocalist for a Dial session before, nor was he keen on recording the inexperienced Coleman with five star soloists behind him. But Parker continued his requests to record with Coleman, so Russell appeased him by scheduling a recording session on 19 February 1947 with Coleman, Parker, and the Erroll Garner Trio.[62] All five musicians showed up on the appointed date, and they set to work. Two pieces, *This Is Always* and *Dark Shadows*, were recorded with Coleman, and another two, *Bird's Nest* and *Cool Blues*, were off-the-cuff yet professional instrumentals by Parker and the Garner Trio. Parker was the session leader, choosing the pieces to be recorded and calling for new takes; as in his previous leader session, Parker allowed Russell to select titles and to pair the master takes for commercial issue. In addition, Russell saved the outtakes of *Bird's Nest* and *Cool Blues* along with their approved master takes.

The 26 February 1947 session was preceded by a rehearsal the previous day.[63] Parker, again the session leader, brought along an untitled blues, whose sinuous theme seemed to take in the entire 12-measure chorus in one long phrase. The piece confounded the other musicians, and Parker had to teach it to them by ear.[64] Trumpet soloist Howard McGhee provided the other three tunes to complete the session: *Cheers*, *Carvin' the Bird*, and *Stupendous*. On the day of recording, Parker approved the master takes but left the titling of

[59]Ibid.

[60]Schaap, in his liner notes to Charlie Parker, *Bird at the Roost*, vol. 3, gives 31 January 1947 as the date of Parker's release from Camarillo.

[61]Letter from Ross Russell to James Petrillo, dated 1 May 1947, in folder "Dial Mechanical Rights," box 6 A, Ross Russell Collection, HRHRC. Later, Russell received some criticism for taking the option: "While we're on the subject, I might say that the Dial contract had reached an option point while he was in Camarillo. Before he came out, I discussed this with him, and I told him that I thought in view of the fact we only made one record date that produced four sides that were considered very good, that he ought to renew the contract for a year. He agreed to do this, and that's the way that went. Some people have kinda put me down on this, I guess, and Bird had another version of it later on, but that's the way it was" (quoted by Reisner in *Bird: The Legend of Charlie Parker*, pp. 200-201).

[62]Reisner, *Bird: The Legend of Charlie Parker*, pp. 200-201.

[63]Russell, *Bird Lives!*, p. 240.

[64]Ibid.

his blues to Russell, who came up with *Relaxin' at Camarillo*, a variation on *Relaxing at the Touro*, a tune recorded on 22 November 1939 by trumpeter Muggsy Spanier after his stay at the Touro Hospital in New Orleans.

Parker returned to New York City in late March 1947, and soon afterwards he formed a working quintet that included trumpeter Miles Davis and drummer Max Roach. Ross Russell and Dial Records moved from Los Angeles to New York City the following July. While setting up Dial's new offices, Russell learned that Parker had violated his Dial contract by recording a session with Savoy Records in June 1947.[65] During the subsequent entanglements between the two labels, Parker was advised by his agent Billy Shaw to record no more for Savoy and to sit out his Dial contract. However, when news came of the impending AFM recording ban—slated to begin on 1 January 1948—Shaw gave Parker approval to continue recording for Dial.[66] Remembering how rough business had been for record firms during the previous AFM recording ban of 1942-1944, Russell hurriedly scheduled sessions with Parker and the other Dial contracted musicians, and he encouraged them to record as many pieces as possible within the studio time limits.

For his own part, Parker set up two sessions with Russell, for October 28 and November 4, filing the AFM union papers on October 25.[67] Since time was of the essence, Parker used his working band instead of a hand-picked all-star ensemble for these two sessions. Fortunately, Parker's working band was an all-star ensemble in itself: Miles Davis (trumpet), Duke Jordan (piano), Tommy Potter (bass), and Max Roach (drums). The sessions took place in WOR Studios in New York City, and they were engineered by Doug Hawkins, a Juilliard graduate with a sharp ear and an ability to capture the full sound on the recording disc.[68]

Parker recorded six pieces during the October 28 session. Three of these, *Dexterity*, *Bongo Bop*, and *Dewey Square*, were Parker originals being played for the first and perhaps the only time.[69] *The Hymn* was an uptempo performance of a blues tune that Parker remembered from his days with Jay McShann.[70] *Bird of Paradise* was a re-recording of Parker and Gillespie's 1945

[65]Ibid., p. 249. Also, Russell kept a running list of Parker's violations of his exclusive Dial contract. The session referred to in this particular instance is the 8 May 1947 Savoy session that produced *Donna Lee* and three other pieces. See folder "Dial Mechanical Rights," box 6 A, Ross Russell Collection, HRHRC.

[66]Ibid., p. 249.

[67]Both AFM contracts are in the folder "Dial Mechanical Rights," box 6 A, Ross Russell Collection, HRHRC.

[68]Russell, typescript account of Charlie Parker, dated 3 January 1956, in folder "Tempo Music Shop," box 4, Ross Russell Collection, HRHRC. Page 12 of this typescript contains glowing remarks on Hawkins's expertise.

[69]No "live" recordings of these three pieces are known to exist.

[70]On 2 December 1940 in Wichita, Kansas, the McShann band with Parker participating recorded

Guild label recording of *All the Things You Are*,[71] only this time Miles Davis instead of Gillespie assists Parker with the introduction. Parker had played *Embraceable You* for many years, but he never had a good opportunity to record his own melodic improvisations in the studio; he performed two takes of the piece, each using a different melodic motif.

Six other pieces were recorded at the November 4 session with the same personnel at the same studio. Parker and his musicians warmed up with a blues later titled *Bird Feathers* before taking up *Klact-oveeseds-tene*. Based on the chords of Juan Tizol's *Perdido*, a seldom used vehicle for improvisation,[72] *Klact-oveeseds-tene* began and ended with a devilishly tricky introduction taken from Wardell Gray and Dexter Gordon's celebrated record *The Chase*.[73] *Scrapple From the Apple* was a hybrid, based mostly on the chords of "Fats" Waller's *Honeysuckle Rose* but with part of the chord sequence from George Gershwin's *I Got Rhythm* dovetailed in the middle. Then, Parker turned his attention to three slow ballads to round out the session: *Don't Blame Me*, *Out of Nowhere*, and *My Old Flame*.

After the November 4 session, there was still a little time for an extra session before the AFM ban was to begin in January 1948. Ross Russell suggested to Parker one more session, this time with trombonist J.J. Johnson sitting in with Parker's working ensemble. Parker liked the suggestion, and he and Russell set a session date for 17 December 1947.[74] A rehearsal was held on December 15 to prepare some very difficult material for the session.[75] Russell caught the flu between the rehearsal and the session, so he sent his wife Dorothy to supervise the recording in his place.[76] The 12-measure blues *Drifting on a Reed* proved difficult to record, requiring five takes. Parker composed a beautiful ensemble chorus for *Quasimado* yet oddly he never seems to have played it in live appearances.[77] *Charlie's Wig* required five takes, most likely because of the 4-measure introduction where Parker, Davis, and Johnson play

what is now known as *Wichita Blues*, which uses a background accompaniment that later became the theme of Parker's *The Hymn*. For additional discographical data, see Koster and Bakker, *Charlie Parker 1940-1955*, entry no. 2.

[71] Recorded 28 February 1945 in New York City for Guild Records.

[72] Leonard Feather, in his remarkable book *Inside Be-bop* (New York: J.J. Robbins, 1949), presents on page 56 a table of "outstanding examples" of compositions based on previously existing songs. Among the models are *Cherokee*, *How High the Moon*, and *Indiana*, but *Perdido* is not included on the list.

[73] Tony Williams, in his liner notes to volume 5 of Charlie Parker on Dial (Spotlite 105), believes that in creating *The Chase* Gordon and Gray had themselves adapted the introduction from one of Parker's solos heard during a 1947 Los Angeles jam session.

[74] Russell as reported by Robert Reisner, in *Bird: The Legend of Charlie Parker*, p. 202.

[75] Russell, *Bird Lives!*, p. 253.

[76] Ibid.

[77] No recordings of *Quasimado* made during live appearances are known to exist.

without the rhythm section's guiding beats. *Bongo Beep*, the second blues recorded during the session, provided some respite. *Crazeology* was indeed "crazy" to record, and it required four takes to get a version to satisfy Parker. The first take of *How Deep Is the Ocean* was acceptable, except that its duration exceeded the three-minute time limit, so a second, shorter take was done.

Two weeks after the *Crazeology* session, the AFM union ban on recording went into effect; it was to last almost eleven months. The ban was of no concern to Parker; in fact, he led clandestine sessions with Savoy Records.[78] At the same time, Parker's Dial contract expired, leaving him free to sign with another company if he so chose. Parker eventually signed with Norman Granz to record for the latter's Clef, Mercury, and Verve labels. This recording association lasted for the remainder of Parker's life.

After his final Dial session on 17 December 1947, Parker took little interest in the label and its issues of his music. On two occasions, though, he provided Ross Russell with titles for his recordings. The first time occurred at the Three Deuces club in New York City, when Parker wrote out the title *Klact-oveeseds-tene* on a charge card on which Russell was taking notes on Parker's career. The second time was on 8 October 1948 when Parker sent a list of titles to Russell; from this list Russell picked *Quasimado* and *The Hymn* for Parker issues on Dial.[79]

In 1948, microgroove recordings at 33 ⅓ rpm speed were being developed, and reel-to-reel tape was becoming available to the public. Dial, and other companies wishing to make their 78 rpm issue holdings available on microgroove records, had to transfer the sound from the original matrix discs to tape, then cut the pressing stampers matrices from the tape. Ross Russell retained Doug Hawkins's engineering services to make this conversion into the new commercial formats, not only with Dial recordings but also with those of other firms as well, for Russell was securing the rights to Parker materials recorded on other labels.

Even when Russell was a record executive, he never stopped being a record collector. He saved many outtakes with fine solos from the Parker sessions, and he kept an eye open for additional Parker recordings that could be issued on Dial. One find was a Comet Records session held on 6 June 1945, in which Parker played with Dizzy Gillespie, Flip Phillips, Red Norvo, Teddy Wilson, and Slam Stewart.[80] Ross Russell bought the approved master discs from Paul

[78]One session was held on 18 September 1948 at Harry Smith Studios in New York City; another was held on 24 September 1948 at the same studio.

[79]Both the Three Deuces charge card and the list are now in folder "Dial Mechanical Rights," box 6 A, Ross Russell Collection, HRHRC.

[80]For musical descriptions of each of the soloists as they performed during this session, see Richard Wang, "Jazz Circa 1945: A Confluence of Styles," *Musical Quarterly* 59 (1973): 531-546.

Reiner of Black and White Records,[81] but later he also found the unapproved outtakes in WOR Studios, where the session had been recorded.[82]

Another find of Parkerana were the so-called "Chuck Kopely" recordings. On 1 February 1947, Chuck Kopely hosted a party celebrating Parker's recent return from Camarillo State Hospital. A joyful jam session took place, during which a home disc cutter, possibly a Packard-Bell model, recorded Parker's solos. Three days afterwards, Russell brought the home discs to Universal Recorders and had durable copies cut, from which the three *Home Cooking* excerpts were selected to appear in 1953 on Dial LP905.[83]

Being a record collector himself, Russell probably anticipated that his buying public was not going to be satisfied with having only the featured artist's name and record title on the label. For this resaon the 78 rpm Dial labels contained the same kinds of recording details as did the Commodore and Blue Note labels. Russell's Dial labels bore such information as title, composer, featured artist and every sideman, "supervisor" (usually Ross Russell), label issue number, and on many issues the recording date and the matrix number assigned to the performance at the recording session.

Label issue numbers differ from matrix numbers, the latter being assigned to all takes recorded during a session. When *Ornithology* was recorded by Parker at the 28 March 1946 session, the composition was assigned the matrix number "D 1012," and the takes of that composition were successively numbered. Thus the first take of *Ornithology* is D 1012-1, the second D 1012-2, and so on. Label issue numbers are assigned to a released performance at the time of issue, in order to fill retail orders and to aid inventory. So when *Ornithology* was released, its label bore the issue number of Dial 1002, the second Dial release.

Awareness of this difference between label issue numbers and matrix numbers is required to assess the Dial series, for Russell did issue outtakes with the same issue numbers assigned to the previously issued takes. For example, Dial 1013 contained the approved takes of *Cheers* (matrix D 1072-D) and *Carvin' the Bird* (D 1073-B) from Parker's 26 February 1947 session; yet some pressings of Dial 1013 had the "D" take of *Cheers* on one side and the unapproved outtake of *Carvin' the Bird* (D 1073-A) on the other!

Russell delighted in issuing collector's items, the strangest of which was Dial 1034. While the approved take of *Crazeology* from Parker's last Dial

[81]Documents related to this sale are in folder "Comet Masters," box 6 A, Ross Russell Collection, HRHRC.

[82]Letter from Ross Russell to Paul Reiner, 3 August 1949, in folder "Comet Masters," box 6 A, Ross Russell Collection, HRHRC.

[83]Details on recording and transfers taken from the mastering sheet and the accompanying re-audition sheets for these recordings are in folder "Dial Mechanical Rights," box 6 A, Ross Russell Collection, HRHRC.

session was being prepared for issue, it was etched into the master disc twice, causing "a little time lag" resulting "in some kind of musical chromatic aberration."[84] An amused Ross Russell decided to release this "doubled" master on the A side of Dial 1034. For the B side, Russell edited Parker's solos from the three outtakes, mastered them successively to fit one side of a ten-inch disc, and titled the side *Crazeology II*. Later, Russell properly mastered the approved take of *Crazeology* for issue on Dial 1055.

In preparation for 33 ⅓ rpm microgroove issues, Russell stopped the Dial 1000 series of 78 rpm records at Dial 1058, even though he was preparing the 59th issue, which was to pair Parker's performances of *Out of Nowhere* and *Bongo Beep*. In place of the 1000 series, Russell planned a 200 "Jazz Series" and a 900 "Collector's Series." The four Charlie Parker ten-inch 200 series albums (201, 202, 203, and 207) appear to have been an attempt to include at least one take of each piece recorded by Parker for Dial.[85] Another four Parker albums were issued in the twelve-inch 900 series devoted to unapproved outtakes and other items, including the 1945 Comet session and three items from the "Chuck Kopely" recordings.[86]

After 1948, Ross Russell was no longer interested in recording jazz, however much of it he was issuing on microgroove; in later years, he regretted not doing so, admitting he had opportunities to record Thelonious Monk and also the Modern Jazz Quartet.[87] But in 1949, Russell launched the Dial Library of Contemporary Classics, recording music by Arnold Schönberg, Anton Webern, Alban Berg, and Bela Bartok, among others.[88] In addition, Russell released eight ten-inch microgroove albums in the Dial 400 "Ethnic Series" using tapes made and photographs taken during a trip to the Caribbean in the spring of 1953.

Dial releases were not expected to sell in the same volume as RCA Victor and Decca issues, but Parker's recording of *Ornithology* sold some 6,254 copies during its first year of issue; by the end of June 1948, it had sold a total

[84]Ross Russell as reported to Tony Williams, in liner notes for *Charlie Parker on Dial* (Spotlite LP106).

[85]Omitted from these four albums were *The Hymn* (matrix D 1104), whose approved take did appear under the title *Superman* on Dial LP212; *How Deep Is the Ocean* (mx. D 1156), whose approved take appeared on Dial LP211; and *Bongo Bop* (D 1102), which was not issued at all on the 200 series albums.

[86]Dial LP 901 was titled *Bird Blows the Blues*. Dial LP903 issued the complete surviving Red Norvo session except for those takes then available on Dial 1035 and 1045. Dial LP904 and LP905 were respectively *Unreleased Masters* and *Unreleased Masters-Volume Two*.

[87]Ross Russell as reported by Martin Williams, "Dial Days," *Downbeat* 31 (17 December 1964): 22.

[88]The Dial classical series has been described by David H. Smyth, "Schoenberg and Dial Records: The Composer's Correspondence with Ross Russell," *Journal of the Arnold Schoenberg Institute* 12 (1989): 68-90.

Dial labels for reissues of recordings by Charlie Parker. *HRHRC Ross Russell Collection.*

Photograph of Ross Russell by Kean Wilcox, n.d. *HRHRC Ross Russell Collection*.

of 13,363 copies in two and a half years to become at that time Dial's best-selling record.[89] Usually a 78 rpm record issue needed to sell a thousand copies at one dollar per copy before it could yield a profit. Parker's recordings did clear the thousand copy mark regularly, but those by comparatively less famous musicians such as Dodo Marmarosa and Howard McGhee sold in smaller quantities.

Dial was an expensive label to run, as it needed to sign top musicians and technicians and to use professional recording studios in order to place listenable recordings on the market. In most respects, retail distribution was limited to record shops specializing in jazz, but geographic distribution extended as far as Europe, where the French label Blue Star was leasing Dial recordings from Ross Russell.[90] The Dial classical and ethnic distributions were somewhat limited, perhaps due to the esoteric nature of contemporary classical music and calypso. The moderate sales, high costs, and the limited distribution of esoteric products may have combined to force Russell to reconsider Dial's place in the record market. In June 1954, Russell sold the Dial jazz catalog to the record firm Concert Hall and closed the Dial business accounts.[91]

For all the microgroove albums of music from the Charlie Parker sessions that Ross Russell released on Dial, he never issued those very sessions complete in the order that the takes were recorded. Back then, however, Charlie Parker was alive and not yet a historical figure, and besides, the original Dial issues of his music were still available. As time passed, though, Dial stock became increasingly harder to find. In 1962, Erik Wiedemann's Parker discography was published in Robert Reisner's *Bird: The Legend of Charlie Parker*, and at the end of the discography Wiedemann notes that "most of the above-listed titles are now out-of-print collector's items. The following is a list of long playing records available when this book went to press."[92] This list contained no Dial issues proper, although it did include some unauthorized reissues of Dial material on Baronet.[93]

---

[89]Memorandum, "Breakdown of Records Sold to Date Including 2nd Quarter 1948 Showing Royalties Earned from DIAL RECORDS by Charlie Parker," folder "Dial Mechanical Rights," box 6 A, Ross Russell Collection, HRHRC. *Ornithology* sold 13,363 copies through June 1948, resulting in royalties of $116.82 for Harris, and $58.41 for Byrd and Parker each. However, Parker and Earl Coleman's Dial version of *This Is Always* (Josef Myrow-Mack Gordon) was cited by Russell as the best-selling Dial recording ever, as reported in Martin Williams, "Dial Days," *Downbeat* 31 (3 December 1964): 17.

[90]David H. Smyth, "Schoenberg and Dial Records," p. 69.

[91]Folder "Dial discography-reference," box 6 A, Ross Russell Collection, HRHRC.

[92]Reisner, *Bird: The Legend of Charlie Parker*, p. 256.

[93]In his interview with Martin Williams, Russell asked Williams "Who was behind Baronet?" Williams admitted, "I don't know." See "Dial Days," *Downbeat* 31 (3 December 1964): 17.

In 1970, British collector Tony Williams was planning the first releases of his reissue label, Spotlite Records. Of special interest to Williams was a comprehensive reissue of Parker's Dial recordings that would organize the performances in the order they were recorded. To achieve this, Williams had to solve many discographical problems that existed among the original Dial issues, and he had to verify dates, locations, personnel, matrix numbers, and titles. Ross Russell was of great assistance to Williams, providing takes that were never previously released, background information, and little-known documents such as the club charge card on which Parker spelled the title for *Klact-oveeseds-tene*.

Tony Williams's "edition" of Charlie Parker's Dial sessions first appeared in Great Britain in 1970 on six long-playing microgroove records as *Charlie Parker on Dial* (Spotlite LP 101-106). The reissue was received with critical acclaim, and more importantly, it was put to scholarly use. In his landmark 1975 Ph.D. dissertation, *Charlie Parker: Techniques of Improvisation*, Thomas Owens adopted Williams's uniform titles and matrix numbers, and he transcribed several Parker solos that were unknown until Williams's reissue.[94] Koster and Bakker also made use of Williams's uniform titles and matrix numbers for the Dial session entries in their monumental discography, *Charlie Parker: 1940-1955*.[95] Williams's reissue, combined with his restoration of the complete surviving "Chuck Kopely" home recordings of Parker, is presently available in a compact disc set on Stash Records.[96]

Although the music from Parker's Dial sessions has been available to general listeners in a logical format, the original Dial issues of that music continue to be sought out by collectors. One reason is that the Dial issues are thought of as "first editions" of important jazz performances. Another reason is that the pressing quality of the original Dials was rather good, if varied. The 1000 series 78s were pressed in shellac, semi plastic, pure plastic, or pure vinyl. Some if not all of the 200 series 33 ⅓ rpm releases were pressed in a plastic compound that was a little noisier than pure vinyl. The 900 "Collector's Series" used vinyl, perhaps virgin vinyl.[97]

Of course, Russell had started Dial primarily not to provide limited numbers of "collectors' copies" but to disseminate music that was otherwise receiving little circulation. All in all, Ross Russell held 16 jazz recording sessions for Dial, from January 1946 to December 1948. Eight sessions

[94]Thomas Owens, *Charlie Parker: Techniques of Improvisation*. Ph.D. diss., University of California, Los Angeles, 1974.

[95]Koster and Bakker, *Charlie Parker 1940-1955*.

[96]Charlie Parker, *The Complete Dial Sessions* (Stash ST-CD-567-68-69-70).

[97]"Note re Parker masters," folder "Discography/Dial/Parker," box 6 A, Ross Russell Collection, HRHRC.

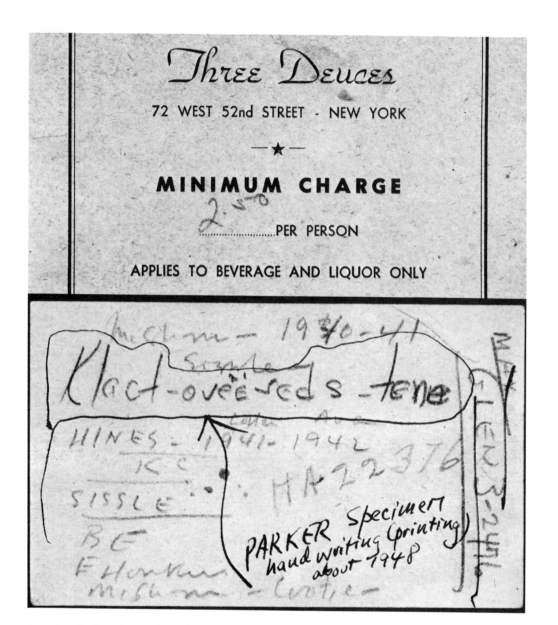

A card from the Three Deuces club with the title of Charlie Parker's tune, *Klact-oveeseds-tene*, printed in his own hand, ca. 1948. *HRHRC Ross Russell Collection.*

included Charlie Parker as a participant, six of them led by Parker himself. By December 1948, Parker had led eleven sessions recording his music according to his own standards with his preferred musicians; five of these sessions were for Savoy Records, the other six for Dial. Through 1949, whenever musicians sought out the latest Parker recordings for study, they usually had to find them on Dial or on Savoy.

Just what was Parker doing musically on those Dial records to gain the attention of his fellow musicians? Most noticeably, Parker showed that many popular songs could be used as harmonic models for new pieces. The models more often used by most of Parker's contemporaries were Gershwin's *I Got Rhythm*, Morgan Lewis's *How High the Moon*, and the 12-measure blues. Parker used these too, but from time to time he based his compositions on other songs such as Juan Tizol's *Perdido* and Sigmund Romberg's *When I Grow Too Old to Dream*.

Parker also showed how to adjust in performance to different tempi. He performed his ballads at the deadly slow tempo of 60 beats per minute, using the full second between beats to render florid embellishments to his melody. At the other extreme, Parker rips through *The Hymn* at the speed of 300 beats per minute, relying on well-practiced fingering and his trademark vibratoless tone to play his solo cleanly through the quick chord changes. On most of his Dial recordings, Parker was comfortable playing approximately at the tempo of 200 beats per minute, whether he was performing a 32-measure song or a 12-measure blues.

When the outtakes of Parker's solos became available on the early Dial long-playing albums, they demonstrated Parker's ability to take different approaches to the same tune. Parker's solos on the two takes of *Embraceable You* have already been mentioned for their treatment of separate melodic motifs that in turn are unrelated to Gershwin's original theme. During the first take of *Bird of Paradise*, Parker plays the theme of the composition's harmonic model *All the Things You Are*, yet for the third and final take Parker creates a different melody altogether. On so many of the performances, Parker's solos are not variations but countermelodies to the composition's theme.

There is one other aspect to Parker as a Dial recording artist that emerges when his Dial sessions are listened to in the order the takes were recorded, which is according to the order Tony Williams organized his reissue. On each succeeding take, Parker seems to play less interesting solos, but the supporting band plays more together during the ensemble theme statements.[98] When

[98]Russell felt this way, also: "[Parker] played his finest solo on the initial take, well before the other musicians had worked out their own concepts, let alone digested the ensemble parts. Because Parker often blew his finest on early takes, much wonderful Parkerana has been lost to the public" (Reisner, *Bird: The Legend of Charlie Parker*, p. 198).

one remembers that Parker could call for additional takes when he desired, one can deduce that Parker was more concerned about his ensemble's performance than his own. The success of a new composition and the reputations of the young artists rested on the clean performance of the beginning and end of a record. Sometimes Parker was patient enough with his backup bands to execute a difficult passage over and over, as with the "break" in *A Night in Tunisia* and the beatless introduction of *Charlie's Wig*. Yet whenever Parker and his recording ensembles perfected a theme performance, they would make it sound as though it were easy to imitate. Parker's approved master takes capture those moments of ensemble perfection, and the unapproved outtakes saved and issued by Ross Russell show how difficult those moments were to achieve.

In such considerations lie a key to why Charlie Parker's Dial recordings are valued by collectors and musicians alike. The best specimens of Dial 78 rpm issues of Charlie Parker-approved performances are supreme models of quality musicianship and professional record-processing craftsmanship. The original Dial microgroove albums and the Tony Williams reissue of Parker's Dial sessions document the process through which those products were developed and recorded. Seeing that Parker sometimes could compose "off-the-cuff" when the occasion demanded that he do so, and taking stock of the outtakes that Russell saved and issued on the Dial label, "product" and "process" seemed to be unified on those days when these two men met in the studio to make what are now their historic jazz recordings.

Photograph of Alain Locke by Carl Van Vechten, dated 1941. *HRHRC Collections*. Reproduced by permission of the Carl Van Vechten Estate, Joseph Solomon Executor.

The Bop Aesthetic and Black Intellectual Tradition

BY LORENZO THOMAS

I. "IF YOU HAVE TO ASK, YOU'LL NEVER KNOW."—LOUIS ARMSTRONG

The music of the late 1940s called Bebop is usually seen, like most avant-garde movements, as an "artistic rebellion." That view, however, often neglects any investigation into the predominant intellectual traditions of the African-American community from which Bebop musicians emerged. The aesthetic concerns implicit in the Bebop style may be traced to the ideological roots of the "New Negro Movement" beginning at the turn of the century which found its grandest expression in the Harlem Renaissance of the 1920s. Howard University philosopher Alain Locke (1886-1954) and other leaders of the Harlem Renaissance saw in African-American folk music and jazz the raw material awaiting "transformation into serious music of high culture by some race genius in the tradition of a Dvorak or a Smetana."[1] Black musicians who developed the Bebop style in the 1940s and '50s were greatly influenced by such ideas, and they also took quite literally Louis Armstrong's statement that the jazz player was a "spontaneous composer" but understood their own relation to musical tradition in a way that Locke was unable to fully anticipate.

In a segment of the recent excellent PBS documentary of her career, diva Marian Anderson succinctly stated the ethos of African-American musicians and their relation to tradition. "I had a special feeling for some of the spirituals," she says, "because they pictured what was going on even as we were singing them."[2] Miss Anderson in her regal way was referring to the fact that the sorrow songs, to the shame of our country, have remained eerily contemporary for more than a hundred years. Inasmuch as all African-

[1]Paul Burgett, "Vindication as a Thematic Principle in the Writings of Alain Locke on the Music of Black Americans," *Black Music in the Harlem Renaissance*, ed. Samuel A. Floyd, Jr. (New York: Greenwood Press, 1990), pp. 29-30.

[2]*Marian Anderson*. PBS. KUHT, Houston. Broadcast 18 April 1992.

American musical genres reflect an African musical origin shaped by the historical experience of the West, her statement might easily be applied to any genre and—in fact—has been by the musicians themselves.

"Africa is the creative source," states pianist and composer Randy Weston. "Wherever African people have settled, they have created a new music which is based on African rhythms."[3] And Dizzy Gillespie reported that "when somebody asked [Cuban percussionist Chano Pozo], 'How do you and Dizzy converse?' he would say, 'Dizzy no peaky pani I no peaky engly, but boff peak African'."[4] It is clear in examining the musicians' testimony that this sense of identity is understood in terms beyond the mere technical requirement of producing sounds in concert. Orchestra leader James Reese Europe made the issue clear in 1914 when he told a newspaper interviewer:

> we colored people have our own music that is part of us. It's the product of our souls; it's been created by the sufferings and miseries of our race. Some of the old melodies we played Wednesday night [at Carnegie Hall] were made up by slaves of the old days, and others were handed down from the days before we left Africa.[5]

And one can trust Duke Ellington to sum up the matter with his characteristic elegance. "The music of my race is something more than the American idiom. What we could not say openly we expressed in music."[6]

It is necessary to establish these artists' idea of a tradition because the place historically accorded African people in this country makes any discussion of African-American aesthetics problematic. What we find is that we must usually filter our discussion through a sociological lens precisely because black people have been so long and so often excluded from the spectrum of discourses assumed to be operational when we examine European culture. It is no secret, for example, that Fernando Ortiz's brilliant turn-of-the-century fieldwork on African traditions in Cuba was undertaken as an exercise in criminology.[7] H. Bruce Franklin has shown that, in our own country, this was

[3]Arthur Taylor, *Notes and Tones: Musician-to-Musician Interviews* (London and New York: Quartet Books, 1983), p. 19.

[4]Ibid., p. 132.

[5]Maud Cuney Hare, *Negro Musicians and Their Music* (Washington, D.C.: Associated Publishers, 1936), p. 137n.

[6]Quoted in Ortiz M. Walton, *Music: Black, White and Blue* (New York: William Morrow, 1972), p. 79.

[7]See for example Fernando Ortiz, *Los Negros Brujos* (Miami: Ediciones Universal, 1973), originally published in 1906 with the subtitle "apuntes para un estudio de etnología criminal." Vernon W. Boggs, "Musical Transculturation: From Afro-Cuban to Afro-Cubanization," *Popular Music and Society* 15 (Winter 1991): 71-83, discusses how Ortiz's research eventually led to a more positive evaluation of the African contribution to Cuban culture.

a period when black Americans—as a race—were being *defined* as criminals.[8] Our recent critical adoption of the French term translated as the Other does not really change the implications of such views.

The African-American intellectuals who launched the "New Negro Movement" at the turn of the century were acutely aware of the pariah status being imposed upon their people. In 1874 William Wells Brown had written of the freedmen, "slavery had bequeathed them nothing but poverty, ignorance, and dependence upon their former owners."[9] The black struggle for recognition as citizens during the last quarter of the nineteenth century was met with increasing hostility and, finally, legalized racial segregation. The black leadership tried to counter these developments, in part, by demonstrating yet again the humanity and aptitude of black people. Often this meant drawing attention to the former slaves' mastery of Western cultural standards.

W.E.B. Du Bois, editor of the NAACP's *Crisis* magazine beginning in 1910, penned numerous accolades for African-American performers of European classical music or skilled interpreters of the spirituals; but nowhere, notes Richard A. Long, "do we find Du Bois mentioning Armstrong, or Ellington, or . . . Fletcher Henderson."[10] Other intellectual leaders of the period such as James Weldon Johnson and Alain Locke were somewhat more approving of black popular music and, of course, such younger members of the Harlem Renaissance as poet Langston Hughes were enthusiasts.[11] In the campaign to win racial respect, however, many African-American intellectuals adopted a decidedly Eurocentric cultural outlook.

Because my own students all take it as a matter of fact that American popular music both owes its origins to African-American creative expression and stands as the unique cultural achievement of the United States—a claim first advanced specifically for the spirituals by Du Bois and James Weldon Johnson—they are aghast when they encounter Maud Cuney Hare's comments on jazz in her *Negro Musicians and Their Music* (1936). Ever the social

[8]H. Bruce Franklin, *Prison Literature in America: The Victim as Criminal and Artist* (New York: Oxford University Press, 1989), pp. 101-104, describes how a combination of peonage, disenfranchisement, and segregation ordinances effectively reduced African Americans in the south to conditions not far removed from antebellum slavery.

[9]William Wells Brown, *The Rising Son; or, The Antecedents and Advancement of the Colored Race* (New York: Negro Universities Press, 1970), pp. 413-414. Brown had been a fugitive slave who turned abolitionist and his writings were widely read and enjoyed great esteem among African-American intellectuals. Brown's *Clotel; or, The President's Daughter* (1853) was the first novel to be published by an African-American writer.

[10]Richard A. Long, "Interactions between Writers and Music during the Harlem Renaissance," *Black Music in the Harlem Renaissance*, ed. Samuel A. Floyd, Jr. (New York: Greenwood Press, 1990), p. 130.

[11]Ibid., pp. 131-133. See also Kathy J. Ogren, *The Jazz Revolution: Twenties America and the Meaning of Jazz* (New York: Oxford University Press, 1989), pp. 117-118.

and intellectual aristocrat, Cuney Hare writes: "So far did the Rag craze and Jazz spread, that in traveling to many institutions of learning, the author found that the musical taste of the youth was being poisoned." Jazz, for her, was most usually the term used to describe "acrobatics and monkey-ish antics on the part of the performers, and the grotesque use of instruments."[12] Maud Cuney Hare's discussion plainly reveals the burden shouldered by the New Negro:

> It has been claimed that Jazz will divide itself and follow two strains— "The Negro and the Intellectual." This aptly describes the situation. Many regard Negro music as synonymous with comedy and buffoon- ery, rhythmic oddities and random lines. But thoughtful musicians differentiate between music as expressed by trained and cultivated Negro Americans and Negro music of the above named style.[13]

Cuney Hare's tone reveals the sort of race consciousness that W.O. Brown, a contemporary sociologist, defined as "oppression psychosis" accompanied by "excessive sensitivity" to insult.[14] Alain Locke was also sensitive to the possibilities of defamatory images and lingering minstrel stereotypes, but, as Kathy J. Ogren points out, Locke "located the controversial qualities of jazz in the white-dominated commercial music industry—not in black perfor- mance traditions."[15]

Locke was, indeed, a perceptive critic and effective advocate. Like Maud Cuney Hare, Locke was properly appreciative of the European classical tradition but he was less interested in adopting it wholesale than in tracing the parallel evolution of an African-American culture from folklore to high art. He was able clearly to distinguish authentic black folk culture from commercial- ized caricature, even if the terms he used seem quaintly romanticized today. In *The Negro and His Music* (1936), Locke wrote:

> Today's jazz is a cosmopolitan affair, an amalgam of modern tempo and mood. But original jazz is more than syncopation and close eccentric harmony. With it goes, like Gipsy music, a distinctive racial intensity of mood and a peculiar style of technical performance, that can be imitated, it is true, but of which the original pattern was Negro. Moreover it is inborn in the typical or folky type of Negro. It can be detected even in a stevedore's swing, a preacher's sway, or a bootblack's

---

[12]Hare, p. 133.
[13]Ibid., p. 131.
[14]W.O. Brown, "The Nature of Race Consciousness," *Social Forces* 10 (October 1931): 90-91.
[15]Ogren, p. 125.

108

flick; and heard equally in an amen-corner quaver, a blue cadence or a chromatic cascade of Negro laughter.[16]

Locke was not, however, content to leave his analysis at a level which could easily be misconstrued as a poetic embellishment of the notion of "natural rhythm." Locke was quite specific in defining what he called the African-American musician's "instinctive gift" for jazz improvisation. "There is a modern delusion," noted Locke's colleague Horace M. Kallen, "cultivated by the lazy and the arty, that originality is the prerogative of ignorance. Nothing could be farther than the facts of record."[17] As an amateur musician himself, Locke understood precisely what made jazz music possible:

> For the process of composing by group improvisation, the jazz musician must have a whole chain of musical expertness, a sure musical ear, an instinctive feeling for harmony, the courage and gift to improvise and interpolate, and a canny sense for the total effect. This free style that Negro musicians introduced . . . really has generations of experience back of it; it is derived from the vocal tricks and vocal habits characteristic of Negro choral singing.[18]

Nevertheless, the Eurocentric element of Locke's thought led him to the scenario that would produce symphonies from jazz in much the way that eighteenth- and nineteenth-century European composers "elevated" and refined simple folk airs into chamber music and symphonic motifs. Locke was also unabashedly academic and these concerns led him to a statement that must have rankled the jazz musicians who read *The Negro and His Music*: "The white musicians, proceeding oftener with a guiding thread of theory, have often been able to go farther by logic in the development of the more serious aspects of jazz than the Negro musicians have, moving too much under the mere guidance of instinct." Thus, Locke concluded with the disappointed tone of a professor prodding his favorite underachiever, "it has been white musicians and critics, who for the most part have capitalized on jazz, both commercially and artistically."[19]

---

[16]Alain Locke, *The Negro and His Music* (New York: Arno Press, 1936), p. 72.
[17]Horace M. Kallen, *The Liberal Spirit* (Ithaca, NY: Cornell University Press, 1948), p. 146.
[18]Locke, p. 79.
[19]Ibid., p. 86.

II.

It is not at all difficult to imagine the black musicians' response to Locke's statement.

Jazz, said Charles Mingus in 1971, is "the American Negro's tradition; it's his music. White people don't have a right to play it, it's colored folk music. You had your Shakespeare and Marx and Einstein and Jesus Christ and Guy Lombardo but we came up with *Jazz*."[20] There's no doubt one might have heard similar sentiments expressed in the 1930s when top African-American bandsmen in Philadelphia were making $10 a night (about a week's wage for an ordinary civilian lucky enough to have a job). Youngsters like Dizzy Gillespie made $2 a gig, but the white commercial jazz men that Alain Locke alluded to were paid like movie stars.[21]

Nor was it merely a matter of locale or reputation. It was as simple as black and white. In a 1938 letter to Abbe Niles, W.C. Handy, composer of *St. Louis Blues*, world-renowned at age 65 and owner of the highly successful music publishing company he established in 1912, reported:

> I had my first aeroplane flight Friday morning to Charleston, S.C. The Carolina Air Line will not carry a Negro, so I could only buy a round trip on the Eastern Air Lines. I drove by automobile from Charleston to Columbia, arriving there in a little more than two hours (120 miles), and witnessed a performance of a play "Cavalcade of the Blues," written by a 17-year-old colored girl around my life and work.[22]

Handy, who had read William Wells Brown's *The Rising Son* in his youth, had achieved both commercial and artistic success in the music business yet was as confined by the system of racial segregation as he had been at the beginning of his extraordinary career. The story of his airplane flight can be set next to a much earlier experience recorded in his autobiography, *Father of the Blues*:

> As a side line in Clarksdale [in 1903] I did a kind of bootleg business in Northern Negro newspapers and magazines. Not only did I supply the colored folks of the town, but also got the trade of the farmers, the croppers and the hands from the outlying country. They would come to my house on their weekly visits to the city, give me the

[20]Quoted in Walton, p. 156.

[21]The pay scale for black musicians in Philadelphia is recalled in W.O. Smith, *Sideman: The Long Gig* (Nashville, TN: Rutledge Hill Press, 1991), pp. 33-34.

[22]W.C. Handy, *Father of the Blues: An Autobiography* (New York: Macmillan, 1955), p. viii.

Photograph of W.C. Handy by Carl Van Vechten, dated 24 May 1932. *HRHRC Robert Downing Collection*. Reproduced by permission of the Carl Van Vechten Estate, Joseph Solomon Executor.

high sign, and I would slip them their copies of the *Chicago Defender*, the *Indianapolis Freeman* or the *Voice of the Negro*. This may sound like a tame enough enterprise to those whose memories are short. . . . But because I was favorably known to most of the white folks as the leader of the band that gave the weekly concerts on the main street, they never suspected me of such dark business as distributing Northern literature to Negroes of the community.[23]

The "New Negro Movement" was, of course, inaugurated by those very publications with the paired objectives of elevating black race consciousness and winning respect and equal treatment from the white community. The Harlem Renaissance merely focused this campaign in the cultural arena, using the arts as both medium and message.

The intellectual leaders of the Harlem Renaissance could not overlook the more practical aspects of the musical profession. The artform soon to be inherited by Charles Parker, John Birks Gillespie, Charles Mingus, Bud Powell, and Max Roach operated within the cruel inequities of segregated America. Though he acknowledged the music's African origins, Paul Whiteman probably did not have any African-American musicians in mind when, in 1926, he envisioned "chairs of jazz in universities."[24] Even in the far less rarified atmosphere of the popular dance music business the disparity of economic reward and critical approval along racial lines was glaringly evident. In his 1926 book, *Jazz*, Whiteman expressed a vision of the music's future that paralleled Alain Locke's; he had, after all, been the conductor of Gershwin's *Rhapsody in Blue* at its 1924 Carnegie Hall premiere. Echoing Emerson's 1844 essay on poetry, Whiteman wrote, "I am ambitious for jazz to develop always in an American way. I want to see compositions written around the great natural and geographical features of American life—written in the jazz idiom. I believe this would help Americans to appreciate their own country."[25] In case this noble patriotism was not enough, Whiteman also tried a little Denver-style "boosterism" to sell jazz to middle America:

> Jazz has affected America . . . in a musical way, and in many more material senses. It is bulking increasingly large in economics. There are today more than 200,000 men playing it. The number of jazz arrangers is around 30,000. Thus two entirely new industries have grown up in less than ten years.

[23]Ibid., pp. 79-80.
[24]Paul Whiteman and Mary Margaret McBride, *Jazz* (New York: Arno Press, 1974), p. 279.
[25]Ibid., p. 287.

They are lucrative industries, too. Players in the best of the modern jazz orchestras have come straight from the symphonies where they were paid $30, $40, or at the most $50 and $60 a week. Now they get $150 up.

Jazz has made fortunes and bought automobiles, country houses and fur coats for many a player, composer and publisher. Indirectly it has filled the pockets of the musicians who are identified with opera and symphony, for it has interested a greater part of the population in music.[26]

The only pockets that were not being filled were the pockets of black musicians; but this annual report from the King of Jazz did not include them anyway.

African-American music historian Maud Cuney Hare complained that "just as the white minstrels blackened their faces and made use of the Negro idiom, so have white orchestral players today usurped the Negro in his jazz entertainment."[27] A somewhat surrealistic historical note (sort of a preview of the *Mississippi Burning* motion picture revision of the Civil Rights era) will perhaps give an indication of exactly how bad things were for the black jazz musician: by the late 1930s *Down Beat* was running a series of articles by Marshall Stearns *arguing* that African-American musicians were the actual originators of jazz![28] Alain Locke tried to find a positive way to describe the situation. Jazz, he wrote, "in spite of its racial origin, became one great interracial collaboration in which the important matter is the artistic quality of the product and neither the quantity of the distribution nor the color of the artist. The common enemy is the ever-present danger of commercialization."[29] It was in this atmosphere of jazz as an "interracial collaboration" with segregated dressing rooms that the first notes of Bebop were heard.

Though it developed out of 1930s big band swing music, Bebop was a radical departure in a number of ways. The players, often with more formal training than their predecessors, thought of themselves as artists rather than entertainers. They sought both respect for their dignity and recognition for their creative genius. "Our rebellion," wrote pianist Hampton Hawes, "was a

[26]Ibid., pp. 155-156.

[27]Hare, p. 148.

[28]Marshall Stearns's "The History of 'Swing-Music'" ran as a monthly serial in *Down Beat* throughout 1936 and 1937 and often focused on the influence of African-American musicians. The debate is reflected in the magazine's pages in other articles such as Paul Eduard Miller, "Roots of Hot White Jazz Are Negroid," *Down Beat* 4 (April 1937): 5; and "White Man's Music Started Jazz—Says Nick," *Down Beat* 4 (March 1937): 1, which quotes leader Nick La Rocca of the Original Dixieland Jazz Band complaining that French critic Hugues Panassié "gave entire credit for swing to early Negro bands."

[29]Locke, p. 82.

Photograph of Paul Whiteman being crowned "The King of Jazz" by Jeanne Gordon of the Metropolitan Opera. From Paul Whiteman's *Jazz* (New York: J.H. Sears & Company, Inc., 1926). *HRHRC Ross Russell Collection*.

form of survival. If we didn't do that what could we do? Get your hair gassed, brothers, put on your bow ties and a funny smile and play pretty for the rich white folks."[30]

The new music was worked out by young African-American musicians in Harlem after-hours joints, nightclubs along Central Avenue in Los Angeles, and in a dozen other black neighborhoods, but it leaped into the spotlight on New York's 52nd Street, remembered by drummer Roy Porter as "the street that never slept."

> There were places like the Three Deuces and the Famous Door on one side of the street. Across the way was the Onyx, Jimmy Ryan's, Leon & Eddie's, the Spotlight Club, and many others. All these spots were featuring name jazz musicians like Papa Jo [Jones], Shadow Wilson, Kenny Clarke, Art Blakey, Big Sid Catlett, Max Roach, Monk, Diz, Bud Powell, Fats Navarro, and one of the greatest trumpet players, Freddie Webster.[31]

The irony was that black customers were unwelcome.[32] America was still very segregated and the unsmiling Beboppers were still playing for white folks. *What* they were playing, however, is something else again.

Louis Armstrong, in his book *Swing That Music* (1936), had confirmed Alain Locke's definition of the jazz musician's "instinctive gift." "To be a real swing artist," said Satchmo, "he must be a composer as well as a player."[33] The younger musicians took this as gospel and many of them had the technical proficiency to make meaningful use of Armstrong's advice. Charles Mingus, for example, "trained his own ear on Beethoven, Bartok, Stravinsky, Richard Strauss. But his earliest and deepest musical influences were 'Duke Ellington records on radio' and his stepmother's Holiness Church, where they sang and swooned and carried on."[34] As for the Ellington band, it included men such as clarinetist Jimmy Hamilton who enjoyed practicing Mozart trios in his spare time.[35] "It's frightening to think of what he could have accomplished," said W.O. Smith, "had he had the college or conservatory experience."[36]

---

[30]Hampton Hawes and Don Asher, *Raise Up Off Me* (New York: Coward, McCann and Geoghegan, 1974), p. 9.

[31]Roy Porter with David Keller, *There and Back: The Roy Porter Story* (Baton Rouge: Louisiana State University Press, 1991), p. 49.

[32]Smith, pp. 76, 151-152.

[33]Quoted in Locke, p. 79.

[34]Janet Coleman and Al Young, *Mingus/Mingus: Two Memoirs* (New York: Limelight Editions, 1991), p. 12.

[35]Smith, p. 198.

[36]Ibid., p. 42.

The 1930s big band, however, was a conservatory in its own right. W.O. Smith (1917-1991), the first band director at Texas Southern University, began his career in Philadelphia in 1935 with the Frankie Fairfax band. Members included Jimmy Hamilton, Shadow Wilson, Charlie Shavers, and Dizzy Gillespie.[37] "Rehearsals," Smith recalled, "were a joy. . . .

> We learned to play hard tunes with difficult chord changes. We played these challenging tunes starting in the original key and proceeding a half step up each chorus until we returned to the original key. Imagine playing tunes like "Body and Soul," "Sweet and Lovely," and "Smoke Gets in Your Eyes" in this fashion. If nothing else, a few weeks of this would give you control of your ax. . . . A year of this with frequent rehearsals and gigs would put anybody at the top of his game.[38]

The brass and woodwind sections would improvise riffs to these tunes in the call-and-response pattern of African-American church singing.

Sociologist Ortiz M. Walton—who is also a bass player who has performed with symphony orchestras and in the jazz idiom—has explained the practical matters of Bebop playing with a clarity that has eluded most critics. Because the Beboppers were veterans of swing bands they were all familiar with the rehearsal style Smith describes and with the "shorthand code" or "head arrangements" such bands used. "Inasmuch as 'standards' (those compositions having greatest popularity during a particular era) were required knowledge of the professional jazz musician," Walton notes, "it was an easy step to their modified usage in the bop aggregation."[39] The Bebop quintet, while reducing the number of instruments, retained the swing big band's organizational approach.

Walton perhaps overstates the case when he writes that "Bop was a major challenge to European standards of musical excellence and the beginning of a conscious black aesthetic in music."[40] In fact, the aesthetic made explicit by the Bebop pioneers was not entirely new. It was the fruit of four decades of African-American intellectual debate. To offer a musical analogy, we might point out that while you can't really hear the drums on many early recordings, jazz fans know that the drums were there. Alain Locke and others were able to hear the polyrhythms of African drumming in the voices of the singers of spirituals, just as the drums of west Africa are able to replicate the voicings of tonal languages such as Yoruba.

[37]Ibid., p. 47.
[38]Ibid., p. 38.
[39]Walton, p. 101.
[40]Ibid., p. 104.

116

There are two major considerations that need attention in order to understand Bebop as more clearly part of an African-American cultural continuum than as an unexpectedly avant-garde "artistic rebellion." On one hand, Bebop challenges Eurocentric standards by aggressively interrogating their hegemonic status. While the musicians themselves accepted Locke's idea of an "evolution" from simple folk forms to sophisticated art, they also moved dance music toward self-conscious artistry without necessarily channeling it through the symphony orchestra as George Gershwin, James P. Johnson, and other earlier musicians had attempted to do. Nonetheless, the relationship of Bebop to the "classical" tradition is complex. If one credits Charlie Parker as an intellectually curious musician capable, even though lacking formal conservatory training, of remarkably advanced composition and improvisation, then Parker's interest in Igor Stravinsky should not be more surprising than Stravinsky's own interest in Woody Herman as expressed in his *Ebony Concerto* (1945). Nor is it logical to dismiss Parker's interest in modern composers of the European tradition as mere pretentiousness or an obsession nurtured by a racial inferiority complex.[41]

On the other hand, Bebop does represent a development of African-American cultural nationalism which *identifies* the evolution of a popular performance style toward a more sophisticated or "serious" artform as a social and political statement. As performed by Gillespie, Blakey, Randy Weston, Max Roach, and others, the style is a creative and explicit expression of racial pride that is logically and inextricably linked to the musicians' desire for artistic recognition and economic self-determination. But it is very clear that the terms of this expression can be found outlined in the aesthetic questions posed by Harlem Renaissance writers such as Alain Locke and Maud Cuney Hare.

Bebop highlights the mixture of resentment and ambition, racial pride and justified anger, that Alain Locke so meticulously endeavored to simultaneously mask and reveal. The Beboppers both fulfilled and rejected the ideals of Harlem Renaissance intellectuals. They pushed jazz further toward the "serious music" that Locke envisioned; they revived a militant race consciousness that had, perhaps, been tactically muted by the accommodatingly genteel pose of the Renaissance aestheticians; yet, accomplished as they were in the European musical tradition, the new jazz created in the 1940s was an astonishingly appropriate and logically instinctive extension of the African way of making music that is the enduring gift of our ancestors.

---

[41]For jazz saxophonist and avant-garde composer Anthony Braxton, the inability to understand the Beboppers' primarily *musical* interest in modernist music is a reflection of "a real interest in suppressing African intellectual dynamics." See Graham Lock, *Forces in Motion: Anthony Braxton and the Meta-reality of Creative Music* (London and New York: Quartet Books, 1988), pp. 92-94.

Photograph of Langston Hughes appearing on 26 March 1953 before the infamous investigative subcommittee headed by Senator Joseph McCarthy. *HRHRC "New York Journal-American" Collection.*

Langston Hughes as Bop Ethnographer in "Trumpet Player: 52nd Street"

By Nicholas M. Evans

In attempting to understand the complicated sociomusical movement of the 1940s called "the Bebop revolution," many different critical perspectives must be considered. The range of these perspectives need not be limited to jazz criticism, or music history, or social science; literature, too, can serve as a medium for analyzing such a cultural phenomenon.[1] Much of the verse of the African-American poet Langston Hughes (1902-1967) documents his interpretations of the sociomusical significance of jazz. Perhaps Hughes's best-known work on Bebop is his book-length poem *Montage of a Dream Deferred* (1951), but "Trumpet Player: 52nd Street," an earlier poem published in Hughes's volume *Fields of Wonder* (1947), also explores his views on this jazz style.[2] In "Trumpet Player: 52nd Street," Hughes offers what might be called an ethnographic account of the subcultural lifestyle of Beboppers and other jazz musicians in New York in the mid-1940s, portraying this lifestyle as a strategy for resisting contemporary racial oppression. Although Hughes does see some features of the subculture as destructive to its members, he nevertheless concludes in the poem that jazz performance is a powerful cultural activity that enables the musicians to survive despite their oppressed condition.

The nature of Hughes's "ethnographic" approach to depicting the jazz musicians in his poem can be elucidated with the aid of James Clifford's *The Predicament of Culture: Twentieth-Century Ethnography, Literature, and Art* (1988), which explores the similar methods of narration employed in the writing of anthropological and literary texts.[3] Further, it is useful to discuss

---

[1] I wish to thank Professor Brian Bremen, who made many helpful suggestions for revising this essay at its formative stage, and Amy Strong, who also offered valuable suggestions for revision.

[2] Langston Hughes, *Montage of a Dream Deferred* (New York: Alfred A. Knopf, 1951); *Fields of Wonder* (New York: Alfred A. Knopf, 1947).

[3] James Clifford, *The Predicament of Culture: Twentieth-Century Ethnography, Literature, and Art* (Cambridge: Harvard University Press, 1988).

119

Hughes's avowed goals for producing his ethnographic-poetic work by examining the audiences to which he often directed his poetry, both in the 1920s (when Hughes established his artistic stance) and in the 1940s (when he wrote "Trumpet Player: 52nd Street"). These discussions ultimately allow for a more incisive interpretation of the poem, since Hughes's "ethnographic" analysis of the jazz musicians' activities is strongly linked to the mode of reception that he anticipated his work would have.

In James Clifford's *The Predicament of Culture* and in his essays contributed to the volume that he coedited, *Writing Culture: The Poetics and Politics of Ethnography* (1986), the critic discusses how both anthropological ethnographers and literary authors confront the complex problem of representing the meaning of cultural experience in narrative form.[4] Clifford asserts that because of the utter complexity of cultural experience—both for the members of a given social group and for critical observers and interpreters of that group—such experience cannot be definitively captured by any single descriptive account. Rather, operating from the assumption that cultural experience is ultimately diffuse, fragmented, and indeterminate, Clifford contends that ethnographers and literary writers selectively assemble and represent only some "truths" about a social group in order to construct a coherently organized and meaningful version of the group's way of life. As a result, both ethnographic and literary texts are partial "lies"—fictions—in the sense that they simplify and reduce lived cultural experience to suppress the "incoherence and contradiction" of that experience.[5]

Clifford further points out that these same writers, in creating their cultural fictions, employ various rhetorical and poetic devices to render their collection of partial truths meaningful. Such writers "cannot avoid [using] expressive tropes, figures, and allegories that select and impose meaning as they translate it."[6] These tropes, figures, and allegories heighten and intensify the

---

[4]James Clifford, "Introduction: Partial Truths," in *Writing Culture: The Poetics and Politics of Ethnography*, ed. James Clifford and George E. Marcus (Berkeley: University of California Press, 1986), pp. 1-26; "On Ethnographic Allegory," in *Writing Culture*, pp. 98-121. At the outset, I should mention that Clifford makes certain assumptions about the functions of literature with which some readers may not agree. He believes (as I do) that, whether or not authors are conscious of it, literary works document some of the workings of cultural ways of life to which the authors are privy or in which they participate. In this sense, the boundaries between genre categories such as literature and ethnography blur. Clifford cites William Carlos Williams as a poet who, in a general sense, is also an ethnographer: "A doctor-poet-fieldworker, Williams watches and listens to New Jersey's immigrants, workers, women giving birth, pimply-faced teenagers, mental cases. In their lives and words, encountered through a privileged [perspective] both poetic and scientific, he finds material for his writing" (*The Predicament of Culture*, p. 6).

[5]Clifford, *The Predicament of Culture*, p. 112. My summary of Clifford's work in this paragraph draws most heavily on Chapter 3 of the book (pp. 92-113).

[6]Clifford, "Introduction: Partial Truths," p. 7.

partial truths portrayed, layering them with additional levels of meaning and significance and hence rendering them "convincing" and "rich." Thus, though ethnographic and literary accounts appear to represent cultural experience "realistically," they actually function as "extended metaphors" or "charged stories" *about* that cultural experience;[7] they do not transcribe so much as recreate the experience by rendering it within limiting modes of representation. The "constructed truth" of such accounts—that is, the supposed accuracy of the culture's portrayal—is thereby "made possible by powerful 'lies' of [both] exclusion and rhetoric."[8]

As Clifford notes, one corollary to this theory of textual construction is that these partially true stories about cultural experience are indeed *meaningful* only to audiences whose modes of reception dovetail with the stories' selective, enhanced representation of reality. A writer's editing and use of tropes, figures, and allegories must be appropriate to the particular "limited audiences" to which the text is directed (whether consciously or unconsciously and implicitly) at the historical moments of its composition and publication.[9] (Of course, the text can be meaningful for later readers as well.) In this sense, ethnographic and literary fictions communicate the "truth" of their cultural descriptions only in particular social contexts, to the "specific interpretive communities" who believe (as the writer does) that the stories accurately document reality.[10]

In Clifford's framework, then, the ethnographic or literary writer effectively acts as a mediator, organizing and translating a limited depiction of cultural experience into a form that is accessible to and meaningful for

[7]Clifford, "On Ethnographic Allegory," p. 100.

[8]Clifford, "Introduction: Partial Truths," p. 7. It may seem redundant to emphasize literature's rhetorically and poetically embellished nature—its "fictional" status. However, Clifford compares literature with more "scientific" modes of writing like ethnography not only to dispel the assumption that ethnographic accounts transparently represent reality but also the assumption that literature is completely fabricated and hence "false." He considers the conventional distinctions between these narrative genres ("imaginative" vs. "objective," and so on) to be unenforceable: the boundaries of literary discourse overlap with those of discourse traditionally considered to be nonfiction, and vice versa. Along these lines, Clifford discusses poets as ethnographers (see note 3 above) and also observes that some ethnographies generically resemble "sociology, the novel, or avant-garde cultural critique" (p. 23).

[9]In her study *On the Margins of Discourse* (Chicago: University of Chicago Press, 1978), Barbara Herrnstein Smith offers arguments that implicitly bolster this point. Smith writes that "the poet, in composing the poem, will have made certain assumptions regarding his audience, specifically that they are members of a shared linguistic and cultural community, and thus able and willing to abide by relevant linguistic, cultural, and indeed literary conventions" (p. 37). Of course, writers often make these assumptions unconsciously, just as (in Clifford's framework) they generally perform their selection and enhancement of limited cultural truths unconsciously.

[10]Clifford, *The Predicament of Culture*, p. 112. Clifford notes that not all writers fully believe in the truth of their representations; some acknowledge the partially true as well as socially and historically contingent nature of their texts' meaning.

particular modes of reception. Performing this role for an audience often simultaneously imbues the writer with an aura of authority; an author whose portrayal is "rich" and "convincing" will naturally be seen as endowed with acute cultural insight. Accorded such authority by the audience, the writer often takes on the dual role of spokesperson for and interpreter of the culture that he or she depicts. One such writer was Langston Hughes.

In his 1926 manifesto, "The Negro Artist and the Racial Mountain," Hughes states that one of his main artistic goals is to portray the "beauty" of working-class African Americans, whom he calls "the low-down folks, the so-called common element."[11] Revealing the applicability of Clifford's framework to the poet's artistic orientation, Hughes implies that portraying this "beauty" involves representing truths about African-American culture in a heightened, intensified, literary form: "These common people . . . furnish a wealth of colorful, distinctive . . . unused material ready for [the black artist's] art." Jazz performance was frequently the "unused material" of Hughes's art, and in this essay he also inadvertently admits that he poetically embellishes truths about jazz in order to ascribe universal racial significance to the music: "jazz to me is . . . the eternal tom-tom beating in the Negro soul."[12]

This artistic process of selectively representing and heightening truths about jazz is evident in "Jazzonia," one of Hughes's most prominent early poems. First published in *Crisis* in 1923 and then reprinted in the Harlem Renaissance collection edited by Alain Locke, *The New Negro* (1925), as well as in Hughes's first volume of poetry, *The Weary Blues* (1926),[13] "Jazzonia" "heightens" the depicted atmosphere of a Harlem cabaret by metaphorically comparing it to primal images of Eden and Africa:

> Oh, silver tree!
> Oh, shining rivers of the soul!
>
> In a Harlem cabaret
> Six long-headed jazzers play.
> A dancing girl whose eyes are bold
> Lifts high a dress of silken gold.
>
> Oh, singing tree!
> Oh, shining rivers of the soul!

[11]Langston Hughes, "The Negro Artist and the Racial Mountain," *The Nation* 122 (1926): 694, 693.
[12]Ibid., pp. 693, 694.
[13]Langston Hughes, "Jazzonia," *Crisis* (August 1923): 162; Alain Locke, ed., *The New Negro* (New York: Atheneum, 1970 [1925]); Langston Hughes, *The Weary Blues* (New York: Alfred A. Knopf, 1926).

Were Eve's eyes
In the first garden
Just a bit too bold?
Was Cleopatra gorgeous
In a gown of gold?

Oh, shining tree!
Oh, silver rivers of the soul!

In a whirling cabaret
Six long-headed jazzers play.

The poem's setting documents a very limited set of truths about "the low-down folks": during the 1920s, in urban centers such as New York, working-class African Americans gathered at cabarets to enjoy jazz, dancing, and other entertainment. But Hughes intensifies these truths by portraying them as manifestations of a much larger historical and racial-cultural tradition. This portrayal is most evident in the similarities Hughes finds between the dancing girl and Cleopatra and Eve; with her bold eyes and golden dress, the girl becomes a present-day symbol of the glory of Africa and even of the origin of humanity. Further, Hughes associates the atmosphere of the cabaret as a whole with Eden by repeatedly invoking the images of the shining, singing tree and rivers. (This repeated reference to "rivers" no doubt also echoes an earlier and even more famous poem by Hughes, "The Negro Speaks of Rivers," in which the poet also emphasizes the influence of African heritage on twentieth-century African-American life.)[14] The jazz musicians in the poem also evoke the African past, since (following early twentieth-century notions of physiognomy) Hughes specifically refers to their "long-headed" African features.[15] Thus, in "Jazzonia," Hughes portrays a 1920s African-American night on the town as a timeless experience, one whose precursors date back to the dawn of history. In this manner, the poet presents the

---

[14]Wilson Jeremiah Moses observes that this effort "to link the black past with the greatness of [African] empires and dynasties and 'high culture'"—a practice that he calls "monumentalism"—was commonly employed by late nineteenth- and early twentieth-century black intellectuals. See Wilson Jeremiah Moses, "More Stately Mansions: New Negro Movements and Langston Hughes' Literary Theory," in *Langston Hughes Review* 4, no. 1 (1985): 42.

[15]On this note, in his first autobiography, *The Big Sea* (New York: Hill and Wang, 1963 [1940]), Hughes recalls wryly that some 1920s anthropologists would venture into Harlem "to stop anyone whose head looked interesting, and measure it" (p. 239). Hughes also describes himself as having "a long head" in a letter to Arna Bontemps dated 2 May 1946. See Charles H. Nichols, ed., *Arna Bontemps—Langston Hughes Letters, 1925-1967* (New York: Paragon House, 1990), p. 206.

"beauty" of "the low-down folks" and portrays jazz as "the eternal tom-tom beating in the Negro soul."

In "The Negro Artist," Hughes specifies that one audience in particular for whom he wishes to reveal this timeless beauty is the "Negro middle class."[16] While some black middle-class readers disliked Hughes's work because of the very fact that it focused on the low-down folks (instead of "respectable" African Americans), others—such as the prominent Harlem Renaissance critic Alain Locke—considered the poet's representation of black working-class life to be authoritative and dubbed Hughes the "spokesman . . . of the Negro masses."[17] Similarly, *Opportunity* reviewer Margaret Larkin wrote that Hughes's second volume of poetry, *Fine Clothes to the Jew* (1927),[18] qualified him as a "poet for the people." To Larkin, the poems in this volume demonstrated Hughes's ability to present the true meaning of "every day [folks']" lives:

> It is a poet's true business to distill th[e] pure essence of life. . . . I think that Hughes is doing for the Negro race what Burns did for the Scotch—squeezing out the beauty and rich warmth of a noble people into enduring poetry.[19]

Larkin found Hughes's poetic cultural fictions to be as "rich" and "convincing" as Locke did, showing that the poet communicated his notions of the low-down folks' "beauty" to at least some members of his target audience; Hughes's cultural portraits were, to use Clifford's words, "meaningful to specific interpretive communities."[20] In much of his 1920s poetry, then, Hughes established his own particular brand of poetic ethnography.

In the 1940s, Hughes continued to play the role of poetic spokesperson for and interpreter of African Americans, though he did so for a wider range of audiences.[21] In 1944, Hughes toured and lectured at a number of predominantly white high schools on the East Coast, and he said that one of his main goals in lecturing was to "interpret Negroes as human beings to white

---

[16]Hughes, "The Negro Artist," p. 694.

[17]Alain Locke, review of *The Weary Blues*, in *Palms* 1 (1926-1927): 25.

[18]Langston Hughes, *Fine Clothes to the Jew* (New York: Alfred A. Knopf, 1927).

[19]Margaret Larkin, "A Poet for the People," *Opportunity* (March 1927): 84-85.

[20]Clifford, *The Predicament of Culture*, p. 112.

[21]I am progressing somewhat ahistorically by shifting my discussion from the 1920s to the 1940s without a transition. Nevertheless, as Arnold Rampersad points out in his biography of Hughes, many in the 1940s still considered the poet to be "someone who understood the problems of the common people" and who could portray these people's experiences with "authenticity." See Arnold Rampersad, *The Life of Langston Hughes*, 2 vols. (New York: Oxford University Press, 1986, 1988), 2:109, 114.

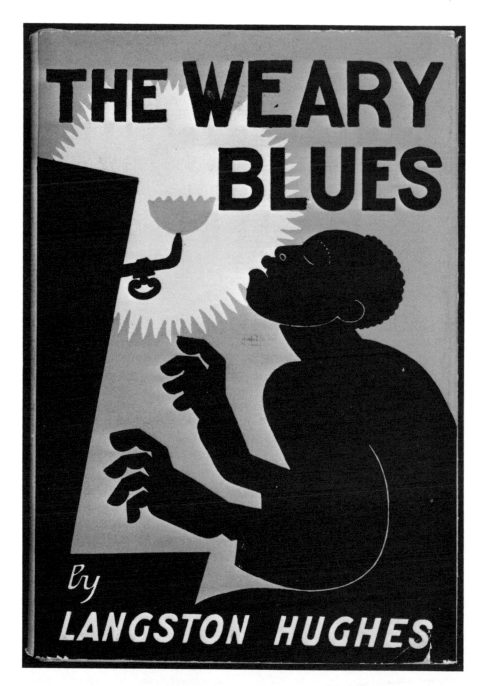

Dust jacket of Langston Hughes's *The Weary Blues* (New York: Alfred A. Knopf, 1945). Jacket design by Miguel Covarrubias. This copy is inscribed by the author. *HRHRC Collections*.

Langston Hughes with students during a tour of Kentucky, 1940. From François Dodat, *Langston Hughes* (Paris: Editions Pierre Seghers, 1964). The General Libraries of The University of Texas at Austin.

students."[22] According to biographer Arnold Rampersad, Hughes successfully "played the role of ambassador of the race" as he spoke to the students and their parents, teachers, and principals, eliciting from the latter praise for his lectures as "the real hope for racial understanding."[23] A similar tour in 1945, during which Hughes lectured and gave readings at colleges throughout the country, was equally well received.

Although we cannot precisely reconstruct Hughes's portrayals of African Americans in these speeches, an essay that he wrote in May 1946 reveals the kinds of representations of black life that he favored at the time. In the essay, Hughes criticizes and responds to the "truths" about African Americans presented in works of Richard Wright and Chester Himes by calling for "a good novel about *good* Negroes who do *not* come to a bad end" (Hughes's emphasis). He elaborates by saying that there are many African Americans

> who never murder anyone, or rape or get raped or want to rape, who never lust after white bodies, or cringe before white stupidity, or Uncle Tom, or go crazy with race, or off-balance with frustration.[24]

In Hughes's view, the "truths" that Wright and Himes present, the versions of black experience that they portray, are distorted and distasteful. Hughes seems to think that they are the kinds of images that reinforce stereotypes and hence do not promote (what he sees as) productive cross-cultural understanding. In contrast, he wants "black writers to stress the brighter, less sordid and defeatist side of their culture."[25] It is presumably this side of African-American life that Hughes presented to his lecture audiences with the aim of "interpret[ing] Negroes as human beings"; it was this kind of partially true cultural fiction that was so meaningful to these audiences that they effusively lauded the lectures as "the real hope for racial understanding."[26] Written at

[22]Hughes quoted in Rampersad, *The Life of Langston Hughes*, 2:90. Hughes lectured virtually year-round during this period; this tour and the later one that I mention are particularly notable examples.

[23]Ibid., 2:96, 97. Rampersad culled the latter quotation directly from a letter written by one of the school principals.

[24]Quoted in Rampersad, 2:119.

[25]Ibid., 2:118. This is Rampersad's assessment of Hughes's general artistic orientation at the time, especially in response to Wright's works.

[26]In arguing that Hughes oriented his works to (what he saw as) white audiences' modes of reception, it may appear—incorrectly—that I am implying that he was a "sell-out," an Uncle Tom. I do not wish to portray Hughes as pandering to white audiences. Indeed, most evidence indicates just the opposite—that Hughes was perceived as a racial-political troublemaker. Principals at some of the schools that he visited were questioned about his lectures "by officials of both the FBI and the Army" (Rampersad, 2:97). My point in emphasizing Hughes's self-contrast with Wright and Himes is to clarify the contours of Hughes's selective representational strategies.

about the same time, "Trumpet Player: 52nd Street" was probably intended to carry a similar meaning for a similar target audience, since it also exhibits an emphasis on representing "less sordid and defeatist truths" about black life and poetically enhances those truths to tell a "brighter" story of peaceful self-redemption.

> The Negro
> With the trumpet at his lips
> Has dark moons of weariness
> Beneath his eyes
> Where the smoldering memory
> Of slave ships
> Blazed to the crack of whips
> About his thighs.
>
> The Negro
> With the trumpet at his lips
> Has a head of vibrant hair
> Tamed down,
> Patent-leathered now
> Until it gleams
> Like jet—
> Were jet a crown.
>
> The music
> From the trumpet at his lips
> Is honey
> Mixed with liquid fire.
> The rhythm
> From the trumpet at his lips
> Is ecstasy
> Distilled from old desire—
>
> Desire
> That is longing for the moon
> Where the moonlight's but a spotlight
> In his eyes,
> Desire
> That is longing for the sea
> Where the sea's a bar-glass
> Sucker size.

The Negro
With the trumpet at his lips
Whose jacket
Has a *fine* one-button roll,
Does not know
Upon what riff the music slips
Its hypodermic needle
To his soul—

But softly
As the tune comes from his throat
Trouble
Mellows to a golden note.

Although the precise composition date of "Trumpet Player: 52nd Street"
is unknown, Hughes most likely wrote it in 1945 or 1946.[27] First appearing in
the volume *Fields of Wonder* (1947), the poem was also included in Hughes's
Selected Poems (1959), though without its subtitle (as simply "Trumpet
Player").[28] Apparently Hughes thought that later readers would not understand the reference to Fifty-second Street, or that the poem would carry more
"universal" meaning without the tag that explicitly identified its original
context. However, interpreting the poem within that very context requires
taking note of the specific social and historical setting to which the subtitle
refers.

"Trumpet Player: 52nd Street" is effectively an ethnographic sketch of
African-American jazz musicians' subcultural way of life, and in particular the
ambience of the Fifty-second Street jazz scene, in New York in the mid-1940s.
Ross Russell has documented in his *Bird Lives!* how, during this period, Fifty-
second Street hosted a wide array of jazz styles: New Orleans saxophonist
Sidney Bechet, stride pianist Fats Waller, swing saxophonist Coleman Hawkins
and trumpeter Roy Eldridge, and, of course, Beboppers Charlie Parker and
Dizzy Gillespie might all be heard performing in different clubs on the same
night.[29] As Russell observes, the Street was like "a chart showing . . . the entire
course of jazz history" up to the current moment.[30]

[27]Hughes submitted the manuscript of *Fields of Wonder* in mid-1946, and Rampersad writes that
"Trumpet Player: 52nd Street" was a "recently composed" addition to the volume (*The Life of
Langston Hughes*, 2:132).

[28]Langston Hughes, *Selected Poems of Langston Hughes* (New York: Alfred A. Knopf, 1959).

[29]Ross Russell, *Bird Lives!* (London: Quartet Books, 1972), pp. 151-152, 164-166.

[30]Ibid., p. 164.

If Hughes intended his trumpet player to represent one specific musician, it was probably Eldridge or Gillespie, but Hughes most likely chose Fifty-second Street as the site of his poem because of the diversity of jazz styles that could be found there; his single musician can be seen to stand for all of the different stylists, as a representative of their shared way of life. The trumpet player's composite identity no doubt stems from Hughes's notion that all jazz styles, including Bebop, belong to a continuous musical tradition. In the preface to his volume *Montage of a Dream Deferred* (1951), he writes that Bebop "progressed" from "[early] jazz, ragtime, swing, blues, and boogie-woogie." Hughes further believed that this musical tradition, and in particular Bebop, signified the resistance of African-American musicians to racial oppression. In "The Negro Artist and the Racial Mountain," Hughes claimed not only that jazz was "the eternal tom-tom beating in the Negro soul" but also that it was the "tom-tom of revolt against weariness in a white world"; he updated and extended this latter sentiment in a 1949 *Chicago Defender* column, wherein his character Jesse Semple asserts that Bebop is a musical response to the police's brutal treatment of African Americans.[31] Within this context, Hughes's goal in setting his poem on Fifty-second Street was to describe the common, oppressed conditions under which the musicians performing there lived and to explore and explain how their subcultural lifestyle helped them to survive.

The truths about the musicians that Hughes represents include various historically accurate allusions to accoutrements of Beboppers and the jazz lifestyle: the trumpet player's slicked-back ("processed") hair, his one-button-roll jacket, his drinking, his drug use (particularly of heroin, as the "hypodermic needle" implies), and, of course, the music itself, performed in the setting of a nightclub. Hughes heightens these subcultural truths by portraying their combination as a coherent strategy for resisting the dehumanizing effects of racial oppression—that is, a method of living through which the trumpet player is able to establish and maintain selfhood within his own social sphere. Hughes does subtly criticize those truths regarding drug and alcohol abuse, but his minor reservations are overshadowed by his ultimate evaluation of jazz performance in particular as a powerful and unreproachable recuperative activity. This portrayal of jazz performance as the subculture's saving grace concludes Hughes's heightened portrayal of the jazz lifestyle: despite the musician's oppressed condition and his somewhat self-destructive behavior, he is able to redeem himself through his own musical creativity. This poetic

[31]Hughes, *Montage of a Dream Deferred*, n.p.; "The Negro Artist," p. 694; *Chicago Defender*, 19 November 1949.

story about phoenix-like self-recovery would be meaningful to audiences like those on Hughes's lecture tours, and Hughes's use of it reveals his effort to interpret his trumpet player to such readers "as a human being."[32]

In the first stanza of "Trumpet Player: 52nd Street," Hughes immediately asserts his view of African-American musical expression as a response to the effects of Jim Crow racial inequality; the poem opens by highlighting the relationship between "The Negro / With the trumpet at his lips" and the history of African Americans' oppression. The "smoldering memory / Of slave ships" is evident in the "dark moons of weariness" beneath the musician's eyes; the legacy of slavery has been burned ("Blazed") into his consciousness by the physical and emotional pain that the historical and contemporary, literal and figurative "crack of whips" has caused.[33] Hughes implies that the discriminatory racial conditions of the 1940s under which the trumpet player lives are merely a modified, updated version of the conditions of slavery itself.[34] By emphasizing the permeating presence of racial oppression in the first stanza, Hughes foregrounds it as the primal force around which the rest of the poem's action revolves: all that follows must be seen in relation to the "smoldering" pain the oppression causes.

In the second stanza, Hughes immediately interprets one feature of the jazz subculture—the trumpet player's hair—as a response to his inherited "weariness." At first glance, the fact that the musician has willingly "Tamed down" his "vibrant hair" appears to indicate that he has symbolically accepted his oppressed condition. However, Hughes also identifies a recuperative strategy in the hairstyle: "it gleams / Like jet— / Were jet a crown." Within the

[32]My interpretation of the poem is based on an attempt to reconstruct the relationship that Hughes believed he had with a target audience when he wrote the work. While different interpretive communities in different contexts will arrive at other readings of the poem, I am trying to approximate Hughes's "intended" meaning by estimating whom he considered to be the poem's primary interpretive communities. My approach implicitly follows that of Wendell Harris, who writes that—in order to try to understand the meanings of a text when it was produced—the text must be read "in the set of contexts in which the author assumed it would be read." See Wendell Harris, *Interpretive Acts* (Oxford: Oxford University Press, 1988), p. 60.

[33]The trumpet player's "weariness" invites comparison of this poem with another of Hughes's famous early works, "The Weary Blues," which could also be productively interpreted as a poetic-ethnographic analysis of black musical performance. Hughes's view on the interconnected relationship between the blues and jazz styles like Bebop reinforces the similarity between these two poems.

[34]Richard K. Barksdale interprets the opening stanza of "Trumpet Player: 52nd Street" in a similar way, viewing the trumpet player as a "folk symbol with deep roots in the racial past" who "remembers [that which] all Black musicians have remembered throughout all of slavery's troubled centuries." See Richard K. Barksdale, "Langston Hughes: His Times and His Humanistic Techniques," in *Black American Literature and Humanism*, ed. R. Baxter Miller (Lexington: University Press of Kentucky, 1981), p. 23.

musician's social sphere, his hairstyle gives him status—it is like a "crown."[35] By using this particular image, Hughes is undoubtedly alluding to the long tradition in jazz of applying royal titles to the more renowned musicians—a tradition evident in the names of King Oliver, Duke Ellington, and Count Basie. The trumpet player's snazzy clothes (mentioned in the fifth stanza) also figure into his subcultural status; his jacket "Has a *fine* one-button roll." Hughes views such stylish, sartorial details as indicators that the musician and his peers have not been completely drained of their creative energy by conditions enforcing racial inequality; he portrays the trumpet player as resisting the contemporary "crack of whips" by reversing the imagery of power and authority so that, instead of his oppressors, it is the musician who wears the "crown."

In the third stanza, Hughes highlights a feature of the musician's subcultural way of life that is an even more powerful strategy of resistance: jazz performance itself. The "smoldering" from the first stanza ignites and is poured forth in the music that is "liquid fire"; the trumpet player expresses the pain of his memory through the music, turning the pain into something more palatable and nourishing: "honey." Playing the music helps the musician to expel his bitterness and reclaim a bearable existence. Further, by figuring jazz's expressive character as "honey / Mixed with liquid fire," Hughes marries his view of the music's social significance to popular jazz terminology of the day: the image alludes to the descriptive adjectives "sweet" and "hot," which were often used in the 1930s and 1940s to denote two common modes of jazz performance ("sweet" generally describing soft and lush musical presentation and "hot" denoting a brasher and more energetic interpretive style).

Jazz's regenerative potential is also evident in the music's "rhythm," which enables the musician to express his expansive, long-held "desires" despite their being restricted by racial oppression. In the fourth stanza, these desires are figured as the trumpet player's "longing" for the moon and sea, two images that in Hughes's work often symbolize the life-dreams that all people wish to have fulfilled.[36] It is clear in this stanza that the trumpet player's ability to fulfill his desires is truncated by his limited opportunities: he is circumscribed by

[35]R. Baxter Miller similarly interprets the trumpet player's hairstyle as a symbol of mixed signification. It can represent "the ambivalence of acculturation"—that is, by adopting the hairstyle, the trumpet player reveals a desire to "resemble Whites whose hair is naturally [straight]"—but its "gleam" also signifies that the musician's energy, his "inner black light," has not dissipated. See R. Baxter Miller, *The Art and Imagination of Langston Hughes* (Lexington: University Press of Kentucky, 1989), p. 63.

[36]Evidence of this symbolism can be found, for instance, in the epigraph of *The Big Sea*, where Hughes metaphorically describes the vast potential of life: "Life is a big sea / full of many fish. / I let down my nets / and pull." Similarly, in a section of *The Big Sea* entitled "Burutu Moon," Hughes writes that the moon signifies the often unattainable yet still "delicious . . . ripe fruit" of life. See p. 117. Richard K. Barksdale similarly characterizes the moon and sea as timeless symbols of human yearning

performance in nightclubs, frequently under exploitative conditions,[37] where the only "moonlight" he has access to is "a spotlight" and the only "sea" available to him is "a bar-glass / Sucker size." Although these restrictive conditions threaten to quell the musician's desires altogether, playing jazz still enables him to hold on to his aspirations. At the end of the third stanza, "The rhythm / From the trumpet at his lips" clearly allows the trumpet player to maintain hope, since it translates his "old" and nearly forgotten desire into palpable "ecstasy" in the current moment. In other words, jazz performance reinvigorates the musician's longing for the sea and moon, his hope that his desires in life will be fulfilled.

Thus far in the poem, Hughes lauds the jazz subculture almost without reservation. However, a second glance at the fourth stanza reveals something of his doubts. By using the bar-glass image, Hughes tentatively tempers his evaluation of the lifestyle: he subtly criticizes the trumpet player as a "sucker" for seeking to assuage his frustrated desires through alcoholic consumption. Similarly, in the fifth stanza, Hughes obliquely alludes to the musician's drug abuse by invoking the image of the "hypodermic needle." These images indirectly register the poet's discomfort.

Nevertheless, at the same time that he hints at these criticisms, Hughes also dilutes them. His reference to the hypodermic needle displaces some of the destructive connotations of the image by simultaneously reaffirming the recuperative power of jazz performance: it is the *music* that "slips / Its hypodermic needle / To his soul." In other words, while Hughes hints that the jazz musician may abuse alcohol and narcotics, he also emphasizes that the trumpet player relies more heavily on the preferable stimulant of the music. Hughes extends this latter point in the final stanza, where he fully dispels any ambivalence he may feel about aspects of the jazz musician's lifestyle. The trumpet player's music "softly" and conclusively enables him to extinguish "the smoldering memory": his "Trouble / Mellows to a golden note." Even if (as Richard K. Barksdale suggests in his analysis of the poem) the musician's relief is only temporary, Hughes definitively presents jazz performance as an important and necessary salve for the musician's suffering.[38]

Close attention to the work's final three lines reveals how Hughes further reinforces the idea of the musician's recuperation through the use of the words "throat," "Mellows," "golden," and "note." The repeated appearance of

(p. 24). In "Trumpet Player: 52nd Street," Hughes appears simply to assume that the images of the sea and moon self-evidently carry such meanings.

[37] Jazz critic Bill Crow writes that Fifty-second Street clubowners often underpaid and took advantage of performers. See Bill Crow, *Jazz Anecdotes* (New York: Oxford University Press, 1990), p. 101.

[38] As Barksdale puts it: "The figure of the hypodermic needle . . . suggests that the music provides only temporary relief from the difficulties of the present: jazz is a useful narcotic to allay the world's woes" (p. 24).

the long "o" vowel sound and of the shape of the printed letter "o" itself in these words aurally and visually evokes notions of wholeness and closure. In terms of both content and form, then, the poem's conclusion clinches Hughes's portrayal of the jazz subculture as a coherent and effective strategy for surviving the hardships caused by 1940s racial conditions.

The conclusion of "Trumpet Player: 52nd Street" also certifies Hughes's attempt to appeal to a readership similar to his lecture-tour audiences, since the resolution ensures that the trumpet player (following Hughes's 1946 essay) is a "*good* Negro . . . who do[es] *not* come to a bad end": though he suffers under conditions of racial inequality, he does not "go crazy with race, or off-balance with frustration." Rather, the musician peacefully resolves his frustration and thus represents "the brighter, less sordid and defeatist side of [black] culture." To put it another way, the poem's conclusion bolsters Hughes's effort to interpret his trumpet player "as a human being" to such a target audience in that it evokes a powerful story about human struggle and survival: to quote Arnold Rampersad slightly out of context, Hughes depicts the musician as a representative of "the uprooted and dispossessed" who "sometimes edges toward despair" but nevertheless manages—via artistic creativity—to achieve "self-redemption in the face of adversity."[39] By following this narrative pattern, the poem translates its portrayal of truths about the trumpet player's subcultural lifestyle—a lifestyle that would be foreign to some readers (especially white ones in the 1940s)—into a more understandable description of generalized human experience. As James Clifford puts it, "Strange behavior is portrayed as meaningful within a common network of symbols . . ., an abstract plane of [cross-cultural] similarity."[40]

Finally, even Hughes's ambivalent portrayal of some aspects of the jazz subculture ultimately supports his narrative authority as an "ethnographer." What Clifford calls a stance of "ethnographic comprehension" involves both displaying sympathy for the depicted culture and analyzing the culture critically.[41] Hughes's presentation of the truths of drug and alcohol use in the

[39]Rampersad, 2:64-65. Rampersad's description actually refers to Hughes's character Jesse Semple, but Hughes would seem to be demonstrating the same principle with his trumpet player. This conjunction between these two fictional figures has a historical foundation: Hughes created Semple in 1943 and developed the character throughout the 1940s. However, it is worth noting that Rampersad identifies Semple's recuperative resilience specifically as a component of "the genius of the black folk" (Rampersad, p. 65). This racially based reading conforms with Barksdale's characterization of Hughes's trumpet player as a "folk music man" of specifically African origin whose role is to anesthetize "Black people . . . against remembered pain" (Barksdale, p. 25). Both of these interpretations can be recast within the framework provided by James Clifford: Hughes's trumpet player can be seen to be figured not only as archetypally "human" (as in my own reading) but also as archetypally "African" or "African American" (like the dancing girl in my reading of "Jazzonia").

[40]Clifford, "On Ethnographic Allegory," p. 101.

[41]Clifford, *The Predicament of Culture*, p. 110.

jazz subculture reinforces his status as a critical, "objective" observer of the musicians, while his overall, sympathetic evaluation of the subculture supports his role of being sensitively attuned to its nuances. Thus, in "Trumpet Player: 52nd Street," Hughes serves both as a spokesperson for and an interpreter of the jazz subculture, since he represents the jazz lifestyle as a coherently meaningful subculture to his target audience in a manner that assures the audience of the well-balanced accuracy of his representation.

The degree of the poem's "success" in culturally representing and interpreting African-American jazz musicians to a white audience can be measured in many different ways. For instance, there is evidence that some contemporary white readers were receptive to Hughes's representation of his trumpet player "as a human being." In 1947, Hubert Creekmore of the *New York Times Book Review* wrote that, of all the "racially inspired" verse in Hughes's *Fields of Wonder*, "Trumpet Player: 52nd Street" was the best: it "shows fine penetration" at its conclusion.[42] This latter opinion would seem to reveal the "rich" and "convincing" nature of Hughes's cultural representation and evaluation, since Creekmore appears to believe that the poet has authoritatively unveiled the truth of the trumpet player's human experience.

On another level, Hughes's conclusion about the significance of jazz performance also coincides with the views of many actual African-American musicians and of "real" ethnographers. Anthropologist John Szwed quotes many black musicians who concur with the notion that musical performance "mellows trouble," and he cites their testimony to support his own conclusion that such "ritual" musical events can "ease personal conditions of stress."[43] In this sense, Hughes's poetic cultural fiction is consistent with other "authoritative" accounts of sociomusical activity.

Finally, "Trumpet Player: 52nd Street" contributes greatly to our understanding of the sociomusical significance of "the Bebop revolution." Even as we recall that Hughes's poetic-ethnographic portrayal of Fifty-second Street jazz musicians tells a story about "the Bebop revolution" that is limited and *partial* (as all accounts of such phenomena are), we can still appreciate the unique, illuminating perspective it provides on such a complex topic. Hughes's portrayal of Beboppers' and other jazz musicians' lifestyle as an effective strategy for surviving the racial conditions of the 1940s can stand equally alongside other efforts to understand the sociomusical significance of jazz in general and of "the Bebop revolution" in particular.

[42]Hubert Creekmore, "Poems by Langston Hughes," *New York Times Book Review* (4 May 1947): 10.

[43]John Szwed, "Afro-American Musical Adaptation," in *Afro-American Anthropology*, ed. N.E. Whitten and John Szwed (New York: Free Press, 1970), p. 223.

Collage of *Down Beat* issues: cover from September 9, 1949; title page from October 22, 1947; page 14 from January 28, 1949. General Libraries of The University of Texas at Austin.

A *Short Stay in the Sun: The Reception of Bebop* (1944–1950)

BY BERNARD GENDRON

FROM POP TO ART

The bebop movement is generally recognized as the major point of transformation in jazz history, when jazz went from being a popular entertainment music, as in the swing bands, to a demanding avant-garde music with a more specialized and sophisticated audience. Bebop signaled the entry of jazz modernism. By turning back to the original reception of bebop, it is possible to reconstruct how jazz modernism was originally interpreted—and indeed constituted—by the swirling discourses of the jazz press and their readership.[1]

However, the bebop revolution did not occur in a vacuum, but rather was born in the midst of one of the most divisive disputes in the history of jazz, between the partisans of swing music, on the one hand, and on the other, the "dixieland" revivalists who were proposing a return to the classic New Orleans jazz of the 1920s. These acrimonious debates, reaching a war-fever pitch, were fueled by a spate of small, sectarian, revivalist journals contesting the hegemony of the two established jazz journals, *Down Beat* and *Metronome*, who were altogether beholden to swing music. The jazz world's reception of bebop—indeed its receptivity to the new music—was strongly conditioned by this revivalist war, which was framed as a titanic battle between Ancients and Moderns. This struggle introduced into jazz a modernist discourse which, though initially confined to the support for swing, soon began to breach the barriers. *Metronome* in particular began to distinguish itself from the uncritically

---

[1] I want to thank Dan Morgenstern and the staff at the Institute of Jazz Studies, at Rutgers University of Newark, New Jersey, for their help, advice, and warm hospitality. I could not have written this article without them.

137

mainstream *Down Beat* as the champion of all that was new and forward-looking in jazz, whatever its stylistic genre. In 1945, not long before the emergence of bebop as a publicly identified movement, *Metronome* explicitly committed itself to the "support of the musicians who stand for the most emphatic experimentation, for the most courageous investigation of new sounds, for musical daring and integrity."[2]

Bebop was initially pigeon-holed as the most recent wave of modernism, after swing, to oppose itself to the traditionalism of New Orleans. The revivalist-swing war so subtly transposed itself into the bebop war that many of the criticisms, once directed against swing by the "anti-modern" revivalists, were now being leveled against bebop, though in different circumstances and with different inflections.[3]

The "Dizzy Rage" (1944–1946)

As the story is told, the bebop movement was born and incubated between 1941 and 1943, during the after-hours jam sessions at Monroe's and Minton's of Harlem, in relative seclusion from the jazz press, whose eyes were focused on the various night club scenes on 52nd Street.[4] In these small and modest venues, the musicians who were to be the charter members of this movement—Dizzy Gillespie, Charlie Parker, Thelonious Monk, Oscar Pettiford, and Max Roach, among others—were honing their new skills, and experimenting with new harmonic and rhythmic devices, in the hothouse atmosphere of no-holds-barred competition.[5]

But the full bebop sound, with the melodic, harmonic, and rhythmic innovations all working together, did not take shape until 1944-45, when the musicians had moved down to 52nd Street with their first combos—at the Onyx, the Spotlite, and the Three Deuces.[6] It was only then that the jazz press

[2]"Jazz Looks Ahead," *Metronome* (October 1945): 10.

[3]I discuss the revivalist-swing war, as a precursor to bebop, in "Modernists and Moldy Figs: Jazz at War (1942-1946)," *Discourse* (Spring 1993): 130-157.

[4]I have found only one, very perfunctory, reference to these jam sessions by the jazz press: Leonard Feather, "Pettiford-of-the-Month," *Metronome* (November 1943): 18.

[5]For accounts of the pre-history of bebop, see Dizzy Gillespie, *To Be or Not . . . to Bop* (New York: Doubleday, 1979), pp. 134-151; Ross Russell, *Bird Lives!* (London: Quartet Books, 1973), pp. 130-144; and Ira Gitler, *Swing to Bop* (New York: Oxford University Press, 1985), pp. 75-117.

[6]For accounts of bebop on 52nd Street, see Arnold Shaw, *The Street That Never Slept* (New York: Coward, McGann, and Geoghegan, 1971), pp. 264-311; Gitler, pp. 118-159; Russell, pp. 162-177; and Gillespie, pp. 202-221, 231-241.

began to take note, though what it first heard was not a movement, but a small stream of new individual sounds joining a rising tide of modernisms, a small group of innovators who were to be added to the ranks of Stan Kenton, Boyd Raeburn, Art Tatum, Coleman Hawkins, and Woody Herman.

Alone among his co-experimenters from Harlem, Dizzy Gillespie was seized by the press as a force of his own, as the most exciting and influential jazz musician of his generation. People spoke of a "Dizzy rage," a "Dizzy movement."[7] He achieved his first publicity breakthrough in two articles by Leonard Feather of *Metronome*, "Dizzy Is Crazy Like a Fox" (1944) and "Dizzy, the 21st Century Gabriel"(1945), each of which had all the earmarks of a hard-sell promotional piece.[8] Dizzy was then defined in the jazz press as a unique new stylist and technical virtuoso, with a "genius for substituting and extending chords in unorthodox but singularly thrilling ways and places," and a facility for playing "incredible cascades of fast notes at breakneck tempos" while making "every note mean something."[9] While praising Gillespie, these writers were most severe in excoriating the "horde" of imitators who "sound like a grotesque caricature," and who have even "been trying to make themselves look and act like Dizzy to boot," with their "goatee beards," "ridiculous little hats," and "apathetic" 'S' postures.[10]

Yet by the end of 1945, the jazz press had slowly shifted from seeing Gillespie as an individualistic prodigy to construing him as only one among many leaders of a revolutionary movement larger than Dizzy, which was also shaped by the contributions of Parker and Monk. Gillespie was now more modestly described as the "symbol" or "focal point" of this new revolution, rather than as a movement unto himself.[11] But the jazz press did not resort to the word "bebop" to denote this as yet unnamed revolution until April 1946, when a controversy erupted over the new music in, of all places, Hollywood California.

[7]"Chords and Discords: Case against Dizzy," *Down Beat* (March 25, 1946): 12; "Influence of the Year: Dizzy Gillespie," *Metronome* (January 1946): 24.

[8]Leonard Feather, "Dizzy Is Crazy Like a Fox," *Metronome* (July 1944): 16, 31; "Dizzy—21st Century Gabriel," *Esquire* (October 1945): 11.

[9]"Dizzy Gillespie's Style, Its Meaning Analyzed," *Down Beat* (February 11, 1946): 14; Feather, "Dizzy—21st Century Gabriel," p. 11.

[10]"Dizzy Gillespie's Style, . . .," p. 14; "Influence of the Year . . .," p. 24.

[11]"Influence . . .," p. 24; Feather, "Dizzy—21st Century Gabriel," p. 11.

"BEBOP" IN LOTUS LAND (1945-1946)

It is generally agreed that the word "bebop" originated, during Dizzy Gillespie's first residency at 52nd Street in 1944, from one of the onomatopoeic scat phrases that he used to remind musicians of the opening melodic-rhythmic line of a newly invented, untitled tune. Soon customers would ask for "that bebop song" or "that bebop stuff."[12] However, the word was not used initially to designate a new musical school or revolution. The tune *Bebop*, composed by Gillespie in 1944 and recorded in 1945, was not presented as the standard bearer of a movement, nor was it so construed in a somewhat unenthusiastic *Down Beat* review, which simply treated it as a failed attempt at "good swing."[13]

The mainstream jazz press initially resisted the term "Bebop," as did the movement musicians themselves, though for different reasons. The first found it too undignified at a time when they were trying to upgrade the image of jazz, and the second resented the naming of their movement by a term devised by white promoters and audiences.[14] Not being so constrained, some revivalists were using the term "bebop" intermittently, before its appearance in the mainstream jazz press, to refer quite indiscriminately to any of the most recent modernisms that they despised, even to the non-bebop music of Lionel Hampton and Woody Herman.[15]

It took a controversy, inspired and disseminated by the mass media, for the name "bebop" to become firmly entrenched, and for the newly designated bebop movement, finally disentangled from other jazz modernisms, to reach the center stage of public attention. In mid-March, 1946, a Los Angeles radio station banned "hot jive," which it equated with "bebop," on the pretext that

[12]For converging, though different accounts, see Barry McRae, *Dizzy Gillespie* (New York: Universe Books, 1988), p. 36; Gillespie, p. 208; and Shaw, pp. 270-271.

[13]Gillespie, pp. 208, 506-507; *Down Beat* (August 1, 1945): 8. This recording was associated with a current fad for songs with scat titles, such as Louis Jourdan's *Mop Mop* and Helen Humes's *Be-Baba-Leba*, which had little to do with jazz schools and ideologies. The Humes piece was sanitized and transformed by Lionel Hampton into *Hey! Ba-Ba-Re-Bop*, a major early-1946 hit which slyly incorporated the term "rebop"—a then widespread, though less "hip," alternative to "bebop." Jim Dawson and Steve Propes, *What Was the First Rock n' Roll Record?* (Boston: Faber and Faber, 1992), pp. 9-13; Lionel Hampton (with James Haskins), *Hamp: an Autobiography* (New York: Warner Books, 1989), pp. 203-204.

[14]As Max Roach put it, "nobody considered the music as 'bop' until it moved downtown. So to derogate the music and make it look like it was one them things, they started hanging labels on the music. For example, don't give me all that 'jazz,' or that's 'bop' talk, this thing or the other. We argue these points because words mean quite a bit to all of us. What we name our things and what we call our contributions should be up to us so that we can control our own destiny" (Gillespie, p. 209).

[15]See Bilbo Brown, "Rebop and Mop Mop," *The Record Changer* (October 1945): 34; Carlton Brown, "Hey! Ba-Ba-Revolt!," *The Record Changer* (May 1946): 12, 20; "Chords and Discords," *Down Beat* (April 22, 1946): 10; and "Chords and Discords," *Down Beat* (October 21, 1946): 10.

140

it emphasized "suggestive lyrics," aroused "degenerative instincts and emotions," and was "a contributing factor to juvenile delinquency."[16] This little, publicity-seeking outburst might have had no repercussions, if *Time* magazine had not given it national attention in an article called "Be-bop Be-bopped." In the process, *Time* gave the first definition of "bebop" to appear in print, when it described it as "hot jazz overheated, with overdone lyrics full of bawdiness, references to narcotics, and doubletalk." It claimed that the "bigwig of bebop" was Harry "The Hipster" Gibson, a "scat" who "in moments of supreme pianistic ecstacy throws his feet on the keyboard," and that the "No. 2 man" was his partner, "Slim" Gaillard, "a skyscraping, zooty Negro guitarist."[17] This most bizarre account was not however totally unconnected with the facts, at least as they existed in California.

In mid-December 1945, Gillespie brought a combo of musicians, including Parker, for an eight-week engagement at Billy Berg's of Hollywood. "Be-Bop invades the West!" proclaimed Ross Russell, the future producer of Parker records, in the monthly publicity leaflet for his Hollywood music store. While promoting Gillespie as the "rave trumpet star," who had been "making history along 52nd Street for over a year," Russell gave a short conciliatory disquisition on the "modern school," which had "dropped melody overboard" while flaunting its "brilliant technique, progressive harmonic explorations, and suspended rhythms."[18]

Gillespie's band was preceded at Billy Berg's by Harry "The Hipster" Gibson and Slim Gaillard, who had achieved considerable popularity and notoriety with their novelty songs, filled with sly allusions to sex and drugs, such as *Cement Mixer* and *Who Put the Benzedrine in Mrs. Murphy's Ovaltine?* Continuing their show on the same bill with the Gillespie band, Gibson and Gaillard quickly became associated with the new movement, more because of the profuse use of "hip" or "jive" talk in their songs than any similarity in music style.[19] This apparent alliance was further reinforced in the public eye by the burgeoning "hipster" subculture regularly in attendance at Billy Berg's, whose members, spouting their "mysterious lingo" and appearing as "high as barrage balloons," were infuriating and shocking the more traditional clientele."[20]

It was in the context of this array of events and perceptions that radio KMPC of Los Angeles imposed the ban on bebop for which *Time* gleefully provided the subtext. *Down Beat* and *Metronome* quickly and indignantly

[16]"Ted Steele Jab at Hot Jive Smells," *Down Beat* (April 8, 1946): 10; Fran Ticks, "The Be-bop Feud," *Metronome* (April 1946): 44-45.

[17]"Be-Bop Be-bopped," *Time* (March 25, 1946): 52.

[18]"Be-Bop Invades the West!," *Jazz Tempo* (December 1945): 1. See also *Jazz Tempo* (April 1946).

[19]Gaillard also recorded with the Gillespie band during their stay in Hollywood.

[20]Ana Ticks, "Jazz à la Billy Berg," *Metronome* (February 1946): 26.

came to the defense of their California colleagues, and in the process introduced "bebop" into their official lexicon. *Down Beat* was especially outraged by the fact that the author of the ban, Ted Steele, was a musician engaged in "a vicious and slanderous attack on his fellows," rather than a mere "press agent" exhibiting "poor judgment and bad taste." However, in defending the newly named "bebop" movement against censorship, *Down Beat* was doing no more, as a trade paper, than expressing solidarity with some of its clientele. It was not interested in contesting definitions, or distinguishing Gillespie's music from that of Gibson-Gaillard. It most emphatically was not endorsing bebop or its perceived life-styles.[21] *Metronome*, on the other hand, was more concerned to correct the distorted image of "bebop" created by *Time*, than to challenge Radio KMPC's act of blatant censorship. Unlike *Down Beat*, the editors of *Metronome* were strongly committed to the legitimation of what was being called "bebop," as a modernist art movement within jazz. In an interview, *Metronome* pressed the censor, Ted Steele, to concede that "he had no argument with jazz," or even bebop, and was in reality only banning the "suggestive" songs of Gibson and Gaillard.[22]

Contesting *Time*'s definition of "bebop," *Metronome* asserted that beyond its musical-onomatopoeic connotations the term was "meaningless," and that if you ban bebop, "you might as well ban the diatonic scale or the Dorian mode." This counter-claim accentuated *Metronome*'s resolution to describe the movement denoted by "bebop" in purely musical terms, in terms of harmonic, rhythmic, and tonal resources, rather than by reference to any life-style or verbal content (e.g., suggestive lyrics). According to *Metronome*, Radio KMPC and *Time* "had confused the frantic antics" of Gibson and Gaillard with the "intense but very different blowing" of Gillespie, Parker, "and their cohorts." The editors distanced themselves from Gibson and Gaillard whose songs, "thick with reefer smoke and bedroom innuendo," "do all jazz musicians a disservice." Hence, "the banning of their records from the air is of little consequence." The villains in this controversy, according to *Metronome*, were not the puritanical censors, but writers and publicists who distort jazz to appear as a "degenerate's paradise" or a "fool's delight," rather than presenting it truthfully as a "serious, disciplined art."[23]

The one concrete result of this controversy was the official promotion of the word "bebop" from a nonsense to a technical generic term, like "swing," and "dixieland."

[21]"Ted Steele . . .," p. 10.

[22]"Steele Bans 'Be-Bop' at L.A. Station; But What He Means by 'Be-Bop' Ain't," *Metronome* (April 1946): 15.

[23]"Feud for Thought," *Metronome* (April 1946): 10; "Steele Bans . . .," p. 15. See also Fran Ticks, "The Be-bop Feud," *Metronome* (April 1946): 44-45.

Photograph of Dizzy Gillespie at Billy Berg's in 1946. HRHRC *Ross Russell Collection*.

The California controversy, lasting barely a month, was followed by an indecisive, two-year interlude in the jazz world—a period of confusion, negotiation, economic anxiety, mild storms, and petty competitions. The bebop movement was now clearly a force to be contended with, bearing an imagery that shocked, titillated, and threatened. But the jazz world was not ready to crown it the heir of swing, or even give it priority over the other modernisms (e.g., Boyd Raeburn, Stan Kenton, et al.).

During this interval, *Down Beat*, *Metronome*, and the revivalist press responded to bebop each in their own distinct, complex, and somewhat inconsistent ways. *Down Beat* provided perhaps the best barometer of the changing whims of the public reception to bebop. As the self-appointed, broad-based trade magazine for band musicians, constantly concerned with the economic welfare of the music industry, *Down Beat* went out of its way to project a moderate and non-ideological image of its practices. However, though apparently allowing for every tendency, this journal was clearly more wedded to the interests of big band swing musicians, and looked at both the revivalists and the beboppers with a mixture of muted hostility and bemusement.[24]

Initially, *Down Beat* responded to the newly baptized bebop movement more with novelty articles that catered to the fad, with catchy titles such as "ZU-BOP NOW," "JACK GOES FROM BACH TO BEBOP," and "CZECHS CHECK BOP," than with critical analyses or substantive news reports. *Down Beat* whimsically asked, for example, "Why must you wear a goatee to play a good hot horn?"[25] Some articles, which otherwise had nothing to say about bebop, would nonetheless use the word in the headline as a hook to lure the reader.[26] *Down Beat* did occasionally transcend such reportage to articulate

[24]Michael Levin, *Down Beat* (August 13, 1947): "New Orleans can't be reproduced out of its environment and . . . bebop is often a poor translation of 1900 classical" (p. 16). That is, Levin asserts that neither New Orleans jazz, which is rooted in a different era and locale, nor bebop, whose supposed novelties are merely derivative of harmonic innovations of early twentieth-century classical music, can be construed as authentic contemporary successors to swing.

[25]See the following articles, all in *Down Beat*: "Zu-Bop Now" (October 21, 1946): 15; "Jack Goes from Bach to Bebop" (September 10, 1947): 3; "Czechs Check Bop" (December 17, 1947): 1; Bill Gottlieb, "Posin'" (June 3, 1946): 3; also, "Kern Music Takes a Beating from Diz" (August 9, 1946): 15; "Bop: The End!" (February 11, 1948): 7.

[26]See the following articles, all in *Down Beat*: "So, Re-bop, etc." (April 22, 1946): 13—a report on the evacuation of the Russian Army from Iran to the tune of a 37-piece band; "Scotch Re-bop" (May 20, 1946): 2—on three drunken musicians playing Scottish folksongs on instruments they stole in a break-in; "Symphony Man Seeks Bebop—Bopped" (April 9, 1947): 1—on the mugging of a famous symphony conductor on his way to hear jazz in the black ghetto of Los Angeles; and "Hears Bop, Blows Top" (February 12, 1948).

its own ambivalent musical views about bebop, as in the response by the regular record reviewer, Mike Levin, to a Ross Russell letter admonishing him for his somewhat hostile reception to bebop discs. In a re-examination of bebop records produced by Russell's Dial label, Levin complained of a "constant, nerve chiseling tension," a disregard for "consistency of tone," and a propensity to "replace genuine improvisational ability with sensational technical figures played at extremely fast tempos." Unlike the followers of "Diz and Bird," he could not rate the latter "as equally important in their time as an Armstrong was in his."[27] *Down Beat* implied, by its statements and allusions, that it objected only partially to bebop, and only on musical grounds. It would rise unqualifiedly in defense of bebop against global and non-musical attacks, such as "worst-than-Uncle-Tom," racial slurs against movement musicians, or gleeful pronouncements that "bebop is dead."[28]

Positioning itself emphatically to the musical left of *Down Beat* on the side of the ultra-modern, *Metronome* was unwavering in its support for bebop. But this journal also made it abundantly clear that bebop was only one, and not necessarily the favorite, among many advanced, modernist movements in jazz that it would support with dedication. Indeed, Barry Ulanov, the chief propagandist for modernism at *Metronome*, seemed to prefer jazz that was more cerebral, more influenced by European avant-garde music, and, in contrast to bebop, less embroiled in showmanship, unusual argot and dress, and suspect life-styles. Amidst a series of warm endorsements of bebop musicians, such as the selection of Gillespie in 1946, and Parker in 1947, as "Influence of the Year," and Gillespie's band as "Band of the Year" in 1948, *Metronome* scattered enough objections to imply serious philosophical disagreements.[29] With respect to Gillespie and his 1947 band, in particular, Ulanov complained of the "senseless screams," the "endless quotations of trivia," "frantic clowning" and "can-can" gyrations—all "acrid" musical effects of a "bitter" personal philosophy driven to avoid any "musical statement bordering on the exalted."[30]

---

[27]Michael Levin, "Diggin' the Discs with Mix," *Down Beat* (October 21, 1946): 21-22.

[28]Bill Gottlieb, "Fouls on Every Line in Collier's Article on Slim Gaillard," *Down Beat* (October 21, 1946): 4+—in response to Ted Shane, "Song of the Cuckoo," *Colliers* (October 5, 1946): 21+; "Champion of Be-Bop Assails Dexter," *Down Beat* (March 26, 1947): 5—in response to Dave Dexter, "The End of an Era; Be-Bop Is Dead in Southern California," *Capitol News* (March 1947): 6; and on the latter diatribe, see also Barry Ulanov, "Who's Dead, Bebop or its Detractors?," *Metronome* (June 1947): 50.

[29]"Band of the Year: Dizzy Gillespie," *Metronome* (January 1948): 17-18; "Influence of the Year: Charlie Parker," *Metronome* (January 1948): 19.

[30]Barry Ulanov, "Dizzy Gillespie," *Metronome* (September 1947): 2; "Dizzy Heights," *Metronome* (November 1947): 50.

In a striking 1947 article, in which he happily proclaimed the death of swing ("the Benny Goodman groove"), Ulanov called upon musicians to create a radically new era in jazz—to rid themselves of the "dead wood," the "banal harmonies," the "fascination" with "merely lush and rhythmic figures," and to study and ground their work in the modern compositions of Hindemith, Berg, Schönberg, Ives, Cage, and Varèse. "It is time for jazz to stop looking in the mirror and fawning upon itself," and to begin "to listen to [these composers] in humble appreciation of what they have done." To accentuate this new symbiosis between jazz and European art music, Ulanov announced that *Metronome* from then on would be subtitled the *Review of Modern Music*. He commended "Dizzy and the Be-Bop crowd" for having initiated this trend. But he was also saying that bebop, innovative as it may have been, was being passed by, as only the first of a whole series of transformations in jazz based on European high culture. The question for the forward-looking *Metronome* was: who would occupy the next stage?[31]

For Ulanov, no one captured the future of jazz as convincingly as Lennie Tristano, whom he championed for three years as the one who was transcending bebop after having learned from it.[32] Tristano obligingly supported this line in two articles for *Metronome* on "what's right" and "what's wrong with the beboppers." He objected particularly to the proclivity of young beboppers toward "pseudo-hip affectations"—they "slouch" rather than "sit," "amble" rather than "walk." Nonetheless, for Tristano, bebop though "not an end in itself" is "unquestionably an excellent means" in the transformation of jazz into an "art for its own sake"—for example, by "its valiant attempt" to replace "emotion with meaning," and by "successfully combatting the putrefying effects of commercialism."[33]

Following quickly on *Metronome*'s heels in the search for a modernist alternative to bebop, *Down Beat* chose Stan Kenton, the winner of their 1947 Reader's Poll, who also proceeded to mouth formulas about the intermediary character of bebop and the relevance of European art music. Though Bebop is "doing more for music than anything else," such as "educating the people to new intervals and sounds," Kenton opined, it nonetheless is "not the new jazz" but only a "hot-foot along the way," because "it lacks emotion" and "hasn't settled down yet." The jazz of the future "will dominate and swallow classical [music]."[34]

[31]Barry Ulanov, "A Call to Arms—and Horns," *Metronome* (April 1947): 15, 44.

[32]"Musician of the Year—Lennie Tristano," *Metronome* (January 1948): 19; Barry Ulanov, "Master in the Making," *Metronome* (August 1949): 14-15, 32-33; "The Means of Mastery," *Metronome* (September 1949): 14, 26.

[33]Lennie Tristano, "What's Wrong with the Beboppers," *Metronome* (June 1947): 16; "What's Right with the Beboppers," *Metronome* (July 1947): 14, 31.

[34]Michael Levin, "Jazz Is Neurotic—Kenton," *Down Beat* (January 14, 1948): 1.

Faced with a bebop movement dominated by African-American musicians, the virtually all-white jazz journals seemed always to be in search of "great white hopes"—white modernists, like Tristano and Kenton, with whom a mostly white readership would feel more at home. There may indeed have been a racial code operating in the white critics' expressed desire for a more cerebral and European modern jazz, as well as a jazz purified of any association with life-styles, argots, or dress.[35]

The contortions around bebop, which both *Down Beat* and *Metronome* underwent at this time, were not unrelated to the sense of economic insecurity which overtook the jazz world immediately after the war, when many big bands had to break up at least temporarily, and jazz clubs on 52nd Street were being turned into strip joints.[36] In good or bad times, *Down Beat* never hesitated to display a blatant preoccupation with commerce, which *Metronome* camouflaged with a patina of aesthetic concern.[37] This insecurity indirectly informed the discourse and debates about bebop. *Metronome* insisted, not altogether convincingly, that bebop, and other post-war modern jazz movements, would create a new market to supplant the declining market for swing.[38] Still wedded to the big bands, *Down Beat* was more confused, and clearly worried, despite its denials, that the public was switching its preference from "swing" music to the "gentle drip of uncontrolled sugar," typical of the "flossy" "sweet" bands.[39] Whatever its musical misgivings, *Down Beat*'s attitude toward bebop would ultimately be determined by how well or badly it affected the market for jazz. During the 1946-48 interval, the results were unclear.

[35]Gillespie, p. 337.

[36]"Zombies Put Kiss of Death on 52nd St. Jazz," *Down Beat* (February 25, 1946): 3; "Worrisome Days along the Street; Biz Is Bad," *Down Beat* (November 11, 1946): 1. See also, Leonard Feather, "The Street Is Dead," *Metronome* (April 1948): 16.

[37]Between 1946 and 1947, a number of scare headlines were emblazoned in large print on the pages of *Down Beat*: "BIG PAYROLLS, LOUD BRASS MUST GO" (August 12, 1946): 1; "MUSIC BIZ JUST AIN'T NOWHERE" (November 18, 1946): 1; "JOB PANIC HITS HOLLYWOOD RANKS" (May 21, 1947); "THINGS ARE GETTING TOUGH EVERYWHERE" (May 5, 1947): 8.

[38]Ulanov, "A Call . . .," p. 15.

[39]"Whose Goose Is Golden, Or the Egg and They," *Down Beat* (January 29, 1947): 10.

Photograph of Charlie Parker with a bebopper's beret, n.d. HRHRC *Ross Russell Collection*.

INTERLUDE: THE MOLDY FIGS REACT (1946–1948)

If *Down Beat* and *Metronome* agreed on anything, it was that dixieland music, and its "reactionary" revivalist supporters, were the natural, and most hostile, opponents of bebop. But this construal was more an invention of these media, with their predilection for simplistic binary oppositions, than a statement of fact. Insofar as they were critical of anything that was "modern," that is, anything since New Orleans jazz, the revivalists, or "moldy figs" as they were derisively called, would of course have little good to say about bebop. But they did not despise bebop more than they did any other jazz modernisms, and indeed, had already spent most of their animus against swing, which for them was the ultimate outrage against "real" jazz.

By the time bebop became an issue, the war over revivalism had already subsided somewhat, in part because New Orleans music was succeeding in carving out a niche in the world of jazz entertainment. Of the approximately 10 "moldy fig" journals that had appeared in the early 1940s, only *Jazz Record* and *The Record Changer* remained, though they spent very little time critiquing bebop.[40] Ernest Borneman, a former editor of *The Record Changer*, and soon a migrant to England, was one of the few "moldy figs"—along with Mezz Mezzrow—to fight systematically and recurrently against bebop. Borneman's main complaint was that the bebop-inspired Europeanization of jazz would make jazz musicians permanently inferior to "legitimate" art composers. He found it outrageous to compare the harmonic experiments of bebop with those of Schönberg and Hindemith. Measured against the achievements of the latter, "Dizzy's harmonic continuity is infantile" and "Bird's contrapuntal patterns are puerile."[41] But this aggressive vendetta was not typical of revivalists (some of whom, including Ralph Gleason, actually converted to bebop).

This did not stop *Down Beat* and *Metronome* from whipping up a publicity campaign on the supposed war between dixieland and bebop. *Down Beat* spiced up its pages with headlines like "POLICE AVERT CLASH OF DIXIELAND AND BEBOP," "A JAZZ PURIST GUILTY OF COLLECT-ING RE-BOP!," AND "BOP GETS MONDAY NIGHT HOME IN DIXIE

[40]During the 1946-48 interlude, *Jazz Record* actually produced two sympathetic accounts, as against one fiercely anti-bebop diatribe: J.C. Heard, "Rebop Is Not Jazz," *Jazz Record* (March 1947): 10; Mary Lou Williams, "Music and Progress," *Jazz Record* (November 1947): 23; Carter Winter, "An Open Letter to Fred Robbins," *Jazz Record* (October 1946): 12, 18; and (November 1946): 12-13.

The Record Changer, for its part, indulged in a few, scattered, negative reviews of bebop records, e.g., a reviewer described Charlie Parker's *Ornithology* and *A Night in Tunisia* as "incredibly dull music," "phoney," with "superficial" effects and an "awful" rhythm section (September 1946).

[41]Ernest Borneman, "Both Schools of Critics Wrong," *Down Beat* (July 30, 1947): 11; (August 13, 1947): 16.

149

HANGOUT," while provoking a public argument between dixielander-turned-bebopper Dave Tough—"DIXIELAND NOWHERE SAYS DAVE TOUGH"—and the revivalist leader Eddie Condon—"CONDON RAPS TOUGH FOR 'REBOP SLOP'."[42]

For his part, Ulanov of *Metronome* organized a "Moldy Figs vs. Modernists" radio show with revivalist Rudi Blesh, involving an "all-star" modernist band made up of Gillespie and Parker as well as Tristano. *Time* magazine, somewhat taken in by these antics, explained to its readers that "moldy fig" was "boppese for 'decadent' Dixieland jazz," though this expression had appeared in print as early as 1944, in a quite different context, before there was any "boppese."[43]

THE REVOLT OF THE MUSICIANS (1946–1949)

Perhaps the most serious challenge to bebop was the growing resentment of musicians outside the movement—mostly from swing bands—who were made doubly insecure by the threat of marginalization in an already shrinking market. The first to complain openly was Benny Goodman who, smarting at insinuations by "modernist" critics that he was becoming passé, responded in an October 1946 interview by striking out against bebop: I"ve been listening to some of the Re-bop musicians. You know, some of them can't even hold a tone. They're just faking. Bop reminds me of guys who refuse to write a major chord even if it's going to sound good."[44] He continued to snipe even after introducing bop elements into his own arrangements two years later—critiquing bebop for being more a "nervous" than an "exciting music," and complaining about the "morals" of the boppers, who have to be "screen[ed]" before being hired, "like [in] the FBI."[45] It was good copy for the jazz press to provoke criticisms of bebop by other musicians, and many obliged, including

[42]All in *Down Beat*: "Police Avert . . ." (July 1, 1947): 3; "A Jazz Purist . . ." (June 17, 1946): 16; "Bop Gets . . ." (November 11, 1948): 4; "Dixieland Nowhere . . ." (September 23, 1946): 4; "Condon Raps . . ." (October 7, 1946): 4, 17.

[43]Barry Ulanov, "Moldy Figs vs. Moderns" (November 1947): 15, 23; "How Deaf Can You Get?," *Time* (May 17, 1948): 76-77.

[44]George Simon, "B.G. Explains," *Metronome* (October 1946): 18. For a contemporaneous "modernist" critique of Goodman, see Tom Connell, "The King of Swing Abdicates," *Metronome* (August 1946): 14.

[45]George T. Simon, "Benny Blows Bop," *Metronome* (August 1948): 12. Goodman later shed crocodile tears over the apparent demise of bebop: George T. Simon, "Bop Confuses Benny," *Metronome* (October 1949): 15, 35.

Fletcher Henderson, Hot Lips Page, Nat "King" Cole, Lester Young, Artie Shaw, and Benny Carter. Most were subdued and careful in their remarks, following a code of peer etiquette, unlike Tommy Dorsey who simply blurted out "Bop stinks. It has set music back twenty years."[46]

The revolt of the musicians peaked in early 1948, when Louis Armstrong, egged on by the media and a few revivalists, launched into a sustained and surprisingly angry diatribe against bebop. After *Time* aired some of his grievances—"Mistakes, that's all bop is" and "A whole lot of notes, weird notes . . . that don't mean nothing"—*Down Beat* and *Metronome* cornered him into interviews which turned stray remarks into a major controversy.[47] The boppers, he said, are "full of malice and all they want to do is show you up."[48] He was clearly smarting from unnamed bebop "cats" who were deriding him for being "old-fashioned" and playing "too many long notes."[49] "All the young cats want to kill papa so they start forcing their tone." He also blamed bebop for the decline of the band business, particularly on 52nd Street, where "they've thrown out the bands and put in a lot of chicks taking their clothes off."[50]

TRIUMPH (1948–1949)

Nonetheless, bebop triumphed. By mid-1948, the jazz press, and crucially *Down Beat*, followed by the mass media, concluded that bebop had acquired artistic legitimacy (however bizarre), that it had a powerful "cult" following that could not be disregarded, and was on the verge of achieving massive commercial success. Most important, it was agreed that bebop, having bested the other modernisms, would occupy the next stage in jazz history as the legitimate successor to swing.

---

[46]Dorsey was upbraided for this breach of peer etiquette in a lead *Down Beat* article: Ralph Gleason, "TD Told to Open Ears to Bop" (September 23, 1949): 1, 12.

[47]"Satchmo Comes Back," *Time* (September 1, 1947): 32.

[48]"'Bop Will Kill Business Unless It Kills Itself First'—Louis Armstrong," *Down Beat* (April 7, 1948): 2.

[49]"Satchmo Comes Back," p. 32; George Simon, "Bop's the Easy Way out, Claims Louis," *Metronome* (March 1948): 14-15.

[50]"'Bop Will Kill . . .'," pp. 2-3. The issue continued to plague Armstrong, even years later. See, for example, John Wilson, "Armstrong Explains Stand against Bop," *Down Beat* (December 30, 1949): 3, when Armstrong jibes the boppers for walking "around with them little hot water bottles on their heads; don't even shave." For Gillespie's more recent assessment of this controversy, see Gillespie, pp. 295-296.

Keenly aware of the dynamics of marketing, Gillespie did more than anyone to assure commercial success for bebop. In early 1948, *Metronome* commended him for organizing a big band with a marketable image, and hiring an activist agent, Billy Shaw, from whose office "streamed reprints of articles about Diz, a steady diet of Gillespie food for editors, columnists, and jockeys." Though it had carped in the past, *Metronome* now applauded Gillespie for developing a "visual personality," imitated "all over America" by "young boppers" who "donned the Dizzy cap," "struggled with chin fuzz," "affected the heavy spectacles," and "with their own little bands began to lead from the waist and the rump."[51] Realizing the importance of cultural legitimation as a marketing device, Shaw organized a very successful Carnegie Hall appearance for Gillespie and Parker in the fall of 1947, and a tumultuous tour of Europe for Gillespie's big band in the spring of 1948.[52] Said *Time* magazine: "In Paris, zealous French zazous (jazz fans) came to blows over [Gillespie]."[53]

But what most impressed the commercially-minded *Down Beat* was bebop's re-invigoration of the New York night club scene. After the demise of 52nd Street jazz, a few very lively bebop night clubs emerged on Broadway between 47th and 52nd Street. The Royal Roost, a chicken restaurant, which in early 1948 had started featuring bebop sessions as a once a week novelty, achieved enough success to transform itself into a jazz nightclub with nightly sessions.[54] The results were spectacular. By August, the Roost was drawing "the biggest jazz crowds in New York . . . many of whom outbopp[ed] the bandsmen, at least in appearance."[55] Other purveyors of bebop soon set up shop on Broadway: the Clique, Bop City, and later Birdland.[56] Bebop musicians even appeared regularly in Greenwich Village, the stronghold of the Dixieland movement.[57]

Buoyed by the surge in the bebop business, *Down Beat* happily stoked up its publicity machine in a supportive role, doubling the number of articles devoted to bebop matters and news. It exulted over the adoption of bebop styles by erstwhile swing musicians, such as Goodman, Charlie Barnet, Nat "King" Cole, Chubby Jackson, and Charlie Ventura who also lectured on

[51]"Band of the Year: Dizzy Gillespie," pp. 17-18.

[52]Michael Levin, "Dizzy, Bird, Ella, Pack Carnegie," *Down Beat* (October 22, 1947): 1, 3; "Dizzy Heights"; Leonard Feather, "Europe Does Dizzy," *Metronome* (May 1948): 19, 35

[53]"How Deaf Can You Get?," *Time* (May 17, 1948): 77.

[54]"Nightly Bop Bashes," *Down Beat* (May 9, 1948): 2.

[55]"Customers Outbop the Boppers," *Down Beat* (August 25, 1948): 3.

[56]See the following articles in *Down Beat*: "Roost, Clique Bopping Mad" (January 28, 1949):1; "Roost Will Switch Bop to New Shop" (April 11, 1949): 1; "City Halts Birdland Debut" (July 21, 1949): 3.

[57]"Huh? Bop in the Village?," *Down Beat* (September 23,1949): 2.

bebop on the radio.[58] It enthused over the rapid spread of bebop to college campuses, foreign countries, and even American rural backwaters (e.g., Greeneville, Tennessee).[59] It promoted the new books on bebop, introduced a series of "technical articles on bebop," and explained the bop argot.[60] Most importantly, after years of parody, *Down Beat* finally produced a few serious, theoretical analyses of bebop, which unanimously supported it as a healthy, inevitable stage in the development of jazz.[61] One article remarked that in the controversies over bebop, "history was repeating itself," since so many of the complaints against bebop—noisy, undanceable, undefinable, shocking—had once been leveled against swing. Born of the swing age, *Down Beat* was nonetheless, for the moment, allowing that the bebop revolution was as momentous as the swing revolution had once been. "Same story, different characters."[62]

The peak of bebop's period of commercial success was probably reached during the critically triumphant, coast-to-coast tour of the Gillespie band in the fall of 1948—from Billy Berg's to the Royal Roost. Surrounded on stage by look-alike cultists, even young women with painted goatees, the band played to enthusiastic, star-studded audiences, including Lena Horne, Howard Duff, Joe Louis, Mel Torme, Benny Goodman, Henny Youngman, and most notably Ava Gardner, "who came out two or three times a week to hear us."[63] In their typically supercilious fashion, *Life* and *Time* took note of these commercial triumphs with feature articles anointing bebop as the musical vogue of the year. Among other fictions, *Life* photographically represented the ritual of a bebop greeting—involving the "flatted fifth" sign, the shout

[58]See the following articles in *Down Beat*: "Bop-Styled BG Septet Stars All But Goodman" (July 14, 1948): 6; Michael Levin, "Barnet Kentonized Crew Bops, Swings at the Same Time" (April 11, 1949): 1; John S. Wilson, "Nat Nominates Himself Advance Man for Bop" (March 25, 1949): 2; John S. Wilson, "Chubby Aglow with Truth and Love" (April 8, 1949): 3; "Charlie Tells Them What's with Bop" (April 22, 1949): 7.

[59]See the following articles in *Down Beat*: "Georgia Hip-Dogs Build Prestige with Bop Touch" (April 22, 1949): 5; "Exciting Bop Ground Found in Pittsburgh" (May 20, 1949): 15; "U. of Washington Crew Bop Pioneers" (July 15, 1949): 6; "Marshall College Crew Bops Sweet" (May 20, 1949): 5; "South America Takes Bop Away" (October 6, 1948): 3; "Bop Cooling Off Tennessee Town" (February 25, 1949): 12.

[60]See the following articles in *Down Beat*: "'Be or Bop' Is a Fine Catalogue" (September 8, 1948): 20; "New Book on Bop Styles an Aid to Progressives" (May 20, 1949): 11; "Moldy or Modern, Folks Should Read 'Inside Bop'" (July 15, 1949): 11; Gil Fuller, "The Bop Beat" (January 14, 1949): 22; Ted Hallock, "Bop Jargon Indicative of Intellectual Thought" (July 28, 1948): 4.

[61]Dave Banks, "Be-Bop Called Merely the Beginning of a New Creative Music Form," *Down Beat* (February 11, 1948): 16; Amy Lee, "Figs Might Do Well to Take a Hint from Bop," *Down Beat* (May 6, 1949): 2.

[62]"Seems We Heard that Song before," *Down Beat* (January 14, 1949): 10.

[63]Gillespie, pp. 342-343; "Improved Dizzy Band Cuts Old to Shreds" *Down Beat* (October 20, 1948): 3.

"Eel-ya-dah," and the "grip" that "ends the ritual," so that the "beboppers can now converse."[64]

Even the "moldy fig" press fell in line before the bebop juggernaut. *The Record Changer*, the only viable revivalist journal remaining, announced in early 1948 that it "refuses to be known as a sectarian publication." New Orleans jazz, though the "best," is not the "only" jazz.[65] Over the next two years, *The Record Changer* would give bebop a great deal of sympathetic attention, including a series of articles by Ross Russell on bebop rhythm, instrumentation, brass, etc., which together constitute arguably the first systematic treatise on bebop.[66]

DECLINE AND DEATH (1949–1950)

Barry Ulanov of *Metronome* declared 1948 "the year of bop"—"the year when the Royal Roost dominated jazz life in New York, when the only jazz acceptable to young audiences around the country was modern jazz."[67] The attention and the plaudits from the press continued another six months into 1949, after which the fortunes of bebop plummeted precipitously.

Down Beat was willing to support bebop only so long as it perceived it to be commercially viable. But quite soon the bebop nightclubs, the only manifestations of bebop's commercial success, began to falter and go out of business—first the Clique and Billy Berg's in early 1949, followed by the Royal Roost in mid-1949, and Bop City at the end of 1950, leaving only Birdland, by this time no longer primarily a bebop establishment.[68] It was clear, at the beginning of 1949, that the jazz industry was facing its worst economic crisis since the depression, from which it might never recover.[69] Ballrooms as well as nightclubs were folding quickly, or indulging themselves

[64]"Bebop," *Life* (October 11, 1948): 138-142; "Bopera on Broadway," *Time* (December 20, 1948): 63-64.

[65]Editorial, *The Record Changer* (February 1948): 4.

[66]Some of these essays are collected in Martin Williams, ed., *The Art of Jazz* (New York: Oxford University Press, 1959), pp. 187-214.

[67]Barry Ulanov, "Wha' Hoppen?," *Metronome* (February 1949): 2.

[68]See the following articles in *Down Beat*: "Clique Bop Folds; Gals Take Over" (April 8, 1949): 1; "Empire, Berg's, Bebop's Hollywood Homes, Close" (May 6, 1949): 9; "Royal Roost Pulls a Fast Fold" (June 17, 1949): 3; "With Bop City Kaput, Birdland Only Broadway Bop Joint Left" (December 1, 1950): 5.

[69]See the following articles in *Down Beat*: "Biz May Be Off but not this Much" (December 1, 1948): 10; "'48 Should Teach a Lesson for '49" (December 29, 1948): 10; "Worst Business in Years, Say Owners, Local Cats" (June 3, 1949): 4.

in the new country-western, square-dance craze, which was causing hysteria in the jazz press—"Hillbilly Boom Can Spread Like Plague," screamed *Down Beat*.[70]

Attempting desperately to re-create consumer interest, *Down Beat* launched a highly publicized contest to replace the "outdated" term "jazz" with a new word "to describe the music from Dixieland through bop." The two winning words, "Crewcut" and "Amerimusic," never gained currency, as *Down Beat* backed down in the face of outraged opposition.[71] By the end of 1949, scare headlines in *Down Beat* announced that the prestigious "modern" bands of Charlie Barnet and Woody Herman were "Toss[ing] in [the] Towel."[72] *Down Beat* decided to take matters in its own hands in dealing with the horrendous "slump in the dance biz." It would spend all of 1950 attempting to fabricate a new dance boom—for example, by devoting a whole issue to dance music, and even to conducting "a laboratory experiment with [an unidentified] dance band to discover what is wrong with the business."[73]

Meanwhile, a scapegoat had to be found, and bebop was the ideal candidate. For the remainder of 1949 and into 1950, musicians and disc jockeys, some of whom had been avid supporters, spilled their recriminations against bop on the pages of *Down Beat*. According to Chubby Jackson, jazz was "plagued" by a "cult" of young musicians causing "bizarre night club spectacles," such as "leaning against walls and staring into space like idiots." Buddy Rich fired the bop "elements" from his band. There was innuendo about the taking of drugs and other behaviors which would give jazz the reputation it used to have "before we picked it out of the gutter and made it respectable." A disc jockey pleaded: "Let's dance, I'm sick of bebop."[74]

Responding to news of a funeral procession for bebop at the University of Minnesota, Charlie Ventura, erstwhile lecturer on bebop, agreed that "Bebop is really dead . . . that is, if you could ever say it was alive."[75] *Down Beat*

[70]See the following articles in *Down Beat*: "Hillbilly Boom . . ." (May 6, 1949): 1; "Music, where Is thy Swing? Cowboys, Barn Dancers Romping and Stomping" (July 15, 1949): 3; "That Hillbilly Threat is Real" (June 3, 1949): 10.

[71]See *Down Beat*: Advertisement (July 15, 1949): 5; "New Word for Jazz Worth $1,000" (June 15, 1949): 10; "Crewcut Contest's $" (November 4, 1949): 1; "Jazz Still 'Jazz' after a Struggle" (November 4, 1949): 10.

[72]See *Down Beat*: "Why Barnet Had to Break up" (December 2, 1949): 1; "Woody Herman Tosses in Towel" (December 16, 1949): 1.

[73]"Why the Slump in the Dance Biz? 'Beat' Plans to Find Out," *Down Beat* (December 12, 1949): 1, 10.

[74]See the following articles in *Down Beat*: Jack Tracy, "Jazz Being Plagued by a Cult—Jackson" (October 20, 1950): 1; "Buddy Gives Boot to his Boppers" (January 14, 1949): 1; "Where Are Cats of Tomorrow?" (August 12, 1949): 11; "Let's Dance, I'm Sick of Bop, Is Deejay's Plea" (May 19, 1950): 23.

[75]"Bop Dead, Ventura Agrees," *Down Beat* (December 16, 1949): 12.

apparently also agreed, since it reduced its coverage of bebop in 1950 to a trickle, dealing mostly with crisis and demise. But it was *Metronome*, formerly the most enthusiastic promoter of bebop, which declared it dead earliest and most decisively. In a December 1949 issue, Ulanov proclaimed "a once-strong edifice is crumbling and the decay is from within." The boppers brought their demise on themselves through the "ugly fights" over the "problem of origins"—was it Gillespie, Parker, or Monk who originated bebop?—as well as the "imitations" that became "apings," the loss of a danceable "steady pulse," and a fetish for breakneck speed. But worse were the "rotten [personal] habits" and mannerisms which "conquered every reserve of decency in jazz," and made "a joke of musicianship and japes of musicians."[76] After bop, Ulanov predicted, "we [will] have a jazz of reflection and restraint, soft statements and extended ideas," music "with mind as well as emotion"—the sure formula for the "birth of the cool."[77]

As the musician most associated with the marketing of bebop, Gillespie also suffered through the downfall of 1949-1950. Fighting against the undertow, he labored to make bop more accessible to "the average guy," by featuring "more bop variations on standard tunes," and introducing a steady four-beat pulse that people could dance to.[78] However, he was rebuked by a reviewer for sacrificing "spark to get his 'bop with a beat'," and contradicted by Parker, who denied not only that bebop had any "continuity of beat," but also that it had any roots in traditional jazz.[79] (Parker's popular reputation was gaining on Gillespie's at the time, and was to peak only after the bebop movement was dead.)

In mid-1950, Gillespie put together a more purist bebop band that drew rave reviews, but had to break up within a month for lack of venues. The foreboding *Down Beat* headline—"GILLESPIE'S CREW GREAT AGAIN, BUT MAY BREAK UP"—was followed two months later by the clincher: "BOP AT END OF ROAD, SAYS DIZZY." In September 1950, Gillespie was "without a band, without a recording contract, and with no definite plans for the future."[80] Thus, bop had come to an end.

[76]Barry Ulanov, "Skip Bop and Jump," *Metronome* (December 1949): 12, 36.

[77]Barry Ulanov, "After Bop, What?," *Metronome* (April 1950): 17, 32.

[78]See *Down Beat*: "Diz to Put Bop Touch to More Standard Tunes" (March 11, 1949): 3; "Bird Wrong; Bop Must Get a Beat" (October 10, 1949): 1.

[79]See *Down Beat*: Pat Harris, "Diz Sacrifices Spark to Get his 'Bop with a Beat'" (January 13, 1950): 8; Michael Levin and John S. Wilson, "No Bop Roots in Jazz: Parker" (September 9, 1949): 1.

[80]See *Down Beat*: Jack Tracy, "Gillespie's Crew . . ." (June 16, 1950): 1; John S. Wilson, "Bop at End . . ." (September 8, 1950): 7; Ralph Gleason, "Dizzy Getting a Bad Deal from Music Biz" (November 17, 1950): 14.

The careers of Gillespie, Parker, and Monk would all revive in the 1950s, and Bebop would be enshrined in the jazz canon as the first great wave of jazz modernism—just as *Metronome* had predicted. But the bop movement never came to life again.

POSTMORTEM

This little narrative raises a number of interesting issues to which it would take a full-length essay to do justice but which I will nonetheless briefly summarize here.

What strikes me most about the story of bebop is the power which the "discourses of reception"—the press, advertising, and promotion—were able to wield in the construction of the meaning of the music. Though having considerable control over their musical product, the musicians seem to have had little control over its public meaning. Their own comments about their music were filtered through the jazz press or—worse—the mass magazines, quoted out of context, and re-distributed in the printed texts to fit the ideologies and marketing strategies of authors and publishers. The bebop musicians neither possessed their own means of discursive dissemination, nor as "mere" jazz musicians were they endowed by society with sufficient cultural credentials to offset those of the critics. Indeed, they were sorely dependent on these critics for increases in their own cultural accreditation.

This leads to the complicated and all-pervasive issue of race. By 1944, even before it had acquired a name, bebop, as an African-American movement, had already migrated from Harlem into the white jazz world, performing in the downtown clubs on 52nd Street and on Broadway, and having its message constructed by white critics. Harlem had not sufficiently recovered from the depression to support the small, specialized jazz clubs and publications that bebop would have needed. The last African- American jazz journal, the *Music Dial*, had died in 1945. Thus, it is not surprising that bebop got smothered in the racially coded discourses of European Modernity, and was constantly stigmatized by racially coded biases about life-styles, mannerisms, and argot. Of course, some beboppers, in particular Charlie Parker, wanted to appropriate European compositional practices, but ran into resistance when trying to accomplish this in their own racial and cultural terms. It seems as if even the most avid supporters of bebop, like Ulanov, were always trying to "civilize" it, particularly on the behavioral level, but also at the musical level. Of course, these critics were not racially prejudiced in any gross sense, for they were in the forefront in the fight against racial segregation in the business. But the fact that bebop got enveloped by the virtually all-white, jazz-culture industry assured that this African-American movement would be to a large extent discursively constructed in a way that reflected the biases of such a racial hegemony.

If swing was the child of a post-depression, post-prohibition, wartime economic expansion in the music industry, bebop was the off-spring of a post-war recession in jazz that never seemed to end but grew into crisis, and even into the threat of death for jazz, from which it would not recover until the mid-1950s. From the beginning bebop was burdened with the obligation to save jazz from its economic miseries. But there was clearly an incompatibility between the imperative to become as European and avant-garde as possible, on the one hand, and to become as commercially successful as possible on the other. Gillespie and Parker personified this tension, the former a genius at publicity and showmanship, the latter operating at the limits of his craft.

Neither the beboppers nor the critics seemed to appreciate the fundamental changes that the music industry was undergoing—the revolutions in recording technologies, the rise of television, the decline of the live music scene, particularly night clubs and dance halls, the emergence of studio orchestras, the increasing popularity of singers at the expense of bands, etc. Unlike swing in its heyday, bebop never made the hit parade, or infiltrated the top ten. It did not even make the "race" charts, which were being taken over by rhythm and blues, by then the dominant musical culture of Harlem, but altogether unseen by the jazz world. In the final analysis, bebop never became "modernist" in the way desired by *Metronome*, and never succeeded commercially to the extent desired by *Down Beat*. Thus, it was abandoned by both parties.

Although dead as a movement and a fashion, bebop would soon acquire a new life as perhaps the most venerated component of the jazz canon and performance repertory. Indeed, the emergence of a jazz modernism initiated by bebop, and thus of a jazz "art music," helped legitimatize the subsequent construction of a jazz canon in the 1950s through a spate of jazz histories and scholarly essays, many of whose assumptions and principles are still held to this day.[81] Thus, though no longer a current contending movement after 1950, bebop re-entered the jazz world as an especially honored part of the perennial repertoire, existing alongside the succeeding waves of new movements and styles (e.g., free jazz). The bebop musicians continue to be revered as the icons

[81]See Barry Ulanov, *A History of Jazz in America* (New York: Viking, 1952); Marshall Stearns, *The Story of Jazz* (New York: New American Library, 1958); André Hodeir, *Jazz: Its Evolution and Essence* (New York: Grove, 1956); LeRoi Jones, *Blues People* (New York: Morrow, 1963); and Martin Williams, *The Jazz Tradition* (New York: Oxford University Press, 1970).

of that great revolution in jazz which made all subsequent jazz modernisms possible. The construction of a jazz canon, following on the heels of the bebop revolution and giving pride of place to that revolution, is itself a complicated cultural event which deserves further scholarly attention.[82]

[82]Two fine attempts in this direction are John Gennari, "Jazz Criticism: Its Development and Ideologies," and Scott DeVeaux, "Constructing the Jazz Tradition: Jazz Historiography," both in *Black American Literature Forum* (Fall 1991): 449-523, 525-560.

Photograph of Charlie Parker's Quintet at the Three Deuces on 52nd St., 1947. From left to right are: Tommy Potter, Parker, Max Roach (hidden), Miles Davis, and Duke Jordan. *HRHRC Ross Russell Collection*.

"Donna Lee" and the Ironies of Bebop

Donna Lee is, as they used to say, Something Else.

Called at a session, it breeds strange behavior before a note is played. Smiles all around, a bit nervous, happy-hostile. Key-poppings, valvings, slidings. Suggestions of tempos, 240 and beyond, to the caller. A pregnant poise, one, two, one-two-three-four-one-two . . . and the always ragged start: no session group comes together on the third-beat beginning at that speed.

Because it's always too fast, a siren tempting swimmers beyond their depths. And, worse, into its idiom, that ceaseless Sargasso of eighth notes. What's more, it's one of those most perverse of bop heads, the tunes that outdo most possible improvisations on their changes. The hacker and the tyro—these run out of eighth-note formulas early, while even the adept is lucky to keep in the decreed style beyond two choruses.

But for all its submersions and drownings, it never loses its fascination. Forty-six years on, it continues to attract and challenge the wary and the unwary alike. More than a test of *machismo,* it's a first-class enigma, ambiguous from its beginning, a genuinely funny tune that is more than funny, ironic to its core. Bebop, of course, was ironic in its inception, the presentation of the familiar in a radical guise, the legitimation of harmonic extensions by presenting them as dissonances, the deliberate unsettling of set categories by using strange names. But even here *Donna Lee* is Something Else. Almost everything generally known about it has been shown, or can be shown, not to be the case.

The title was wrong, the standard attribution was wrong, the composer couldn't play the head, the significance of the piece was wildly misconstrued, and it remains an open question whether it is to be seen as an act of homage to a contemporary or a slick joke played by a non-virtuoso on posterity. The ironies are, let us say, *layered*—and assessment is not made easier by the tune's humor: in spite of—or perhaps because of—the contentiousness built into it, *Donna Lee* is that rarity, a genuinely *witty* piece of music.

I. Who?

> Charlie Parker All Stars
> Miles Davis, tpt; Charlie Parker, as; Bud Powell, pno; Tommy Potter, b; Max Roach, dms. New York, 8 May 1947
> *Donna Lee* [five takes]; *Chasin' the Bird* [four takes]; *Cheryl* [two takes]; *Buzzy* [five takes] [all on Savoy S5J 5500 and on BYG 529 130 and BYG 529 131; master takes on Savoy 2201; alternate takes on Savoy 1107]
>
> —Jack Chambers[1]

> You dont expect me to know what to say about a play unless I know who the author is, do you?
> —George Bernard Shaw, 1911[2]

There is a Japanese word *wabi*—defined as "a flawed detail that creates an elegant whole"—which may be taken as an index of artistic authenticity, the irruption of the quotidian into the high seriousness of creation. If the concept is at all valid, the Savoy studio was awash with *wabi* that eighth of May, 1947, and the results were very, very elegant. They are certainly as *authentic* as could be wished.

Bird was under contract to Dial, but, as often for him, contracts were only pieces of paper. Still, the hole-and-corner status of the Savoy date may well have affected its procedure. It was a dogged session. They started with *Donna Lee,* gave it five takes at varying tempos, finally went back to the first for the keeper. The trouble is Miles. Solos aside, he has, shall we say, difficulty with the head. Responsibility for the wretched intonation must be shared by both hornmen, of course, but the abundant clams are all Miles's. This might well be put down to the crowded account of the Early Miles of the Bird days, still toiling to find his voice, and his chops. Often, however, this is glossed over, or rather given a heavy coat of spar varnish. Here is Ross Russell on this Savoy session:

> . . . a session for Savoy . . . revealed the superb instrument that Charlie had assembled. The rhythm section was smooth and light, even on the fastest tempi, and infinitely flexible. Miles Davis, improved over

---

[1]Jack Chambers, *Milestones I: The Music and Times of Miles Davis to 1960* (Toronto: University of Toronto Press, 1983), p. 61.

[2]George Bernard Shaw, epilogue to *Fanny's First Play,* in *The Shewing-Up of Blanco Posnet* and *Fanny's First Play* (Harmondsworth, Middlesex: Penguin, 1987), p. 177.

his Savoy outing [the *Ornithology* date], *continued to play his ensemble parts elegantly* and contributed meaningful solos.[3]

Elegance—except, perhaps, in the sense conveyed by *wabi*—is scarcely in question here. Russell is sinning against the light, as is Ira Gitler, though he waffles around the clams much more obviously:

> Miles Davis had not yet reached full maturity (the years with Parker had helped him greatly towards his goal), but he had improved tremendously since 1945. His light, middle-register sound was a perfect foil for Bird; if his solos were not up to Parker's on the very fast numbers, his personal lines were refreshing at medium tempos, and his tender, sustained-note ballad performances were an apt contrast to Parker's darting, intricate interpretations of standards.[4]

Which is to say, Miles played slow and low. For a real assessment of the situation, we have to go to Thomas Owens:

> The initial recordings of "Donna Lee" date from a recording session with [Parker's] own quintet. Four [*sic*] takes, each containing two choruses by Parker, are preserved. *The four takes were necessary because trumpeter Miles Davis made several mistakes in attempting to play the convoluted theme in unison with Parker.* Also, perhaps because this was the first piece attempted at the session, the two lead players had not warmed up, for they had many intonation problems that they attempted, unsuccessfully, to eliminate as the takes proceeded.[5]

If this seems severe, well, there is nothing despicable in a tyro's toiling to perform the mature creations of the master, which is how Owens read the situation: He held to the view, common until recently, that Parker was the author of *Donna Lee*. In fact, he was not. In *Donna Lee*, the 5/8/47 Savoy date produced the first recording of a composition by . . . Miles Davis.

This fact has never been absolutely unknown, in spite of Savoy's attribution of the piece to Bird. Writers on Miles, at least as far back as Bill Cole in the

---

[3]Ross Russell, *Bird Lives! The High Life and Hard Times of Charlie 'Yardbird' Parker* (London: Quartet Books, 1973, 1988), p. 246. (emphasis added)

[4]Ira Gitler, *Jazz Masters of the Forties* (New York: Collier Books, 1966, 1974), p. 36.

[5]Thomas Owens, *Charlie Parker: Techniques of Improvisation*, Ph.D. dissertation, UCLA, 1974 (Ann Arbor: University Microfilms International, 1974), Vol. I, p. 60 (emphasis added).

early '70's,[6] have insisted on the correct attribution, but only Jack Chambers' exhaustive tracking of the truth in 1983[7] promoted anything like general acceptance—though, given the endurance of the error, it may yet rise again.[8]

No one, however, seems to have unpacked the implications of the true authorship as it reflects on the recording. Even Ian Carr's careful assessment of the composition *qua* composition avoids the obvious, the fundamental clash between piece and performance.[9]

There is, quite happily, no musical law that decrees that composers should be able to perform everything—indeed, *anything*—that they write. But this hardly holds for early bop heads, which are canonically written-down improvised lines, crystallized and possibly regularized expressions of the sort of chorus that the composer/performer plays when wearing his other hat. But, not only is *Donna Lee* not conceivably in any of Miles's styles on that date or any other time, but it is, flatly, beyond his capabilities. Why should Miles Davis write *and then record* a piece of music that he couldn't play?

And then there is the *ontological* question: What *is* this thing? How are we to take it? As things stand now, *Donna Lee* is still treated as one of a group, a shining jewel—or whatever—in the stunning necklace of Bird's creations in his Great Period 1944-1948. But this is by *Miles, not Bird*. Work by analogy: What would happen if it were incontrovertibly shown that one of Haydn's greatest symphonies, the 102nd, had been written in 1794, not by the master, but by his 23-year-old pupil, Ludwig van Beethoven?

II. NAME THAT TUNE

> We did replace Duke Jordan with Bud Powell on a record for Savoy around May of 1947. I think the record was called the Charlie Parker All Stars. It had everyone in Bird's regular group on it except Duke. I wrote a tune for the album called "Donna Lee," which was the first tune of mine that was ever recorded. But when the record came out it listed Bird as the composer. It wasn't Bird's fault, though. The record company just made a mistake and I didn't lose no money or nothing.
>
> —Miles Davis, 1989[10]

[6]Bill Cole, *Miles Davis: A Musical Biography* (New York: Morrow Quill, 1974), p. 45.

[7]Chambers, *Milestones I*, p. 61.

[8]In fact, it has. David Rosenthal perpetuates the Parker attribution in his 1992 *Hard Bop*. See note 13 below.

[9]Ian Carr, *Miles Davis: A Biography* (New York: William Morrow, 1982), p. 26.

[10]Miles Davis with Quincy Troupe, *Miles: The Autobiography* (New York: Simon & Schuster, 1989), pp. 103-104.

The titles of early bebop heads—especially Parker's—never cease to amaze and delight. They foster fascinated conjecture: What has *Anthropology* in common with *Thriving From a Riff*—except that it's sometimes the same tune?[11] Was *Moose the Mooche* Parker's LA connection? If *She Rote*, who was *She*, and what did *She Rite*? What about *Quasimodo*? Why, oh, why does a lyric effusion on the changes of *Embraceable You* masquerade under the lumpy Latin appellation of the Hunchback of Notre Dame? And—a bit lickerishly—who are these women who sashay through Bird's *œuvre*—the *Kims*, the *Alices*, the *Cheryls*, the *Lees*, the *Donna Lees*? And, even if Miles did write it, who was *Donna Lee*?

It must first be noted that Miles, as frequently in his autobiography, is editing the past when he says "I wrote a tune for the album called *Donna Lee.*" Not falsifying it, but editing it, collapsing time in the interests, we will suppose, of concision. He wrote a tune, and he may have written it for the Savoy album, but he did *not* write a tune called *Donna Lee*. He *may* have written a tune called *Cheryl*—another of Parker's women-tunes, we note—but he did *not* write a *Donna Lee*. That ultimate name was assigned by the record company. Let Chambers tell it:

> The confusion over authorship has not been helped by the fact that *Donna Lee* is named for bassist Curly Russell's daughter, whereas *Cheryl*, written by Parker, is named for Davis's daughter, but these titles were assigned, apparently quite arbitrarily, by producer Teddy Reig.[12]

It may be illuminating to the practice to underline the fact that Russell was not on this particular date. In any case, naming-day at Savoy must have been an exhilarating, if rather random, experience. One visualizes Reig somehow casting a fistful of titles over the products of this and other sessions and assigning the ones that stuck.

But if the lubricious conjecture that Parker, or even Miles, somehow used titles as seduction ploys *à la* George Gershwin has departed, the irony remains. Russell's small daughter's name is all wrong for the piece: The tune is hell-for-leather, deserving its frequent epithet *rambunctious,* but the name conjures cotillions, or better proms, the damped shuffles of the early forties— *Candy* and that ilk. In early bop titles, *Tempus Fugit* fits. *Chasin' the Bird* fits.

---

[11]As to the *source* of *Anthropology*. . . . Well, this is a question I don't really want answered; I have more fun with conjecture. Given its bridge quotes from *Ornithology* and *Hot House*, it might well have been an early summing-up of Bird & Diz's progress to eminence in bop. A brief *Bildungsroman*, if you will, ontogeny recapitulating phylogeny, and all that jazz. Don't confuse me with facts.

[12]Chambers, *Milestones I*, p. 61.

But *Donna Lee* only waves a well-bred pom-pom from the sidelines as the mad stampede thunders past. Tune and title, taken together, constitute a staggering musical oxymoron.

And, it must be confessed, Miles's recorded reaction sounds more than the least disingenuous. If he became Prince of Darkness, he was evidently always Duke of Diffidence, but this sang-froid—"The record company just made a mistake and I didn't lose no money or nothing"—though conceivable from the grizzled campaigner forty years on, hardly seems a possible reaction from a young musician who has just had the first recording of a composition and has placed the name of his infant daughter in the producer's hopper. Stoic isn't the word.

III. The "Classic Bebop Melody"

As a style, bebop was remarkably of a piece, best played by the nucleus of musicians who had been responsible for its technical and aesthetic breakthroughs. Because of the school's compactness, many if not most bebop tunes are also "typical" ones. For instance, Charlie Parker's [*sic*] composition "Donna Lee," which he recorded for Savoy Records with Miles Davis, Bud Powell, bassist Tommy Potter, and Max Roach, is based on the chords to the popular song "Indiana." This in itself was a standard bebop procedure, and "Donna Lee" is a classic bebop melody: serpentine, eccentrically syncopated, and based more on improvisational phrasing than on a simple "songlike" theme. . . . On "Donna Lee" and dozens of other masterpieces of the era, everything is off center, almost perversely so. . . .

—David H. Rosenthal[13]

The piece is fast, difficult, and typical bebop in its rhythmic drive and the way the melodic line flows through the chord changes. Only the symmetry of the phrases suggests that Miles, and not Bird, was the composer.

—Ian Carr[14]

Donna Lee features very long unison lines by the two horns, based on the chord changes of *Indiana*. Neither Parker nor Davis preserves

[13]David H. Rosenthal, *Hard Bop: Jazz & Black Music 1955-1965* (New York: Oxford University Press, 1992), pp. 12-13.

[14]Carr, *Miles Davis: A Biography*, p. 26.

166

Publicity photograph of Miles Davis, 1960. *HRHRC "New York Journal-American" Collection.*

the structure of the opening melody in his solo, and Parker's solos on all takes consist of several short phrases strung together, a distinct contrast to the unbroken phrases of the written ensemble.

—Jack Chambers[15]

The sobriquet of "classic"—which is to say, "typical"—is easier to assert than prove. The surviving early monuments of any artistic movement are *of course* "classic": they are, after all, *there,* and have themselves become established as fit sources for development and reaction. Take a look at *Donna Lee:*

Miles Davis, *Donna Lee* (1947)

---

[15]Chambers, *Milestones I,* p. 61.

By and large, Rosenthal's assertions are correct: the tune does wind around, its odd syncopation starts with the two-beat delay of the entrance, and the whole does evoke improvisational phrasing—though not the phrasing of any participant on that Savoy date. But Rosenthal's global observation— "everything is off-center"—needs to be tempered with the observations of Carr and Chambers: *Donna Lee* is *symmetrical*,[16] almost compulsively so, and its very long lines, whether they flow through the changes or not, husband the squared-off structure of the piece with a care that is nothing less than loving. It is, *mutatis mutandis*, suprisingly faithful to the *melody* of its traditional model, Ballard Macdonald and James F. Hanley's *(Back Home Again in) Indiana* of 1917—and even, as we shall see, to its model's model—and in this, and in its off-center symmetry, *Donna Lee* is hardly a touchstone of early bebop tunes; in this regard, it is typical of nothing but itself.

IV. DONNA LEE MEETS SISTER CARRIE

Donna Lee is a charter member of that class of bebop heads best known as "contrafacts."[17] That is, melodies based on the changes of well-known popular standards, largely composed for recording by working musicians, in order to preserve familiar harmonic structures while avoiding the payment of royalties. Gershwin's *I Got Rhythm* is the prize example, spawning numberless adumbrations. By its sheer existence, any contrafact performs an act of fealty to the original piece . . . but only to its harmonic structure. Since the Urmelody, which might be recognized, is precisely the reason for the new creation's existence, any reference, much less any subservience, to the original tune is rarely encountered. And yet, on examination, Miles's first tune proves to be, not mere salvage of the chords and no more, but a thoughtful exploration of Hanley's *melody*, making its principal features into the structural elements of his composition. And, just to add the resonance here, *Indiana* is itself a reworking, an act of homage to the refrain of Paul Dresser's well-known song *On the Banks of the Wabash*, which appeared in 1899.

---

[16]Carr's observation—though it is rather strong to say that this is the feature that confirms Miles's authorship. *Quasimado*, Parker's contrafact on the changes of Gershwin's *Embraceable You* (a tune of the same structure as *Indiana*), is at least as symmetrical as *Donna Lee*.

[17]A restatement, using the Latin roots, of *counterfeit*, which made its way into English through French, this was coined by James Patrick in "Charlie Parker and the Harmonic Sources of Bebop Composition," *Journal of Jazz Studies* 2.2 (1975): 3, and has reached a wider audience through the instructional and analytical works of David Baker—*e.g., How To Play Bebop*, Vol. III (Bloomington, IN: Frangipani Press, 1985).

The most obvious of the elements that *Donna Lee* preserves from nonjazz music is the ABA´C configuration, one of the two great favorite shapes of American popular song. Four sections of equal length, where the first, A, is followed by a differing one, B, and then restated as A´, to be closed with a final strain, C, which may or may not resemble B. Not merely an ordering of harmony, this falls neatly into two halves, and may occur in a number of sizes—eight, sixteen, or thirty-two bars. In the refrain of *Wabash* we have the short version; even here, the C section is a distinct entity on its own, and closes the entire piece with reversed rhythm.

Paul Dresser, *On the Banks of the Wabash* (1899)

Simple enough . . . though by no means simple-minded. I print here all of Dresser's carefully varied dotting,[18] a deliberate strategy which he uses *throughout the refrain* and very selectively in the verse, to establish an oldtimey feeling and induce nostalgia.[19] But the melody is ingenious and tight: at A, it states a close four-note figure, WAB,

moves it down a step scalewise, then flips it over and does the same at B; then repeats A and remakes the figure into the core of a cadence at C.

---

[18]NB, for example, the reversed dotted rhythm on the fourth and fifth notes of the next-to-last bar.

[19]*Wabash* suffers quite a bit in fakebooks: the verse is lost, the key changed, the dottings obliterated. This text of the song, with the rather suprising key of B-flat, is taken from the collected edition, *The Songs of Paul Dresser* (New York: Boni & Liveright, 1927), pp. 72-75.

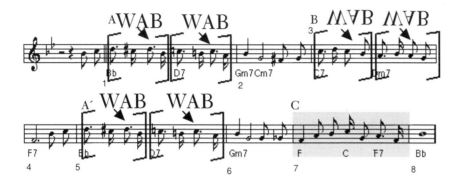

Immortality in eight bars, an immortality that Hanley honored when, 18 years later, he produced his homage. But Hanley made something new: In *Indiana*, the sixteen-bar version was used, and the resultant structure emphasizes subdivisions:

A1-A2—B1-B2—A′1-A′2—C1-C2

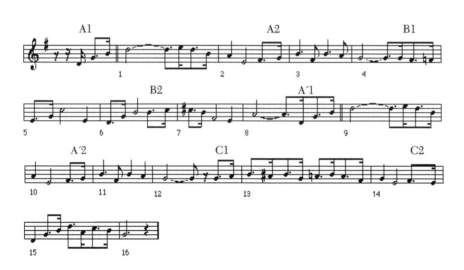

James Hanley, *(Back Home Again in) Indiana* (1917)

171

Photograph of Paul Dresser, n.d. *HRHRC Theatre Arts Musicians File.*

The debt to *Wabash* is considerable, but, while keeping its overall structure (ABA´C) and the oldtimey dotting,[20] Hanley has moved beyond: the listener must fare through a forest of arpeggios to reach Dresser's scalewise figure, and there it shines the brighter for its very difference. The arpeggios may well be due to Dresser also; he employs them skillfully in his verse to counter scalewise passages:

Paul Dresser, *On the Banks of the Wabash* (1899), verse, measures 1-4

What Hanley has done is to reverse the order, first playing with the arpeggio, "running the change" up and down, and *then* proceeding scalewise:

The upward arpeggio is established from the beginning of the strain: *Indiana's* "hook," the figure with which it grabs the hearer, is a rising tonic triad, 5-1-3-5; lest anyone forget it, it is repeated at the beginning of A´1 and recapitulated at the end in C2, in bar 15. This tracing of the basic chords seems to have been quite a common, and indeed effective, practice in starting popular songs in the early part of this century. George M. Cohan, for example, never tired of it. To take some of his blockbusters: The chorus of *Mary* (1905) begins with the same rising arpeggio as *Indiana*—5-1-3-5—but drops back to 3:

George M. Cohan, *Mary's A Grand Old Name* (1905)

---

[20]If fakebooks harry *Wabash,* they positively brutalize *Indiana.* The dotting—deliberately archaic even for Hanley—goes early; keys are chosen at random; the tune itself is smoothed into vapidity.

You're A Grand Old Flag (1906) takes the tonic, descends, and camps, 5-3-1-1-1:

George M. Cohan, *You're A Grand Old Flag* (1906), measure 1 with pickup

When Cohan returns to the fray, quite literally, in 1917, his war song *Over There* begins with the same three notes of the tonic triad, but makes them into a bugle call, 3-5-1 and repeat and repeat and repeat:

George M. Cohan, *Over There* (1917)

But if Cohan was usually satisfied with stating his tonic hooks by themselves to start, and then building lines to the end of a longish section, Hanley made the confrontation of ascending arpeggio and descending line the central constantly stated feature of *Indiana*: Five of the seven arpeggios which stud the piece rise; the descending scalewise line is hinted at in measures 4, 7, and 12, and then highlighted in the *Wabash* quote in the C1 section.[21] And this feature of *Indiana*'s melody marks the entire length of *Donna Lee* . . . since the same feature is one of the characteristic improvisational structures of early, and even later, bebop.

There is then the matter of *Indiana*'s quote of *Wabash*—and, particularly, of its placement. When we look for the placement of the quote from *Wabash*, we find it nestled firmly at the beginning of the C-section, in C1, measures 13-14 of a 16-bar tune, or 25-28 of a 32-bar tune. And, if we look further afield, we find that this position is a favorite for what might be termed the Defining Quotation, that fealty shown to an earlier tune which *places* the later one. And, even where there is no quote in songs of this type, C1 is an especially *sensitive* location. It is the tune's self-referential section, the defining difference; something happens here that throws the rest of the melody—and indeed its harmony—into relief. It performs something like the function of the *bridge*, the B-section of the most favored structural type, tunes of the form A-A-B-A.

[21]There is even more underlining: The last statement of the tonic arpeggio in *Indiana* is set off by its variation on the scalewise cadence of *Wabash*, which would certainly be expected by the average listener.

174

Here are the bridge's redefinitions, departures, extensions, and qualifications, the information that both encapsulates and *locates* the entire tune, but with an especial breathless *urgency*: even in the large 32-bar size, the tune has very little time left before it ends. To give a name to this extraordinarily significant part of a tune, since "C-section" bears an unsuitable connotation,[22] I would suggest a term that literature has already adopted from heraldry: *mise en abyme.*

Multiplication of jargon—especially by importing jargon from another field—is an odious practice, and should doubtless be prohibited by law. Still, when this is said, the term has advantages. The heraldic source is effective: originally, *mise en abyme* was applied to a small shield represented centrally on a larger one, a miniature replica of the shield that contains it. Lucien Dällenbach begins his authoritative work on the *mise en abyme* with an extended meaning for literature: "Any aspect, enclosed within a work, that shows a similarity with the work that contains it."[23] Putting off the rationale until another occasion, I would extend *similarity* to include something as far afield as *significant difference:* in my formulation of it, the *mise en abyme* may be the mirror that Dällenbach's title claims—*Le récit speculaire,* translated as *The Mirror in the Text*—but it is a mirror that may distort. It supplies a *context* for the tune—a source for it, an attitude towards it, a criticism of it—which locates, defines *what it is.* Further, I would like to limit its placement, for the time being, to the C1 section of ABA′C melodies.

This is an especially good place for quotation. To turn to Cohan again: In *The Yankee Doodle Boy,* the title's source is quoted at C1:

George M. Cohan, *The Yankee Doodle Boy* (1901), measures 25-28

Grand Old Flag quotes *Auld Lang Syne* at C1 to set its nostalgic ambience firmly:

George M. Cohan, *You're A Grand Old Flag* (1906), measures 25-28

---

[22]Given the sensitivity involved here, "G-spot" was also considered . . . but only very briefly.
[23]Lucien Dällenbach, *The Mirror in the Text* (Chicago: University of Chicago Press, 1989), p. 8.

In *Indiana,* the *mise en abyme* could hardly be more obvious: a note-for-note quotation of the most famous segment of *Wabash,* heightened by an accompanying direct quotation in the lyrics: "When the moon is shining bright upon the Wabash. . . ." Overall, *Indiana* breaks down something like this:

James F. Hanley, *Indiana* (1917)

The interplay of arpeggio (ARP) up and scale (SC) down, the locating quote in the *mise*—these are the primary features of *Indiana,* and certainly the ones that Miles employs in *Donna Lee.*[24] The fidelity, in its way, is thorough. To the *Indiana* items, he adds a boppish triplet figure to be varied as needed (TRI)

[24]The third-based arpeggiation of *Donna Lee,* among other bebop heads, is pointed out by Steven Strunk in his "Bebop Melodic Lines: Tonal Characteristics," *Annual Review of Jazz Studies* 3 (1985): 107-110. The same article gives an in-depth investigation of the structural levels of *Donna Lee* on pp. 113-117.

and, thus fitted out with a kit, he makes his melody:

Miles Davis, *Donna Lee* in terms of *Indiana*

Davis begins with TRI, then reverses the order of ARP vs. SC: The descending SC in bars 1-2 is countered in 3, after TRI, by a rising ARP on B-flat7, 3-5-7-9, and this ascending chord-spelling persists through the entire A section, occurring four times. B1 concentrates on descending SCs, but then an ARP asserts itself at 12, and is in the ascendant by the end of B2. The A1a section is repeated at A´1a, but the first *rising-falling* SC takes over at A´2a, bar 21, setting up TRI's moment of glory, its double appearance at bar 22. Section A´2b, after all the frenetic movement, supplies nearly two bars of dead silence, and then the madness renews at the *mise:* a scalewise figure, not previously encountered, *ascending,* and then going back down at C1b, stopping for a TRI at 27 and then moving on to the diminished chord spelled out in bar 28, the longest rising ARP of the piece. But this is countered by *Donna Lee*'s longest descending SC, which begins in measure 28 and ends on the first note of measure 30. In that measure, there is a final statement of both items: the rising ARP on B-flat7 and the falling SC on E-flat, coming to rest on the final note.

I apologize for the impressionistic flavor of the above account of 32 bars of bebop, but if it rather sounds as though a battle were going on, well, it *is:* a contention, a *war,* in fact, between two opposed sorts of musical phrase, a conflict that is finally resolved at the end. And the knowledge that by far the greatest share of those melodic items have their source in a down-home monument to heartland nostalgia—Hanley's *(Back Home Again in) Indiana*—adds an ironic undercurrent to the madness that is happening.

There remains the matter of what happens at the *mise en abyme*. It may have been prepared for slightly by the rising-falling SC at bar 21, but there is really nothing else like it in the piece. After the (relatively) interminable rest, it charges off madly in another direction, with an effect rather like that of the standard circus march:

from Fucik, *Entrance of the Gladiators*

But for the source of Miles's quote—it *is* a quote—we should look nearer home. Or, rather, nearer *Home,* the idyllic midwest celebrated by his source and his source's source. Davis has taken Dresser's essential figure

Sheet music edition of James. F. Hanley's *Indiana* (New York: Shapiro, Bernstein, & Co., 1917).
HRHRC Theatre Arts Collection.

removed its dots and bars, squeezed it slightly, and flipped it over in a different way:

He then repeats it twice, moving up a full step each time:

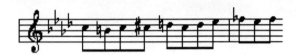

And then takes the scale back down. Whether from *Indiana* or *Wabash,* the result is more or less the same. The Classical Bebop Melody has, at its heart, something like mush, a tripled quotation, however varied, from Ye Olde Tyme Classick Nostalgic Ballad—Paul Dresser's *On the Banks of the Wabash.* And there is one more turn of the screw: The inspiration and part of the words for *Wabash* were given by Dresser's brother, who recounts the 1896 event with disarming false modesty:

> "Why don't you write something about a State or river?" I retorted.
> ". . . . Take Indiana, what's the matter with it—the Wabash River? It's as good as any other river, and you were 'raised' beside it.". . . .
> "That's not a bad idea," he agreed. "Why don't you write the words . . . ?"
> After a little urging. . . . I took a piece of paper and scribbled the first verse and chorus of that song almost as it was published. . . .[25]

This would signify nothing at all, were it not for the fact that Dresser's brother was the American novelist Theodore Dreiser. The resultant connection between two creators in the throes of making, the author of *Sister Carrie* and the author of *Donna Lee,* two individuals as different as possible—this may not mean very much, or indeed anything, but, like many other events associated with *Donna Lee,* it affords a simple joy to the beholder. Still, such fringe benefits should not obscure what Miles has done—*adapted Indiana,*

---

[25]*The Songs of Paul Dresser*, Introduction, p. viii.

not looted it of its chords, transmuted the melody into something very different which insists, in a number of ways, on declaring its heritage.[26]

One can hardly call *Donna Lee* nothing more than an *Indiana* thirty years on. Whether "typical" or not, it is a bebop melody, and ties into 52nd Street as well as into the Heartland. *Donna Lee* has two sources, one traditional, one new, and for the new one we must look at the New York jazz scene in 1947.

V. "ICE FREEZES RED": A LICK AND A PREMISE

SIDE C
Fat Girl
Ice Freezes Red
Eb Pob
Goin' to Mintons
C 1-4: Fats Navarro: trumpet, Leo Parker: baritone sax, Tadd Dameron: piano, Gene Ramey: bass, Denzil Best: drums. 1/16/47.
—Dan Morgenstern[27]

... [I]n his solos, [Fats Navarro] clothed the genuine departure from swing inherent in bebop with logic and beauty. Set against the background of his often dishevelled peer, a Navarro solo was like an immaculate fairway flanked by ankle-deep rough. His solos compare extremely well with Dizzy Gillespie's most famous effusions of the time. . . . [T]he fact is, Navarro was the better trumpet player. . . .

[26]There are other forms of fealty: Dizzy Gillespie's *Groovin' High*, a contrafact of *Whispering*, is faithful to its source by being a *countermelody*—keeping the original everywhere in view, silent during its active parts, active during sustained holds. See the sensitive analysis by Joan Wildman, "The Evolution of Bebop Compositional Style: 'Whispering' / 'Groovin' High'," *Annual Review of Jazz Studies* 3 (1985): 137-146. This is not at all the approach taken by Miles, who adapts features and structure, but is never—except, possibly, at the half-bar delay at the very beginning—waiting on *Indiana* to say its piece.

[27]Dan Morgenstern, liner notes to the omnibus 1977 rerelease of Navarro's Savoy sides, *Fat Girl: The Savoy Sessions* (Arista/Savoy, SJL 2216).

Sometimes Navarro's phrases lasted ten or twelve bars: they crossed meadows and stiles and corpses before landing.

—Whitney Balliett[28]

[Navarro's] strength was in molding long, flowing lines composed largely of eighth notes. The line rises and falls easily and calmly, and there is a constant if subtle play of accent throughout. . . . The music seems at times to rustle gently like leaves in the wind.

—James Lincoln Collier[29]

To return to Rosenthal's remarks on *Donna Lee*:[30] As he asserted, it *is* based on improvisational phrasing—but not the phrasing of any participant on the Parker/Davis date. Neither Bird nor Miles ever recorded a solo remotely like the *Donna Lee* line. Rather, the prime source was the trumpeter Theodore "Fats" Navarro, Miles's running mate, who, on January 16, 1947, had recorded an *Indiana* contrafact he had put together with Dameron, called *Ice Freezes Red*.[31]

Contrafacts, by their very nature, aim at the preservation of traditional changes, but not all go about the job in the same way. They fall roughly into two classes, metamorphic and minimal. The first type, the thorough transmutation into something new, is what we have seen in *Donna Lee*. The second serves merely to display the changes before the soloists are turned loose on them; it can employ the simplest, and often the tritest, formula that fits, and, in advanced cases, abandon it for short improvised sections when it proves inadequate. The compositional scheme here might be termed "a lick and a premise"—where the *lick* is any formula that accords with the *premise,* or inherited changes. The melody of *Ice Freezes Red,* recorded nearly four months before *Donna Lee,* is an almost perfect example of this *ad hoc* minimalism.

[28]Whitney Balliett, *Night Creature: A Journal of Jazz, 1975-1980* (New York: Oxford University Press, 1981), pp. 166-167.

[29]James Lincoln Collier, *The Making of Jazz: A Comprehensive History* (New York: Delta, 1978), p. 399.

[30]Rosenthal, *Hard Bop*, pp. 12-13.

[31]A great title, engendering metaphysics in the gullible or the wishful. The truth, as supplied by Dexter Gordon, is more prosaic than any conjecture: "Ice" and "Red" were the nicknames of two of the Billy Eckstine band's most limpet-like fans. Gordon is quoted in Ira Gitler, *From Swing to Bop* (New York: Oxford University Press, 1985), p. 133.

opening head, Fats Navarro, *Ice Freezes Red*, January 16, 1947

A sandlot creation, drawn in the dirt like a pass play in pickup football,[32] this seems to have been composed—if that is the word—on site. To start, after Dameron gives four bars, Fats and Leo Parker intone a hoary traditional lick known (from its rhythm) as "I Get the Neck of the Chicken":

(I   get the neck of the   chick- en)

Stated four times, with each repetition starting a half-step lower, this fills the eight bars A´1 and A´2 sections. At B1, another doddering pensioner is pressed into service:

---

[32]"Iggy, you hold off the big guy. Stash, you run out in the flat to the the trash can, count three and cut straight across, and I'll get the ball to you. Okay, guys, on two."

Twice on this, with the repetition also descending a half-step, and the tune arrives at the modulatory necessities for returning to start. Neither lick fits the changes, so a moratorium is declared for section B2, which Fats fills with two bars of improvisation. Chicken-licking fills the first two bars of the A´ section, but is inadequate for the modulation to the *mise* and the *mise* itself, so Dameron tinkles through the modulation and Fats fills out again with more improvisation. A hurried job, but it serves. As in most bebop tunes, the *service* function is uppermost. The head sets the key and the changes, and defines the space, builds a varnished knotty-pine frame to set off the glories of the solos.

So here—but with a difference. The frame includes a glory or two, and they are to be found in the admissions of compositional defeat: the breaks. This was Fats's date, and the improvised insertions show him playing his signature, his characteristic: the unbroken phrase cunningly crafted to arrive at just the right place at just the right time. His first break fills the 3 ½ bars of the first half, and runs seamlessly out of its section into the second half, the restatement of the chicken's neck. His second fills, without stuffing, both *mise* and end, eight bars of flawless filigree dovetailing incongruously with Leo Parker's joyous Johnny-one-note galumphing.

Ultimately he even drags the bary into the act. At the piece's end, after the solos are done, a half-chorus takes all the time that remains of the 78's 2:38. For this, Fats modifies things a bit, *fixing* the improvisation that ends the head so that both horns[33] can play it, and we have the unforgettable spectacle of the behemothian bary in a tutu, charging up and down in tandem on a Navarro line, albeit broken for breath:

out half-chorus, Fats Navarro, *Ice Freezes Red*, January 16, 1947

[33]Respect must be paid to the other horn, the baritone saxophone of Leo Parker, who would have been anyone's choice for least compatible partner for the fleet, controlled Navarro. But a good deal of the date's wonder is due to Parker's bary, which thuds and slaps and snorts around the foundations while Fats patterns his unflappable spirals up top. One of the great feel-good gigs.

The head on *Ice Freezes Red,* then, is a *double* frame. It includes glories, forecasts and then recapitulates the leader's solo, which is *all* line:[34]

Fats Navarro, solo on *Ice Freezes Red* January 16, 1947

If the tune—what there is of it—has been skeletal, Navarro's improvisation is certainly not. This is baroque bebop, Arcangelo Corelli at the Royal Roost, carpeting most of the available room with eighth notes. Miles, and even Bird, are pointillists beside him, dotting their canvas with bursts where Navarro fills

---

[34]The transcriptions of the *Ice Freezes Red* head are from *Fat Girl: The Savoy Sessions;* my transcription of the solo given here on page 25 is based heavily on David Baker, *The Jazz Style of Fats Navarro: A Musical and Historical Perspective* (Hialeah, FL: Studio P/R, 1982), pp. 32-33. All quotes from *Ice* and *Donna Lee* are given in the concert key of A-flat.

his with friezes. He thinks in *swatches*—stretched eighth-note phrases, the longer the better, separated by glorious silences. His 48 solo measures contain only eight phrases, most unbroken, but with the rare eighth rest to leaven the eighth notes (90+%) and adjust the rhythmic placement of the next note. The most distinctive manifestations of this completist approach to improvisation are those lines which "play through the changes"—that is, they *enjamb*: keep going into the next section at the big junctures, or ride right over the spaces within sections.

To see him at work, take one for all:

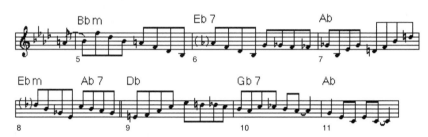

Fats Navarro, solo on *Ice Freezes Red*, measures 5-11

Not a break. Its elements are "typical" bebop, of course, but how atypical, really. The chords rule, but such a *tasteful* serfdom it is. The first three clusters of eighths in 5-6 merely "run the changes," one could say, play the standard arpeggios, two on the B-flat seventh chord and one on E-flat seventh, but they're the same three notes, F-D-flat-B-flat, but look at the ordering: each arpeggio is firmly pegged to successive notes of a downward chromatic phrase, B-flat to A to A-flat, and this movement continues by half-steps, G to G-flat, when the arpeggios give way to the chromatic scalewise passage that leads into bar 7. Having given two signals for the next note, Fats slides into the A-flat chord via the flat seventh, then runs, not the basic intervals of his ruler, but its higher intervals, 9-5-natural 7-sharp 4-6-9-sharp 4, parodying a B-flat seventh to get him in position for the E-flat minor seventh arpeggio and A-flat seventh scale phrase that *enjambs*, leads *through* the division between bars 8 and 9, the dividing line between the large A and B sections, where bar 9 is a collapsed [middle element out] and stretched version of the phrase that runs from the last half of bar 7 and all of bar 8. For bar 10, he plays around the G-flat chord's third, the B-flat that is also the ninth of the coming A-flat chord, hits the A-flat before its time as root has come, and then staunchly refuses to play it at all during the cadence. It is very like the mime's walking-in-place: keep moving but don't run out of the allotted space, or indeed of horn. Everywhere *order*: governing line, anticipations, variations, sideslips, articu-

186

lated in the careful alternation of our old friends, arpeggio and scale. These strategies were becoming, and quickly became, the common stock, but this was January 1947. And the really characteristic element, played by successors or not, is the combination of all this management in the long line—Fats's essence, what he did that others didn't.

That governed long line, given its occurrence in the heads, in and out, and its dominance in Navarro's solo, is certainly what *Ice Freezes Red* is *about*. And it is just as certainly what Miles picked up in early 1947, whether from recording or performance, and used as the second source and inspiration for *Donna Lee.*

VI. An Act of Homage

A: Like Fats

> [1944:] Then there was Fats Navarro, who came through from Florida or New Orleans. Nobody knew who he was but that motherfucker could play like I never heard nobody play before.
> [1945:] I ran into Fats Navarro again up at Minton's and we used to jam there all the time.
>
> —Miles Davis[35]

If Davis never played a solo like the line of *Donna Lee,* he *did* try. Consider his half-chorus on its first take:

---

[35]Davis, *Miles: The Autobiography,* pp. 45, 54.

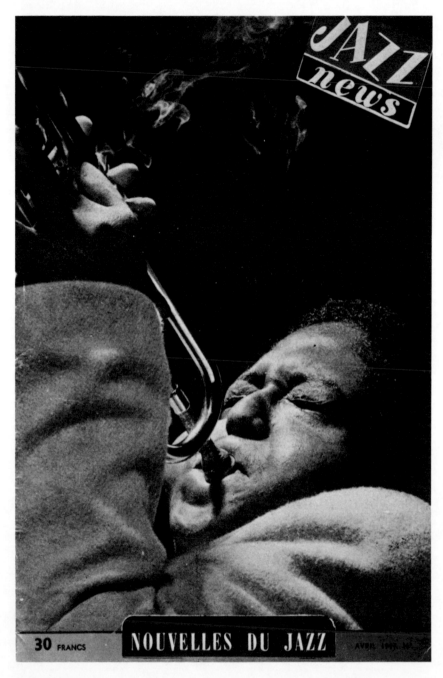

Photograph of Fats Navarro pictured on the cover of *Jazz News* for April 1949. *HRHRC Ross Russell Collection.*

Miles Davis, solo on *Donna Lee* (first take), May 7, 1947

On solo as on head, the tempo is too fast. Miles rises on a Navarresque straight-eight passage, but by the second measure is in trouble and descends on what is certainly the composer's prerogative: he quotes the head. This only lasts until the middle of the next bar, where he fluffs what seems to be a misplaced triplet, and then has trouble getting back on track, such trouble that he lays out for a bar, then hangs onto the high A-flat until he can formulate a way of getting through to bar 15, where he enters on a comfortable cliché, and then goes out. Transcribed, it looks much too neat:[36] though the solo is not an utter disaster, it certainly shows the wreck of lofty intentions. What looks to have been about to be a pastiche, or parody, of Fats's lyrical doggedness has become an assemblage of disject members. On his second-take solo, Miles manages a better line, playing through the changes at 8-9 and the lesser break at 12-13:[37]

[36]Transcription (concert A-flat) is from Charlie Parker, *Bird: The Savoy Recordings, Vol I* (Arista/Savoy CD ZDS 4402, 1976).

[37]Transcription is from *The Immortal Charlie Parker* (Nippon Columbia Savoy Jazz CD SV-0102, 1991).

Miles Davis, solo on *Donna Lee* (second take), May 7, 1947

A surer thing, really, even if bars 11-13 of the solo are an exact quote from the same bars in the head. Still, Davis's deftness this time through is only made possible by the retarded tempo tried after the crash of the first take, and at ♩=210 rather than =240, the essential rapid freneticism of *Donna Lee* vanishes. Bird is positively *strolling;* he easily double-times at the end of his second chorus.

But if Miles couldn't play a Fats performance, he could certainly write one. *Donna Lee* is the perfect Navarro solo, long lines and all. How can we be sure it's Fats? The debt is not left to inference. *Donna Lee* declares its source from its very beginning:

Above: Navarro, solo on *Ice Freezes Red*, pickup bar and bars 1-3. Below: Davis, *Donna Lee*, bars 1-4.

190

The evocation is delayed for half a bar, but observe that Fats is quoted *at start*, quoted *directly* except for the substitution of the triplet figure, to be repeated at the beginning of the head's second half (measures 17-20). Lest we forget what is going on, and whose this is, the descending scale is reprised at the piece's end, after the apocalyptic rising diminished arpeggio at bar 28, leading into the cadence:

Miles Davis, *Donna Lee* final cadence

And this hammered homage is merely the skeleton, the underpinning for an extended exercise in Navarronian phrase structure, a building of a second *Indiana* contrafact from the materials and style of the first.[38]

One longs for colors, somehow, to represent the solos on top of one another, to reproduce an impossible exercise in musical intertextuality and see Fats's ghostly solo (in red, of course) behind Miles's celebration, a study in brown. But monochrome will have to serve:

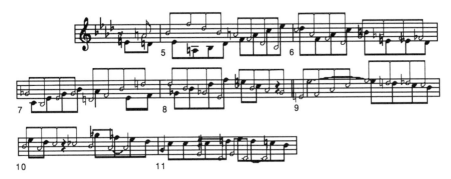

Donna Lee, bars 5-11, superimposed on Navarro's *Ice Freezes Red* solo, bars 5-11

[38]And, of course, the key. Hanley's original G didn't sit well with horn players, who preferred flat keys. A-flat was well-established by the Original Dixieland Jazz Band's version, which fronted *The Darktown Strutter's Ball* on Columbia A2297 in 1917, the year of the song's publication. But the key has wobbled over the years: Red Nichols and His Five Pennies, for example, recorded *Indiana* on 4/18/29. The band starts in B-flat, Nichols and Benny Goodman take choruses in Hanley's G, but Jack Teagarden returns to B-flat for his chorus, and the ensemble takes it home in that key. From the CD *Jack Teagarden Vol 1: 1928/1931*, "Jazz Archives No. 51" (Paris: EPM, 1992). The basic under-the-counter fakebook prints *Donna Lee* in its standard A-flat, but consigns *Indiana* to F.

Early on, tune dogs solo, but not slavishly. "In his master's steps he trod," sings the carol, but Fats was not King Wenceslas, and Miles, even in 1947, was nobody's squire, not even Bird's. He sticks close, but with significant alterations. In bar 5, Fats takes his B-flat minor arpeggio down from the second note, 5-3-1-7-5-3-1; Miles takes the same figure *up,* and changes to the B-flat minor seventh: 7-1-3-5-flat 7-9-11. In bar 6, Fats plays a descending B-flat minor seventh arpeggio, 7-5-3-1, followed by a descending chromatic bit, B-flat, A, A-flat, jump to G-flat; Miles uses the same pattern, but the arpeggio hits the root and then goes *up,* 5-3-7, and the chromatic bit occurs a fourth lower. And so it goes throughout, a strange *pas de deux,* with the dancers performing sixteen weeks apart, Davis sedulous but not aping, keeping out of Fats's way: Only rarely do the two find themselves occupying the same note at the same time.

Miles Davis, *Donna Lee* in terms of Fats Navarro.

In *Ice,* Fats negotiated 48 bars in eight phrases; in *Donna Lee,* Miles uses eight phrases for a mere 32 of the head. Yet the later piece gives the more seamless impression: at times, it appears to be one long single phrase that never stops. The reason is not far to seek. Here's Balliett again: "He [Navarro] would punctuate these serene juxtapositions with silence, and shift back into his parade of eighth notes."[39] Navarro's interstitial tacets were substantial: in *Ice,* the favored length of a rest is a bar and a half. Miles behaves almost like the thievish architect in the Christian Morgenstern poem who steals the *Zwischenraum,* the space between the pickets of a picket fence, till it's all fence.[40]

Oh, he leaves a little space, but not much; he squeezes the rests to less than half their length, to become the odd quarter-stop and half-stop that partition the lines. Of Navarronian silence, only that "magic void," the two-bar *Ginnunga Gap* at 23-24, remains; the rest is sound, all sound. Of the slowed rises to glory, nothing but the prolonged E-flat at bar 9. But the lines, the phrases—these are pure Fats, formed and arrayed with additional order. To see this in action, look closely again at measures 5-14:

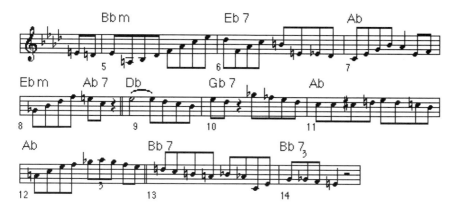

Miles Davis, *Donna Lee,* bars 5-14

[39]Balliett, *Night Creature,* p. 167.

[40]Christian Morgenstern, "Der Lattenzaun" ("The Picket Fence"), lines 1-5: "Es war einmal ein Lattenzaun / mit Zwischenraum, hindurchzuschaun. / Ein Architekt, der dieses sah, / stand eines Abends plötzlich da / und nahm Zwischenraum heraus. . . ." A translation by Max Knight: "One time there was a picket fence / with space to gaze from hence to thence. / An architect who saw this sight / approached it suddenly one night, / *removed the spaces* from the fence. . . ." Christian Morgenstern, *The Gallows Songs: A Selection,* translated and with an introduction by Max Knight (Berkeley: University of California Press, 1963), pp. 16-17 (emphasis added). Morgenstern's architect goes on to build a house *out of the stolen space;* Miles, an architect in his way, chucks it.

This is an analytic sketch of Navarro, outlining the Fats of *Ice Freezes Red*.
Miles's composition fills the bars with the interplay of arpeggio and scale,
enjambs over the standard melodic gap at 12-13, runs back and forth and
encapsulates notes with sidewise flanking movements to keep going without
running out of space, and packs them in in quantity. But there is a difference:
For all their extravagant proliferation, the Navarrisms here have been *disciplined,* subjected to even more control than Fats imposed. First is the
essential idea taken from Hanley's *Indiana*: in *Ice,* change-running and scalar
passages both run up *and* down, in what looks after a while to be a celebration
of free will, but the determinism of *Donna Lee* is quite stern and thorough-
going: arpeggios *up,* lines *down.* And the other order is a matter of shrinkage,
of all things: Fats's range, with its stratospheric high F, is lopped at the top,
and the tune directed to stay within Miles's compass: no note above concert
A-flat. Finally, the portrait is signed, and signed, and *signed* with what seems
to have been *Miles's* signature in 1947, that ubiquitous triplet figure TRI: [41]

But a regularized Fats, signed and sealed, was still Fats, and he is very
recognizable here. Of possible conclusions, let me put forth the most obvious:
In *Donna Lee,* Miles abandoned his "introspective, spare lines" for Navarro's
"powerful, long statements,"[42] and produced an act of homage to Fats—but
then blew take after take, and had to be content, for public consumption, to
abide by Savoy's onomastic and attributive errors, to let his wrongnamed
firstborn find a foster-home with Bird.

Scarcely the scenario one would choose. *At least,* the narrative instinct cries
out, *let the hero realize the tribute,* or confront *his celebrator,* or, *if all else fails,*
play the piece *that exalts him.* As it happens, reality provided an approxima-
tion: Navarro recorded *Donna Lee* as sideman with Bird in November of 1947
. . . but took no solo.[43] How he handles the head, though! This is Navarro
playing himself, and the head has been around The Street for more than half

[41]In the above form or a transposed version, this occurs *nine times* in *Donna Lee* (bars 1, 3, 12, 16,
17, 19, 22 [twice], 27) with an effective cadential variant ♫♫ at 14. Triplets may be the most
obvious feature of the bebop language, but this is not the famous or infamous "Woody Woodpecker"
triplet on beats 2 or 4, usually fastened by enemies of bop such as Philip Larkin, *All What Jazz* (New
York: Farrar-Strauss-Giroux, 1970, 1985), p. 94. That rises to a stress. What we have here is the *Red
Cross* type on beats 1 or 3. Davis used it in other compositions of 1947, especially *Half Nelson,* where
it is not too much to say that one of the tune's goals is to explore this very lick.

[42]The stylistic characterizations come from Chambers, *Milestones I,* p. 141.

[43]The performance is on *Charlie Parker: The Great Sessions 1947/1948* (Jazz Anthology 550082).

a year. He is crisp and certain, no fluffs, incomparably surer than the composer on the tune's maiden outing, and this at what may well be the optimum tempo, up forty beats since May, ca. =280. The ensemble comes across brilliantly, *Alles in Ordnung*. Thomas Owens's judgment that "this is the best recording of *Donna Lee*"[44] probably applied only to recordings by Bird, is nearly twenty years old now, and there have been many versions since, but it may well stand as an accurate assessment of *all* performances of *Donna Lee*.

Jazz, that mixture of the hardest realities and the softest legends, specializes in failed scenarios, and this is as near *das Happyend* as we're likely to get: The honoree records the head, and the act of homage is complete. Slow fade.

B: *Like Sonny*

And yet. Homage is a difficult thing to assess. One musician's congratulation may, without the change of a note, be another's satire. The alternative interpretations, for example, of Coltrane's 1958 Rollins pastiche, *Like Sonny*, may well have the innocence attributed to them by Zina Carno in the first liner notes:

> LIKE SONNY is so-called, says Coltrane, because he once heard Sonny Rollins play the little figure on which the tune is built, and he liked it so much he decided to use it in one of his own lines. I've always called it his impression of Sonny. Either way, it's a very attractive little theme, Latin-flavored at the beginning, then going into straight swinging.[45]

Well, maybe. But something here is disingenuous, since the Coltrane line, Caribbean ambience and all, involves the madly compulsive *over-use* of that "little figure," dragged up and down, variously extended but always recognizable. We hear

---

[44]Thomas Owens, *Charlie Parker: Techniques of Improvisation*, p. 61.
[45]From the original notes to 1960's *John Coltrane: Coltrane Jazz*, recently reissued (Atlantic Jazz 1354-2).

thirty-two times in twenty-four bars.

It is difficult to avoid thinking that Coltrane, even as Rollins himself, had read Gunther Schuller's famous article, "Sonny Rollins and Thematic Improvising," in the first issue of *The Jazz Review* in 1958,[46] and, with a wicked wit, decided to run Rollins's thematicism into the ground. Coltrane was having fun with Rollins in late '58 and early '59, as his performances of Rollins's *Doxy* and *Oleo* show, booted along as they are by the other horn, Ray Draper's *tuba*. Draper was certainly an agile tubist, but his instrument has a built-in elephantiasis that pretty well undermines any serious third-stream soloing, and gives the two pieces a firm foundation in the halls of the ridiculous. Not to rake up the hyped contention between the two titans, but if this is also part of Coltrane's "impression of Sonny," that impression was not wholly adulatory, not by a long shot.[47]

So. What is going on in *Like Sonny*? Innocent homage to a brother saxophonist treated with extreme seriousness in the jazz press—or perhaps a satirical challenge? "Thematic Improvisation—taking a figure and playing with it? Hell, I can do that, too. Just listen." An exaggerated evocation of an established musician's characteristic style leads to a statement that is ambiguous, perhaps designedly so.

Change the instruments, choose another characteristic, and we can perhaps see Davis making the same sort of statement on Navarro eleven years before.

C. Blood Lines

> Under the circumstances, it might have been natural for Navarro and Davis to have emerged as competitors. Both were highly regarded on The Street a few years earlier [*sc.* than 1950], and listeners debated their relative merits; both were young . . . and both started out as disciples of Gillespie. But Navarro seems to have had no competitive

[46]Gunther Schuller, "Sonny Rollins and Thematic Improvising," reprinted in Martin Williams's *Jazz Panorama* (New York: Crowell-Collier, 1962), pp. 238-252.

[47]See, or rather hear, the collected evidence on EMI's 1990 Roulette reissue, *Like Sonny* (B4-93901)—which includes the tubized *Doxy* and *Oleo*—and the already noted *Coltrane Jazz*, whose CD version includes the earliest recording of *Like Sonny*—the April Fool's Day (!) 1959 version with Cedar Walton on piano.

196

instinct, even before his addiction drained away all his worldly ambition, and his benign personality seems to have defused any competitive instinct in those around them.

—Jack Chambers[48]

"When I was with Bird," [Miles] told Michael Watts, "Fats Navarro used to say I played too fast all the time, but I couldn't swing with Max Roach 'cos he couldn't swing." As an attempt to revise the history of bebop, the comment is simply ludicrous.

—Jack Chambers[49]

(*Re* Art Tatum:)
[S]urely nobody else in jazz ever combined such an active sense of humor with pure musicality. Tatum loved to demolish moods, slaughter clichés, parody other pianists, toss in hilariously irrelevant snatches of familiar classics, and develop insane clashes of line, accompaniment and style. . . . [His] ability to conceive and execute compound musical ideas at such a dizzying rate of speed is hardly to be believed, and it makes for savage stride sendups of James P. Johnson and especially Fats Waller. . . .

—John Litweiler, 1992[50]

Besides, what sort of a play is this? thats what I want to know. Is it a comedy or a tragedy? Is it a farce or a melodrama? Is it repertory theater tosh, or really straight paying stuff? . . . [H]ow am I to know how to take it?

—George Bernard Shaw, 1911[51]

Donna Lee is, of course, no "savage sendup" of Navarro. And there is no good reason to doubt Davis's affection for his running mate. Everyone loved Fats, the childlike, non-competitive Fats. But one does wonder about the defusing of Miles the Contentious, especially the young Miles, who, though *Down Beat*'s New Star (trumpet) for 1946, still found many who felt that "It didn't sound like Miles had any chops," and whose cooption by Parker for his first line was still a matter of debate, debate based largely on his shortcomings

[48]Ibid., p. 141.
[49]Jack Chambers, *Milestones 2: The Music and Times of Miles Davis Since 1960* (New York: BeechTree/Morrow, 1985), p. 250.
[50]John Litweiler, "Tales of Tatum" (a retrospective review), *Down Beat* (March 1992): 48.
[51]George Bernard Shaw, *Fanny's First Play*, pp. 177-178.

in the Trumpet King department, Navarro's long suit.[52] Miles's affection for Fats the Child may have been tempered, just a tad, with resentment. Even as Coltrane's *Like Sonny*, when you back away and take a good, hard look at it, *Donna Lee* is not uniformly complimentary. It is, among other things, *funny*. And the basis of humor is attack by incongruity.

First, there is the dislocation. As shown, the initial phrase of *Donna Lee* is the initial phrase of Navarro's chorus on *Ice Freezes Red*. But Miles delays the beginning until the third beat of the first measure, when he substitutes the triplet figure and goes into Navarro's descending scale, half a bar late. The result is out of phase, upsetting the listener,[53] who keeps trying for a bit to make sense of an orientation, half a measure or more off, which rapidly becomes intractable. It is a trick that Miles would use again, notably in the "staggered syncopation" of his 1956 *Steamin'* recording of Monk's *Well You Needn't*.[54] The disorienting effect is on the order of that musical *Spass* where *Take Me Out To The Ball Game* is started two beats *early*, on the pickup:

/ Take me OUT / to THE ball game TAAKE MEEE OUT / to THE crowd buy MEEEEE

and so forth, relentlessly manhandling word-meter, till the game is suddenly over before the last two notes are out. Disturbing and funny; one laughs, but wants to scream.

Navarro's was a quite various talent, his invention prodigious, and it gets hard, within a small compass, to pin him down to formulas, but there was at least one antiquated lick he used in his lines on *Ice Freezes Red*—one which might as well be called HSL for *HoneySuckLe*, since it reproduces and repeats the 5 notes that watermark Waller's tune:

[52]Chambers, *Milestones I*, pp. 48, 59-60, 62. The "chops" quotation was made later by Med Flory.

[53]It might be suggested that performances of *Donna Lee* should be started *from silence* on the first measure's third beat, without the warning quarter notes that Powell puts on the Savoy takes. Disorientation is sometimes valuable.

[54]In the *Steamin'* album, Coltrane is brought in late on the theme at the bridge, and Miles and Coltrane then finish the head half a measure apart. "Staggered syncopation" comes from Paul Scanlon's liner notes to Prestige's omnibus reissue in 1974, *Miles Davis: Workin' and Steamin'* (P-24034).

198

Miles gets hold of this and shakes it twice in 13-15, recalling, and perhaps teasing, Fats the dude.[55] And with the TRI, he signs the portrait almost everywhere. Not content with that, he insists on another of bebop's stigmata: the two eighths, on the beat, followed by silence (*be*bop!), occur 4 times in *Donna Lee*.[56] With the imposed orders, he somehow *tames* Fats, the technician, brings him within the fold—which is also funny.

Even silence is funny in this piece—that rest, that near-grand pause at 23-24, the lonely single occurrence of *nada* in the whole piece. There's nothing else like it; the tune runs as hard as it can and then stops absolutely dead. All Fats's between-spaces have been condensed into one hyper-zero that, even at ♩=240 and beyond, gapes like the pit of the abyss in the *Revelation of St. John,* throwing the madness of all the notes into relief.

And that is the real joke: the frantic *profusion.* By collapsing the rests and continuing the lines through hell and high water, Miles—like Coltrane with his thirty-two dozen repetitions of the Rollins figure—has made too much of a muchness. What we have here is more than Navarro's baroque, more even than mannerism: It is a Peano curve of sound, a Perpetuum-Mobile fractal that aims to fill, with bebop's patented hurry, every bit of available space (except, of course, for the two-bar rest at 23-24, the gap that yawns and throws into high relief everything that is going on)—downright obsessive, an eighth-note *compulsion.*

And obsessive-compulsiveness is *funny*: Wile E. Coyote doggedly—or coyotedly—pursuing Road Runner again and again, at whatever the cost to himself, or, perhaps, H.G. Wells's comparison of Henry James, trudging the labyrinth of his style, to a hippopotamus trying, over and over, to pick up a pea. If this is the definitive Navarro imitation, it is also the definitive Navarro parody, the glory proliferated into a tick. Miles could—*see?*—encompass Fats the technician in his style. . . .

But, as things turned out on May 8, 1947, he couldn't play like Fats. *Donna Lee* couldn't be taken public as *homage* because of the vagaries of Miles' chops. And these same chops vitiated the *satire*: If Davis fluffed while mounting his attack—however mild it may have been—the point was turned right around: Miles would be shown as just what many said, no technician, not a *real* trumpet player, certainly not a Fats.

Confronted with a choice that was no choice, sandwiched between ironies, the only thing to do was follow fairly outrageous fortune: Savoy had messed up, but *stet*: Let it stand under the title of Curly Russell's daughter and the authorship of Bird. Swallow the whole business and soldier on.

[55]This lick, in various forms, occurs in *Ice* at bars 15 and 26 in the breaks of the opening head, the *mise* of the out head, and bars 29, 31, and 47 of Fats's chorus.

[56]At measures 4, 8, 10, and the repeat of 4 at 20.

The joke might be spoiled, but there was always the bottom line: He didn't lose no money or nothing.

VII. Miles Smiles

> Let's get down to the real heart of the matter: wit. . . . We've already discussed this aspect of humor in connection with a symphony by Haydn [*Symphony 102*, Movement 4]. I am sure you all noticed his wit: how he surprised you all the time; how he got fun into the music through sudden pauses, sudden louds and softs; and how he made humor through using those fast, scurrying themes that remind us of a little dachshund puppy skittering around the floor. . . . [H]ow fast that Haydn movement flies by! Speed has always been one of the main things about wit; fast and funny—that's the rule for jokes.
>
> —Leonard Bernstein[57]

> For one of the great things about purely musical jokes is that, unlike most jokes you tell, they are even better fun as they grow more familiar.
>
> —Leonard Bernstein[58]

But the joke worked, in a way that Miles could not really have foreseen in 1947. It was a simple thing that did it. *Donna Lee*'s tempo went up. And up. This began fairly early, as witness Bird's ♩=280 (from the beginning 240) in December 1947. Fats could play that. But, sooner or later, *Donna Lee*, which it is only a bit too strong to call Davis's Revenge—revenge on the technicians, the trumpet kings, the teachers who valued the fat tone and the flashing valves, the critics who savaged a young trumpeter after the *Ornithology* date—well, *Donna Lee* became a *Classic*, not so much a Classic Bebop Melody as a school figure and rite of passage to be mastered at the highest speed, a gig warmup and cloutmaker to astound and amaze one's section mates of the evening. Tempi inflate, and go through the roof, and sooner or later the most agile new Fats must yield.

---

[57]Leonard Bernstein, "Humor in Music," in *Leonard Bernstein's Young People's Concerts for Reading and Listening* (New York: Simon & Schuster, 1962), pp. 71-2. (From a CBS telecast of 1959?)
[58]Ibid., p. 71.

In the saddest irony connected with the piece, Miles's first recorded composition became Clifford Brown's last performance. On June 25, 1956, the night before he died in a turnpike crash, Brownie finished his appearance at Music City in Philadelphia with, of all things, *Donna Lee*.[59] He handled the idiotic pace, around ♩=290, with aplomb during his long, long improvisation ... but came to grief on the head going out, missing the beat and only making it back by an effort of will—rather like Miles improvising nine years before at fifty beats less.

And that 290 must be the upper limit for trumpeters; beyond lies strictly saxophone territory, till it tops out at the ridiculous ♩=350 or so performed— if that is the word—by Richie Cole and Phil Woods in a Denver frenzy in 1980.[60]

But hackers have aspirations, too, and the process keeps on, in the jam-session subculture which keeps up a standard inflation of the tempi of standard bop numbers, whose very familiarity breeds attempt.[61] It is the joke that keeps on giving, lighting the ever-exploding loaded cigar. Somewhere, Miles may be smiling.

Marked cross from the womb and perverse, misnamed and misattributed, misconceived and misconstrued, a feisty emblem of the new music that respectfully preserved the old, homage and satire at once, an affirmation of the composer's performance ability that he was unable to perform, a mighty monument with a moppet's monicker misused to measure *machismo*—this is *Donna Lee,* a grab-bag of ironies that spring from many curious sources, ironies that interbreed and somehow continue in effect as time and distance increase.

---

[59]*Clifford Brown: The Beginning and the End* (Columbia LP PC 32284, 1973).

[60]Richie Cole, with Phil Woods, *Side By Side* (Muse CD reissue MCD 6016, 1991), recorded July 25-6, 1980.

[61]So it is that, for example, Clifford Brown's *Joy Spring*, recorded by its composer at a leisurely ♩=165 MM or so, which sets off well the beauty of its changes, is frequently called at a hundred beats more per minute. I write ruefully as a trombonist who has learned the hard way never to let a guitarist set the tempo.

Photograph of Charlie Parker and Dizzy Gillespie with two Chileans, Mr. and Mrs. Jorge Guinle, pictured between the two jazz greats. On the left are record producer Ahmet Ertegun and jazz historian Rudy Blesh, and standing with his baritone saxophone is Sahib Shihab. *HRHRC Ross Russell Collection.*

The Bebop Tradition in South America

BY JOSÉ HOSIASSON

Interviewed by biographer Alan Lomax in 1938 for the Library of Congress, Jelly Roll Morton, the New Orleans jazz pioneer, spoke of the early days in his hometown: "Then we had Spanish people there. I heard a lot of Spanish tunes and I tried to play them in correct tempo...."[1] Certainly what Morton referred to as Spanish included all kinds of "Latin" elements which were to be found in the Crescent City by the end of the nineteenth century. Living in New Orleans in 1880, Lafcadio Hearn had already written that "the melancholy, quavering beauty and weirdness of the negro chant are lightened by the French influence, or subdued and deepened by the Spanish."[2] In *The Story of Jazz*—perhaps the finest book written on the subject—Marshall Stearns traces the common roots in the development of Afro-American music, both in the United States and in the West Indies.[3] In a recent article on bebop trumpeter Dizzy Gillespie, reviewer-critic Gary Giddins has remarked on "a marriage of Cuban music and American music" that demonstrates how the Caribbean influenced such a piece as Gillespie's *Manteca*, which in turn had an impact on both "Latin" music and jazz in creating a fusion that brought together the music of the Americas.[4] Indeed, there is a sizable body of writings on the huge mutual feedback between American jazz and the music of the Caribbean area, yet little has been written on the musical exchange that—since the inception of jazz—has gone on between the United States and the South American republics.

From as early as the 1920s, sailors and musicians on passenger ships brought records to South America and participated in jam sessions in port cities like Guayaquil, Callao, Valparaíso, Buenos Aires, Montevideo, Santos, Rio de Janeiro, and La Guaíra. American jazz musicians toured the South

---

[1] Alan Lomax, *Mister Jelly Roll* (Los Angeles, CA: University of California Press, 1950), p. 57.

[2] H.E. Krehbiel, *Afro-American Folksongs* (New York: G. Schirmer, 1914), p. 134.

[3] Marshall W. Stearns, *The Story of Jazz* (New York: Oxford University Press, 1956).

[4] Gary Giddins, "Dizzy like a Fox," in *Faces in the Crowd* (New York: Oxford University Press, 1992), p. 179.

American continent and hired local sidemen along the way. Although Charlie Parker never played south of the U.S. border, American bop musicians did tour South America in the early 1950s, many of them with "Latin" bands like that of Pérez Prado. At the same time, South American artists who performed in "Latin" bands in the United States were mastering the new jazz idiom—and contributing to it.

When we speak of South America, we are talking about an area which is more than twice the size of the continental United States and which has over twenty percent more population. In spite of the similarities in their origins, the cultural differences among the thirteen South American countries cannot be overestimated. Although it is true that—except for the Brazilians and the Guayanans—we South Americans all speak Spanish, the difference between Spanish spoken in Chile and the one used in Venezuela, for example, is at least as large as the difference between the English of Birmingham, Alabama, and the language of a native of Birmingham, England. Not only do we speak differently, we also eat different foods, we keep different timetables, and our ethnic makeups are different. Thus, the development of jazz also took a different path in each South American country.

The bebop influence in South America is best represented by the South American artists whose names have appeared on the international jazz scene since the 1950s. Most of these world-famous musicians came from Argentina and Brazil, and obviously they did not emerge out of a vacuum but rather from environments which had important jazz traditions.

Argentina is the second largest and most populous country in South America, and jazz has been played there since even before the 1920s. The late Argentine poet and jazz pioneer Evar Méndez recalls how "jazz music awoke my interest through the music-hall shows which I attended in Buenos Aires between 1910 and 1916."[5] A "Bop Club" was founded in Buenos Aires in 1950 and it attracted most of the young Argentine musicians and many of the older ones who had been active in the old "Hot Club."[6] Pianist Boris "Lalo" Schifrin, born in 1932, and tenor saxophone player Leandro "Gato" Barbieri, born in 1934, have both made successful jazz careers in the United States: Schifrin is remembered—among other achievements—as the pianist with the Dizzy Gillespie quintet in the early 1960s; Barbieri for his recordings with Carla Bley, Don Cherry, and under his own name. Both of these musicians are known by a larger non-jazz audience, however, because Schifrin wrote the theme songs of the popular television shows, *Mission Impossible* and *Mannix*,

[5]Luciano Díaz, "Evar Méndez, reportaje póstumo," *Jazz Magazine Buenos Aires* (April/May 1956).

[6]Sergio Pujol, *Jazz al Sur—la música negra en la Argentina* (Buenos Aires: Emecé Editores, 1992), p. 189.

and Barbieri wrote the score for *The Last Tango in Paris* and his tenor saxophone playing was heard in that 1973 film.

In the early 1950s Schifrin assembled at the Buenos Aires "Bop Club" a big band which was modeled on Gillespie's band of 1946-47. He also wrote the arrangements for *Enigma para Boppers* (*Slow Boat to China*) and *Nunca supe* (*I Never Knew*), which were recorded in Buenos Aires with the sponsorship and supervision of the "Bop Club Argentino" on 12 December 1952 and were issued the following year on a 78 rpm record.[7] These two pieces constitute a superb early example of bop-influenced playing by Argentine musicians. They contain some very fluent and inspired performances in the bebop idiom by Rubén Barbieri (Gato's elder brother) on trumpet, Luís María Casalla on trombone, Luís Horacio "Chivo" Borraro on clarinet, Carlos Dato on alto, Enrique Varela on tenor, Julio Darre on baritone, Lalo Schifrin on piano, Horacio Malvicino on guitar, Emilio Méndez on bass, and Rudy Lane on drums. The arrangements are clearly inspired by the Miles Davis Nonet's "Birth of the Cool" recordings made in New York in 1949-50.

Among other internationally known Argentine bop-influenced musicians, aside from Schifrin and Barbieri, are trumpet player Gustavo Bergalli, who lives in Sweden;[8] saxophone player Jorge Anders[9] and pianist Carlos Franzetti,[10] who work out of New York; and the late pianists Jorge Dalto, who performed with Tito Puente,[11] and Enrique Villegas, who in the 1950s recorded in the United States for the Columbia label.[12] Also well known are Argentine bandoneon, or squeeze-box, players Dino Saluzzi, who recorded with the George Gruntz Concert Jazz Band (an international all-star orchestra which operates out of Switzerland),[13] and the late Astor Piazzolla, who recorded with Gerry Mulligan.[14]

[7]Odeon (Argentina) 55533, matrixes 18736 and 18737.

[8]*Lars Sjoesten Plays the Music of Lars Gullin*, Dragon (Sweden) DRLP 66; *Gustavo Bergalli Quintet*, Dragon (Sweden) DRLP 119.

[9]*Jazz en Embassy*, Dial (Argentina) DRM 15003; *Jorge Anders y su orquesta*, Redondel (Argentina) SL 10503; *Como tiene que ser*, Redondel (Argentina) SL 10517; Rubén López-Furst Quartet, *Jazz argentino*, CBS (Argentina) 8695; *The Buenos Aires-New York Swing Connection*, Famous Door HL 152.

[10]*Prometheus*, Audiophile AP 187.

[11]Tito Puente, *On Broadway*, Concord CJ 4207; Tito Puente, *El Rey*, Concord CJ 4250; Gato Barbieri, *Bolivia*, RCA PD 89559; Machito, *Afro-Cuban Jazz Moods*, OJC 447; *Urban Oasis*, Concord CJ 4275.

[12]Columbia CL 787; Columbia CL 877; *Villegas en cuerpo y alma*, Trova (Argentina) TL 6; *Metamorfosis*, Trova (Argentina) TL 8; *Tributo a Monk*, Trova (Argentina) TL 10; *Porgy & Bess*, Trova (Argentina) TL 19; *Encuentro*, Fresh Sound Records FSR 72; *60 años*, Trova (Argentina) 80064; *Tributo a Kern*, Aleluya Records (Argentina) AR 17000.

[13]The George Gruntz Concert Jazz Band, *Theatre*, ECM 1265; Enrico Rava/Dino Saluzzi, *Volver*, ECM 1343.

[14]*Gerry Mulligan/Astor Piazzola 1974*, Accord 556642; *Tango: Zero Hour*, American Clave AMCL 1013; *Piazzolla!*, American Clave AMCL 1021; *Live in Wien*, Messidor 15916.

Roughly half the South American continent and half its population belong to Brazil, which is also one of the world's richest countries so far as musical tradition is concerned. The early bop influence in Brazil can be traced to a photograph in which a well-known Brazilian personality, Jorge Guinle, who in 1953 wrote a book entitled *Jazz Panorama*, appears with his wife at a New York club sitting between Dizzy Gillespie and Charlie Parker.[15] So many Brazilian artists are known abroad that listing them would be endless. João Gilberto, Antonio Carlos "Tom" Jobim, Sérgio Mendes, and Milton Nascimento are practically household names in the Western world. Tânia Maria, Astrud Gilberto, Flora Purim, Laurindo Almeida (who joined the Stan Kenton orchestra in 1945 and recorded with Bud Shank and Shorty Rogers as part of the West Coast jazz scene of the mid 1950s), Luiz Bonfá, Baden Powell, Raul de Souza, and Egberto Gismonti have all performed successfully in the United States and elsewhere. Also, percussionists Airto Moreira, Nana Vasconcelos, Guilherme Franco, and Dom Um Romão have been members of top American groups. Instead of playing straight-ahead jazz, as most of the Argentine players do, Brazilian artists have tended to integrate the bebop elements within the mainstream of their own country's music. An outstanding exception to this rule was the late saxophone player Victor Assis Brasil, who had been trained at the Berklee School of Music in Boston and who—influenced by Charlie Parker, Lee Konitz, and Paul Desmond—developed a highly individual jazz style.[16] Several of the compositions and arrangements on Miles Davis's 1970 album *Live/Evil*[17] belong to Brazilian multi-instrumentalist Hermeto Pascoal, who also recorded with Duke Pearson and with his own group.[18] Pascoal is, I believe, one of the most influential and creative artists in Brazil, and indeed one of the most creative musicians performing in the world today.

Both in Argentina and in Brazil there are many, many more bop-derived players who are only known locally within these huge countries' borders. For a better insight into these scenes I suggest that the reader turn to Sergio Pujol's *Jazz al Sur—la música negra en la Argentina*[19] and to Zuza Homem de Mello's chapter "O Jazz no Brasil" in the Brazilian edition of André Francis's *Jazz*.[20]

[15]Chan Parker & François Poudras, *To Bird With Love* (Poitiers, France: Wizlow, 1981), p. 257.

[16]*Brasil Instrumento*, EMI-Odeon (Brasil) 364 795273.

[17]Miles Davis, *Live/Evil*, Columbia G 30954.

[18]*Slaves Mass*, Warner Bros. (Brasil) BR 36021; *Hermeto*, Imagem (Brasil) 6001; *Live at Montreux*, Atlantic (Brasil) 20052/3; *Zabumbe-Bum-A*, Warner Bros. (Brasil) 36104; *Cérebro magnético*, Atlantic (Brasil) BR 30127; *Lagôa de Canôa*, Som Da Gente (Brasil) SDG 021/84; *Hermeto Pascoal & Grupo*, West Wind 2009; *Por diferentes caminhos*, Som Da Gente (Brasil) SDG 039/88.

[19]See footnote 6 above.

[20]André Francis, *Jazz* (São Paulo: Martins Fontes Editôra, 1987).

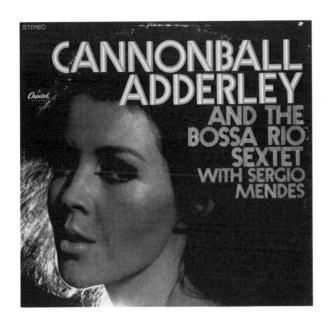

Above: album cover for *Cannonball Adderley and the Bossa Rio Sextet with Sergio Mendes*, from Capitol Records, 1962. *HRHRC Ross Russell Collection*. Below: album cover for Gato Barbieri's *Caliente!*, from A & M Records, 1976. Courtesy of Pat Fox.

There is only one other country in South America which has a jazz-related musician with a claim to international fame. Percussionist Alejandro Neciosup "Alex" Acuña was born in Pativilca, Perú, in 1944, and, among others, he has recorded with Weather Report,[21] Ella Fitzgerald,[22] Dave Grusin,[23] Tânia Maria,[24] and also with his own group, "Alex Acuña & The Unknowns."[25] Although not known internationally, the late Peruvian pianist-composer-arranger Jaime Delgado-Aparicio, who was trained in the 1960s in Boston at the Berklee School of Music, worked extensively in Lima and thus contributed to the spread of the bop idiom in his homeland. "Perú Jazz," a group that plays a fusion of bop, rock, and South American music, has performed at international festivals in Italy, Canada, and elsewhere and is made up of Jean Pierre Magnet on tenor, Enrique Luna on bass, Manongo Mujica on drums, and Julio "Chocolate" Argendones on various native percussion instruments.

Apart from Argentina, Brazil, and Perú, no other South American country has added any well-known names to the international jazz roster. For certain, each of the remaining countries has its own jazz scene and some of the local musicians are talented indeed. As an example we can take my own country, Chile, where a "Jazz club" has existed since the late 1930s. In Chile a small contingent of bop-derived musicians is still quite active today and there is even a new generation of bop players.[26] Among the youngest of this new generation, the shining examples are twenty-year-old trumpeter Cristián Cuturrufo, guitarist Angel Parra (grandson of the late Violeta Parra, Chile's best-known folk performer and composer), and tenor player Marcos Aldana, son of a local jazz pioneer and a semi-finalist at the 1991 Thelonious Monk Institute saxophone competition in Washington, D.C.

Jazz is an amazing cultural phenomenon. At its best it is a sublime art form, which can express the highest and noblest qualities of exceptional human beings. In the process, it also reflects the circumstances of their time and place. I never cease to marvel at the universality of jazz. Born at the turn of the century as a local occurrence in the southeastern United States, in less than twenty years it became the musical esperanto of our time, a really universal musical language. Just a few years after Charlie Parker recorded *Tiny's Tempo* on September 14, 1944, musicians all over the world started to incorporate bop lines into their playing. South America was no exception, as

[21]Weather Report, *Black Market*, CBS 32226; Weather Report, *Heavy Weather*, CBS 32358.
[22]Ella Fitzgerald, *Ella abraca Jobim*, Pablo Today 2630201.
[23]Dave Grusin, *Harlequin*, GRP 9522; *Havana*, GRP 2003.
[24]Tânia Maria, *Love Explosion*, Concord CJ 230.
[25]JUC 3322.
[26]*Jazz Chile*, Alerce (Chile) 0121.

demonstrated by recordings made locally in the 1950s, as well as by the South American artists who joined the international jazz roster in the 1950s and 1960s.

¡Viva el bop! ¡Viva el jazz!

Album cover designed by William Claxton for *Laurindo Almeida Quartet featuring Bud Shank*, from Pacific Jazz Records, 1955. Courtesy of Martha and Hubert Campbell.

Participants in the 1992 Bebop symposium panel discussion, posing with symposium speaker José Hosiasson: from left to right, Thomas Owens, Red Rodney, Hosiasson, Gary Giddins, Dan Morgenstern, and Carl Woidek.

Bebop in the 1990s: A Panel Discussion

Moderator: We have a fantastic group of musical minds here: Dan Morgenstern, Thomas Owens, Gary Giddins, Red Rodney, and as a kind of "traffic cop," I'm Carl Woidek. The topic I thought we would start off with, that's not to say we won't depart from, is "Bebop in the '90s—A Vital Form or a Museum Piece?" And I'd like to begin by asking Red, How's the state of health of Bebop right now? How's the patient? What's the state of Bebop in 1992?

Red Rodney: Well, there aren't many of the original group left. There are very few of us left. But there are a lot of *younger* players who have grown up with this music. They have *developed* it and modernized it; made a little more of a melodic bed to it; added all of the condiments of the '60s, '70s, and '80s. And I think there are some bands like mine, which you may have heard last night, and there are some others, that are playing Bebop of the '90s. Now, of course, the young men in the quintet, some of them weren't even born. Most of them weren't at that period. And they came up with more modern forms. But they quickly learned the roots and traditions of the Bebop form and [what came] before, which is very important to make a complete, well-rounded player. We were very lucky because I was able to give them roots, traditions, and a little discipline of the original Bebop, and they were able to bring to me all of the nuances of the new. And if you're wise enough to listen to the youngsters and learn from them, then you're going to get better, as I've gotten better because of that. And, so, there are other groups like this today; even the young ones like the Harper Brothers, maybe now they're starting to play more modern. When they first came out they were playing the '40s Bebop and most of us would say, "Well, they do it but they don't do it as well as we did it." Well, how could they? We didn't give them a chance. Now I think they're just starting to come up with their own version of Bebop. I think this music is going to continue growing and growing and adding all new forms, because Bebop is still the most intellectual, the most difficult idiom of jazz to play. More than the modal thing was, more than the free thing was, but put all together, it's magnificent! That's how I feel about it.

CW: I'd like to ask the same question of Dan Morgenstern in terms of music that is Bebop derived, swinging chord-change music. How healthy is that scene today?

Dan Morgenstern: Well, I think part of the answer is what we heard last night, which certainly was healthy indeed. But I think in a way what we heard last night may not be, unfortunately, a common denominator. Because what we have here is Red, who is a veteran, and we have the young musicians. Most of the groups now playing in a Bebop tradition lack what I think is very important, which is a generational meld. Because they're all young guys playing together, what they do is very interesting, but it doesn't have that guidance, maybe, or that mix, which is very creative, of not really the old and the new but of the generational thing which always was the case in this music. And so we miss Art Blakey, who was like a whole university producing all these people. The only thing we can wait for now is for some of the young guys to get a little older and hire younger people. In a way we have that with Wynton, who I believe is already going to hit 30 this year.

RR: He's 30!

DM: There was a time when you wouldn't have been able to trust him anymore (laughs). But obviously what has happened is something quite remarkable, which *is* that the music called Bebop, because everybody calls it that, it made such a strong comeback, which is to say that the tradition, which is infused with new blood and so on, has made a return after a prolonged absence. We had a lot of very interesting and sometimes very weird and also sometimes very boring things going on. We had the freedom and so on, and we had fusion, which I think still exists and has produced some things of interest, but basically, I mean to me at least, it was pretty boring. Now it's very interesting to see what these young musicians can do with the tradition and, as Red pointed out, Bebop in itself, in its pure form, is one of the most difficult jazz disciplines. It's awfully hard to play, I mean, it was hard even for Bird and Diz. Right? So, maybe what we call contemporary Bebop may not be quite as rigorous, and it has new elements in it—it has to have, because a lot of things happened. Sometimes it also is looking back beyond Bebop—we are seeing a little bit of this—but not necessarily in this very sort of academic repertory form, but reaching back to role models like Johnny Hodges, and Benny Carter, who's still very much with us, and Coleman Hawkins, Art Tatum, and

212

Ellington, which is, I kind of think, some of the seminal stuff that went into making Bebop. But whatever is happening now, it's fascinating, it's something that is entirely unpredictable. You don't want to stick your neck out, but sometimes you're asked to forecast what's going to happen in the next decade. I wrote something awful for *Downbeat*, at the end of the '70s, I think. They asked me to say something about the '80s. I haven't dared to look at it. I'm sure it's pretty awful. Anyway, I don't think that you can ever predict what's going to happen in a living art form and I think the most important thing is that jazz is *very* much alive and the Bebop tradition is certainly a very important part of that life.

CW: I have a question for Thomas Owens, which is, the music that we heard last night with Red's group, I guess the age range, not counting you [Red], is 21 to 40-ish or so?

RR: [Gary?] Dial [the pianist] is 38. . . .

RR: But he came to me when he was 22 or 23!

CW: Is the music heard last night, if not a carbon copy, if not identical, is it consistent with Bebop, the music of Parker and Gillespie?

Tom Owens: Oh yeah. . . . Well, that brings up an interesting point. I think that there have been implied, during the last couple of days, different points of view about just *what* is Bebop. There are people who would say that Bebop basically was the style defined by Parker and Gillespie in the '40s and early '50s. Then you have to add different labels for whatever came after, and I think that's an awfully narrow point of view. And, maybe, is almost belittling to what we know as that music, because it says that it's very limited and doesn't have room for expansion. But I think we've seen *in* [Red's] band there are three generations of beboppers represented. And they're, as you say, bringing in the younger ones, bringing new points of view, adding elements. . . . Coltrane *lived* and all those who come along after Coltrane, if they're saxophonists, probably have Coltrane in them. Well, was Coltrane a bebopper? *I* think so. He brought in some new elements to the language. Now, the young guys are building upon that and adding to the vocabulary. Just as English is the living, growing language, there are living, growing musical languages too. There's another band that represents the same sort of thing that is not a working band like [Red's] is. I live in the Los Angeles area, and once a year a band assembles at Catalina Bar and Grill in LA. It's a quartet. The leader is Milt Jackson. Cedar Walton and Billy Higgins and John Clayton complete the group, and when

213

they can, they just come together, they block out that time, so they can be together for that week. I don't think that band has ever played in New York City, because three of those guys live on the West Coast, so it's easier for Milt to come out to them. And when that band gets together, it is pure joy and pure love on both sides of the bandstand. And it occurred to me the first time I heard them, which was four years ago I guess when they started doing this, that here again is just about three generations of Bebop. There's Milt from Red's generation carrying on the tradition, then a second generation represented by Cedar Walton and Billy Higgins, and John, almost literally young enough to be a grandson of Milt Jackson, holding up the bass and quite nicely, thank you, and the music that those guys play together is just phenomenal. Cedar Walton and Billy Higgins have a communication that is un*earthly*. You wonder, how can those two guys, how can Billy Higgins read Cedar Walton's mind like he does? And the joy that's in everybody's eyes as it's happening, certainly when that band plays in town, Bebop lives in a brilliant way, and I think it lived on this stage last night in a brilliant way too. I guess I've kind of gotten off the track, but yeah, I think that Bebop is a much bigger language, musical language, than it was in the '40s, but it's still, given the fact that it's a lousy word that many musicians really kind of cringe at, and some really hated to use, but we're stuck with probably forever, by whatever you call it . . .

Gary Giddins: Jazz itself!

TO: That's true, but whatever you call it, it's alive and well and flourishing.

CW: In my Jazz History Class, toward the end I've played most recently some comparisons between some very young artists and some earlier, more established artists, for example, Ralph Moore and John Coltrane, or Vincent Herring and Cannonball Adderley, Bennie Green and Bobby Timmons, Marcus Roberts and a particular Thelonious Monk cut, a particular Branford Marsalis and Ben Webster at one point. What I'd like to ask Gary Giddins is, in the '70s it was often said that the musicians who were drawn into fusion were not very aware of the roots of jazz, that many of the youngest fusion artists have not really studied where the music came from, and I'm wondering if you think that could be the opposite problem in today's young Bebop-derived music, that the musicians have gone to the opposite end of the pendulum swing and are doing justice to the roots, are showing respect, homage to the roots, but then are not looking beyond, or at least at this stage of their career, don't show signs of moving ahead. Could we have gone to the opposite extreme of showing roots and not showing as much individuality?

GG: I think there's a useful analogy in what's happened to jazz over the last 25 years and the history of modern painting. We got to a point where it became so abstract that there were black on black canvases, white on white canvas, I mean you have a canvas that is completely covered with black paint or white paint. It's almost an invitation to go back to the *beginning* and do some kind of a representational painting, which is exactly what happened—we got the pop art, the op art, and the same thing is happening in classical music now, a return to David Del Tredici and other composers in that idiom. I think what we're seeing in jazz is a response to the fact that it went all the way out. We had the black on black canvas. We had musicians standing on a stage and playing without—attempting to play without—bar lines, trying to defy the tempered scale without chords. . . . Booker Ervin, for whom Dan and I share a great admiration, was playing during the late '60s in a club called the La Boheme with Ted Curson and I was asking Booker at intermission about some of the players, about these techniques, and he said, "Anybody could do that. You know how they do that?" And I'm thinking about harmonics and all this stuff I've read and he said, "You bite on the reed!" (Laughter), and he bit on the reed and he squealed sitting at the table in the club. So we're seeing a response that I think is very healthy. Tom said he wondered how Cedar Walton and Billy Higgins read each other's minds. . . . The answer, of course, is that they've played together for twenty years. Why did the band sound so great last night? Because that's a band, there's just no substitute for that, there's no replacement for that. And I think that one of the most exciting things going on in jazz is that there's an attempt to have bands. When you go to see Tommy Flanagan's trio, it's a trio. Not just Tommy Flanagan and a couple of guys. There's no replacement for that. I've been involved with a group called the American Jazz Orchestra, and the first time we played I was just very proud of the way the band was sounding until I heard the tape and I heard all these clams, and John Lewis, who was the conductor, said, "Don't ever think about this sounding like a real band for two or three years," and, of course, he was exactly right and all of a sudden it started to sound like a band. And it's the magic of musicians playing with each other, understanding each other, reading each other's minds, figuring out how they think. And a lot of the musicians who are coming up now can play with each other. In the avant-garde period of the '60s, nobody played with each other. Ornette Coleman and Cecil Taylor played together *once* and they've never allowed the tape to be released, and I'm sure there's a good reason for that. There was the Coltrane school, there was the Ornette school, the Cecil school. Now you have a whole generation of musicians who can get on a bandstand—they know the tunes, they know the rules, they have a whole history of the music to draw on, and they're going to be inventive in the amazing way that, say, Chris Potter is, or a bass player in New York named Chris McBride, who is something! Unbelievable! He's also 20, 21.

DM: 19 . . . he's not 20 yet.

GG: 19, and everybody wants to work with him! Because he's just got it all! The timbre and the sound, the strength, the brains, and he just has a tremendous feeling for the music. When Wynton first came up, [Carl Woidek's] question was much argued about because of the feeling among a lot of people that he didn't have anything of his own. And I think it's taken Wynton ten years to figure out where he's going. You know, some of the recent things, there's definitely more Ellington in there than there is Miles, and a lot of the younger players who have come up since Wynton are not satisfied with just reading the licks off of records. It's an educational process. [Red's] band last night, what really amazed me was that one would say, "It's a bop band, in the bop tradition," yet it sounded very contemporary—very vital. I don't know if there's something about the rhythm section, but it just had a radiance about it and it just really illustrated to me how *totally* contemporary that bebop is when it is played by musicians who are *thinking* together. Gary Dial's piece was wonderful!

TO: Who was it who said, "Bebop is the music of the future?"

RR: Joe Segal! Joe Segal, I'll answer that! How it's done. I'm a romantic at heart and I'm a melody man. And Dial, of course, has been writing for us for thirteen years, and Chris brought some things in, and *other* writers. Bob Belden comes to mind, because he brings *a lot* to us. And he's our producer, for this next date and our last one. But in the final analysis, the final arrangement is *mine*. I tell them, "You can go as far out as you want," because youth will have their way, they will go out, and this is fine, but I say, "I want the melodic *beat*, no matter how far you go," so, what you heard last night, some of those things, were *very* far out, they were quite modern, they were very difficult for me to play, but there was that melodic beat in there. *That* is *my* doing, the rest of it is theirs. So it's a good match. That's the reason for that!

CW: Just as a kind of follow-up, and I certainly don't want to belabor this point, do you feel that the young artists that you're hearing in New York are not only paying homage to the masters and exploring roots, but also have a feeling for individuality, exploration?

216

Above: Red Rodney and his band during their concert at The University of Texas at Austin for the 1992 Bebop symposium; below: Red Rodney conducting a master class in the University's Department of Music.

GG: Yes, it seems to me that one quality that really good young musicians have—tell me, [Red], if you disagree with this—is a feeling that they know what they're doing and that they have something to say. And as you get older and wiser I think that it may become a little bit modified. But I look for that, I want to see that in young musicians; I want to feel that they're showing off and that they've got something to say. And I see a lot of that. McBride has it. He loves to do little flourishes to show you his dexterity and a number of the younger piano players. There's a very good piano player—he's not that young anymore, but . . . John Campbell.

RR: John Campbell?

GG: Yeah.

RR: Oh, yeah! He's wonderful!

GG: He's all over the keyboard. David Murray is somebody who's become more and more involved with his roots, but he's also gone through the whole history of it, of the modern period. He's trying everything. He's got a big band. He just did a quartet—it's a blues album with Don Pullen on organ. And in fact there was a cutting contest which I regret that I wasn't there for. Albert Murray, the writer, had a party and I guess it was in November or early December, and there was a jam session and it got to a real old-fashioned cutting contest between Wynton and David. Wynton's always putting David down, and apparently David just blew him off the stage and totally won the whole audience there. So, you know, I think that there are a lot of surprises. I'd like to see more of that. I'd like to see more of this kind of jamming and trading ideas on the stage, and not just a kind of this is my school, this is their school. And I think when you have musicians who are studied, who know the rules and the fundamentals of the music, then you have that possibility, you can actually stage a jam session and have people come by and intermingle. Red has participated in a party that goes on at the end of every year. It's a sixty position Gibson Jazz party, and they're all musicians of a couple of generations who can get up on the bandstand and call a tune and play it. We haven't really seen that kind of situation with younger players in a while, but I think in this generation you *could* do something like that because, I remember in the early '70s I was doing a piece for *Esquire* on young players and I went to a loft where there was a jam session going on and there was a guitar player from Japan named Rio Kawaski, and he said, "Let's play 'Body and Soul'." They didn't know the changes. They were trying to hear it. I thought, Wow! how are they going to communicate on this music. That's not true anymore!

RR: No more.

DM: I think things have come to a pretty pass when a tenor player can cut a trumpet player! (laughter) But aside from that, I think that one really fundamental difference, which has happened gradually, is the attitude of musicians toward music itself, or tradition. There was a time we went through, which maybe was a necessary time, when the music was so overlaid with political and social issues and agendas that a lot of things were lost in the shuffle. One of the most important things that has happened in terms of jazz is that it has now become a music that can be seen whole and that is something that should always have been the case, but for various reasons it couldn't be. Now it seems perfectly natural, and [GG] mentioned Marcus Roberts, a pianist who's interested in the music of Jelly Roll Morton, in James P. Johnson, in Monk, and yet he plays like himself. A drummer like Harlan Rowley plays with those New Orleans re-creations and plays wonderful press rolls, and he's also a great modern jazz drummer. [GG] mentioned Chris McBride. He seems to be one of these people who's especially gifted, who can step into any musical situation. I mean, he listens to records and stuff, but he hasn't listened to everything. He isn't old enough! My God, there's hundreds and hundreds and hundreds of hours. But he can step into almost anything and do right by it. And the idea that a jazz musician today should be familiar with and able to play in all of these different, but related languages, it's probably something that has to do with the maturity of an art form. It also has some dangers and some people have raised that point. Some say that you should be a complete musician and acquainted with the tradition, you should be able to play all kinds of styles, but doesn't that mean losing your own identity? I don't think that that is necessarily the case. But I do think that we have to look at jazz in a slightly different way than we've looked at it before. And that is, that we are probably going to get musicians now who are similar to classical players, and there's never really been that much difference. I mean the idea that some jazz-oriented people have, that classical music is reading music off a sheet of paper, I think we need to dispense with that, for there are so many different interpretations of that paper. If you are a pianist there are so many ways of playing Chopin, so many ways of playing Debussy. And what about the interpretations of conductors! So I think what we might get for the first time is jazz musicians who are conversant with a lot of different styles but may prefer a certain one to play in. I mean, we have guys like this now in New York, somebody like Dan Barrett, who's an excellent trombonist, but who prefers to play in a certain mainstream group. And I think that's fine. I think everybody now also feels that everybody else has the right to exist. It's no longer a matter of questioning whether some form of music has a right to be

219

there or whether it should lay down and die or whatever. And there were times when people were insisting that that was the case. You know, "Get out of the way!" But, getting back to the issue, which is Bebop, Bebop today, of course, can't be the Bebop of 1945, because of all the things that have happened since then, but this afternoon, when Red's rhythm section was doing a clinic, Gary Dial said something that interested me. When he was demonstrating, he was talking about the Bebop scale—he demonstrated Bebop scales. He said, when we play Bebop, that's what we use, but you wouldn't use that when you're playing something that's more modal oriented. So, the fact is you can go in and out. You have different vocabularies and you can use them. Sometimes you can use them at the same time. It's just simply becoming a more varied and more mature musical language and some of it is going to be alike. You know, you don't have to be an innovator in order to be a respectable player.

GG: I was just reminded of an anecdote in Bill Crow's endlessly useful book. He tells the story about a musician, I can't remember who it is, but he's on stage, and he plays in the Lester Young style and he walks off the bandstand and some guy says, "Hey man! All you're doing is playing Lester Young!" And the guy hands him his saxophone and says, "Here, you play Lester Young!" (Laughter) Now, that's ok, but I remember a time when somebody came along and he was playing some Bud Powell and it was like oh (shruggingly), you know, like that didn't count for anything.

CW: I wanted to pick up on something Dan said and probably on something that Gary touched on. Not everyone has felt this way, but I think that among some critics, some musicians, there was a feeling that each successive generation of musicians has made the preceding generation obsolete. Of course, there are many, many exceptions among musicians who are innovative and yet have had respect for what has come before. But a lot of people seem to organize jazz in the sense that we were improving the breed, that harmonically, melodically, rhythmically the music would become more sophisticated. What Dan is suggesting is a view that integrates all the areas of jazz, all the styles of jazz, where a musician would be conversant, as he said, with the various styles. And what I noticed—Gary was talking about the David Murray album—where they're playing enriched gut-bucket music with Don Pullen on organ. How much of the integration that you see on the scene today looks back to Bebop and even the Swing Era and yet bypasses the explorations of the '60s, and do you feel that there is a meaningful integration that can happen, that would not ignore the explorations of the '60s, but integrate them into an even wider palette?

220

GG: They're not ignoring it as much as people think. Wynton, for example, is a great admirer of Ornette. He doesn't have use for a lot of other people in the avant-garde, but he quotes from Ornette. I think if Tom were to do one of his analyses of Wynton, or you [Carl], you'd keep finding Ornette phrases that he steals. Sometimes he writes them into the heads. I'm trying to think, George Lewis, well he's kind of an avant-garde figure, and he's also associated with the classics. I remember being with him in Europe and he had nothing but Coltrane tapes. He listened to them over and over, the same two or three records. I think most of the musicians that have been coming up in the last fifteen to twenty years have some idea of the major figures of that period and of the Bop period. What they probably don't know, and I don't know that this is a bad thing, are the musicians who kind of fall by the wayside because they haven't ultimately stood the test of time. I mean, Coltrane's place in this music is . . . Mount Rushmore. You can't get around it. But there are a lot of other figures that *we* remember who were playing that, it could be debated that, people in fact aren't listening to anymore. They simply have not necessarily enriched the vocabulary, but that doesn't mean that their music was worthless.

CW: Vocabulary, does this mean that you're not doing a discography of Giuseppe Logan? (Laughter)

GG: It's interesting that you mention that, because I like Giuseppe Logan's records because Don Pullen is on them and I think Eddie Gomez was the bass player and there are actually some interesting sounds there. But I would say, however, that when you listen to Giuseppe Logan, that his music is dated in a way that ultimately you listen to it and say, "Ah yes, the '60s, my youth!" You don't listen to it with the same kind of attention that you're going to listen to Coltrane's *Alabama* or something which is this incredible, emotional, overwhelming force.

DM: There is, you know, a place where this *tradition* of the '60s, for lack of a better word, is still alive, for instance, in what Richard Abrams is doing. Mostly what he has done on records now has been Big Band. I think the third Big Band CD has just been released, and there are also ways of incorporating that. I mean, there are things that were played on this bandstand last night that couldn't have happened if the '60s hadn't taken place, but they're in a different context. There was one alto thing when there was just rhythm behind it. That was out, but you can go out and still be *in*. I think much of that music of the '60s was so oriented toward protest that even people get tired of playing it. And some of the key figures, of course, died. Who knows what Albert Ayler would play like today if he had lived! Don Cherry is still around . . .

Charlie Parker (far left) and Red Rodney (second from right), after a jam session in Kansas City, 1951. HRHRC *Ross Russell Collection*.

GG: That raises a question that I want to ask Red. What would Charlie Parker be doing if he were here?

RR: You know, a lot of people have asked me that. I firmly believe that he was put here for that little ten-year period, or twelve-year period, to give us what he did, the legacy that he left, the music that he influenced everybody to play. I mean he was the creator and the progenitor of the Bebop style. But I was with him toward the end of his life also, and there was nothing new, everything was repetitive. He recorded the same things over and over; he just played his things so well that he was able to do it. That was unique, because that was a ten-, eleven-year period. On the other hand, Miles had many, many years as a great innovator, throughout the modal period, throughout the avant-garde period. The only period that I personally didn't like was his rock-and-roll period. But sometimes you take away that rhythm section, and you still heard Miles Davis playing Miles Davis. So, Bird I don't think would have done anything different. I think that he would have stayed the same. And that leads me to answer one more question. Many of my great heroes, my idols, and my dear friends stayed in their comfort zone because they were great all their lives in that comfort zone, and that's fine. That's fine. However, jazz doesn't belong in that comfort zone. We need to grow, we need to take chances. I don't care if I made thirty mistakes on that bandstand. If I tried something new and it worked, it was Great! If it didn't work, then next time we'll get it! I think it's incumbent upon us to keep growing and developing and taking all the newer forms and putting them in with your own specific style. My dear friends who remain in their comfort zone, I don't like to play with them anymore! I feel like I've had "yesterday's warmed over mashed potatoes" playing 1940s and '50s Bebop. And I came from that era. I think that we should all *continue growing*. That's my own personal observation and my own personal feeling, but some of those people who played *beautifully* sound *tired* because they won't try to make anything else. And the new guy that comes along, "Ah, man, he don't make any sense!" How can you say that if you don't listen to him? That's my one beef. On the other hand, I think we have better circumstances now for jazz coming ahead in the next generation than we ever did before, because there're jazz societies coming up all over the country. And we're not going to have to play—I won't see it perhaps, but the younger ones will—we're not going to have to play in the clubs, sit in smoke-filled rooms, start at 10 o'clock at night, and all to sell whiskey. That's the criterion. The more whiskey you can sell the better. We're gonna play in auditoriums like this. Two hundred-, three hundred-seat auditoriums. Like Kleinsinger has—whatever we think of Kleinsinger he's got the formula! Sell subscription concerts. Now, these Jazz Societies are springing up in every city. Willie Jenkins is trying very hard to put

223

them all together and have block booking. So, I think the next decade, the next generation, we're going to have much more employment, more dignified employment, and jazz is going to benefit from it. The music itself will benefit.

CW: One of the things I heard [Red] saying is that for you, exploration is important, that exploration is not inconsistent with staying true to yourself, that one does not have to be complacent in order to be true to yourself, but instead, you can be true to yourself by seeking new sounds that are, as I said, consistent with your values.

RR: I believe that, I firmly believe that! When Don Cherry first came along, all the trumpet players said, "Hey man, what's he doing!" I thought it was great! I became the Jewish Don Cherry! (Laughter) I thought it was great! Other guys come along and they're not playing traditional forms that we know or the Bebop forms that we know. That's wonderful, but you have to learn to take this and use it for your *own* particular style. That's growing!

DM: For those of you who are not from New York, which is a number of you I think, that Kleinsinger is Jack Kleinsinger, who is a New York City jazz concert producer who has been presenting a series of monthly concerts now for what, about twenty years?

RR: Twenty years!

DM: Yeah, an interesting footnote.

TO: One thing that I would like to follow up on is what [Red] said earlier about the musician wanting to explore the tradition. Maybe more at least in the early years in their lives, than carving their own individualist niche. And I wonder if it doesn't follow from that, that those of us who write about the music have an obligation to be guided by that attitude. That is, the books that say first there was New Orleans, then there was Swing, then there was Bebop, then there was Cool, and then there was Funky—implicit in all this is that there is always change, always change, always change. . . . Of course, the labels didn't come from musicians most of the time. They came from the writers. Maybe it's time for the writers to kind of listen to the musicians and look at their attitudes and say, "Okay, we don't need change every ten years." Let's just take Wynton Marsalis as a . . . Oh, let's not try to find a pigeon hole for him. Let's just say that he's a great trumpeter and that he's doing this and doing that, and that's the same with Chris Potter and so on. And maybe we don't have a *label* for these guys. Maybe we don't need one.

224

DM: This word "eclectic." Wynton seems to be an eclectic, and there's room for that, and Gary pointed to the other arts. We don't have the dominant style or any real innovation in *any* art form today, since the great innovators of the first three or four decades, the first half of this century. No Picassos, not even any Jackson Pollacks. There are no George Bernard Shaws or even Samuel Becketts. Who is the great living poet? I mean, there's nice work being done, everywhere, in a multitude of styles. But the tremendous thrust of innovation and upheaval, that went hand in hand with all of the things that happened historically in our time, it seems to have abated, and maybe that's a good thing too, because it gives us a chance to look back at all the things that *were* done, and sort of sort things out and say, "Hey, this was great, and this fell by the wayside." And also as a listener—I came to this music as a listener—I never had any plans to become, you know, a "jazz critic." What the hell was that? Besides, you can't make a living (laughs), and so, it's not something that you plan to do. You know, we've managed, but we do a lot of different things. What drew me to this music was that I loved the way it sounded. I'll be damned if I can't try to enjoy Sidney Bechet and Louis Armstrong, and I can enjoy Duke Ellington and I can enjoy Charlie Parker and I can enjoy Ornette Coleman. What I'm saying, you know, is not very popular these days, but take your pick! There was a time when you could do that without being accused of being politically incorrect. Thank God, let's not have any political correctness in jazz, please. (Laughter)

RR: Um-hmm. Very good!

CW: Maybe that would be a good note on which to conclude, the spirit of integration. I'd like to thank Red Rodney . . .

RR: Thank you!

CW: Gary Giddins, Thomas Owens, Dan Morgenstern, and I'd like to thank everyone in the audience.

Transcribed by Al Hood

NOTES ON CONTRIBUTORS

NICHOLAS M. EVANS received his B.A. in English in 1989 from Oberlin College and his M.A. in English in 1992 from The University of Texas at Austin, where he is currently working on the Ph.D. in English. The prospective topic for his dissertation is the U.S. Ethnic Minorities' Literary Representations of the Meaning of Jazz.

GARY GIDDINS writes for *The Village Voice* and has published a number of important collections of essay-reviews on jazz, including *Riding on a Blue Note: Jazz and American Pop* (1981), *Rhythm-a-Ning: Jazz Tradition and Innovation in the '80s* (1985), and *Faces in the Crowd* (1992), all from Oxford University Press. In addition, he is the author of *Celebrating Bird: The Triumph of Charlie Parker* (1987).

DELL HOLLINGSWORTH received an M.M. in musicology from Texas Christian University in 1979. As a staff member at the Harry Ransom Humanities Research Center, she is responsible for music reference and research assistance, as well as the cataloging of books, music scores, and recordings. Her special field of interest is musical performance practice in the baroque period, and she and her husband perform regularly with La Follia, a baroque chamber ensemble.

JOSÉ HOSIASSON is a past president of the Jazz Club of Santiago and a contributor to *The New Grove Encyclopedia of Jazz*. He has published articles on jazz history in *Revista Musical Chilena* and has written liner notes for jazz recordings issued in Chile. He and his sons are active musicians on the Chilean jazz scene.

EDWARD KOMARA received the Masters in Library Science and an M.A. in Music History from the State University of New York at Buffalo. He is Music Librarian/Blues Archivist in the Music Library at the University of Mississippi and a regular columnist for *Living Blues*. His book, *The Dial Recordings of Charlie Parker: A Discography*, is forthcoming from Greenwood Press.

RICHARD LAWN, who holds the Marilyn and Morton Meyerson Centennial Professorship in Music, is Chair of the Music Department and director of Jazz Studies at The University of Texas at Austin. He has recorded with the Nova Saxophone Quartet, and performed with such jazz greats as Lionel Hampton and Dizzy Gillespie. Before coming to Texas, he was the director of the jazz program at the University of Northern Iowa.

GEORGE LEAKE is in the Preservation section of the Conservation Department at the Harry Ransom Humanities Research Center. He has written on music for *The Austin Chronicle* and the *Texas Music Association Newsletter* and has been active in the South by Southwest Music and Media Conference.

DOUGLASS PARKER, a Professor of Classics at The University of Texas at Austin, occasionally performs on campus with Cadence, his own bebop combo. As a teacher, he is noted for his course on Parageography, a study of everything from Homer's *Odyssey* to Edmund Spenser's *The Fairie Queene* and from imaginary to real utopian societies. His verse translations of comedies by Aristophanes and Terence are widely performed.

ROSS RUSSELL is the author of *Jazz Style in Kansas City and the Southwest* (1967), the standard study of Southwestern jazz, and *Bird Lives!* (1973), the foundational biography of Charlie Parker. Dial Records, the label established by Russell in 1946, accounted for a series of important recordings made by Charlie Parker on the West Coast and in New York and by other vital figures in the Bebop movement. The Ross Russell Collection at the Harry Ransom Humanities Research Center came to The University of Texas at Austin in 1980.

LORENZO THOMAS received the B.A. from Queens College in 1967. A writer in residence in the English Department at the University of Houston, he has published widely, both essays and poetry, and *The Bathers*, his selected poems, appeared in 1978.